---------------- ★ ----------------

Morrissey stood in silence and took in the kind of horror that was becoming familiar to him. No misplaced cuts. Somebody who knew his work; somebody who'd had practice.

His eyes picked out the two bottles near the body, one empty of cheap wine, the other holding a third of its volume in industrial spirits. Close up by the brick wall an old oil drum made a brazier, hole-punched sides nearly burnt through.

Some enterprising mechanic keeping warm before the place closed.

Now there were new ashes, underneath and around.

And a body naked as Duffy's.

Somebody trained to kill or who'd trained himself?

---------------- ★ ----------------

show you the short-cut path," said Barrett. "If anything hap-

Also available from Worldwide Mystery by
KAY MITCHELL

ROOTS OF EVIL
IN STONY PLACES
A LIVELY FORM OF DEATH

STOCKHOLM • ATHENS • TOKYO • MILAN
MADRID • WARSAW • BUDAPEST • AUCKLAND

A PORTION FOR FOXES

KAY MITCHELL

WORLDWIDE.

TORONTO • NEW YORK • LONDON
AMSTERDAM • PARIS • SYDNEY • HAMBURG
STOCKHOLM • ATHENS • TOKYO • MILAN
MADRID • WARSAW • BUDAPEST • AUCKLAND

for Peter
my one true love

A PORTION FOR FOXES

A Worldwide Mystery/April 1997

First published by St. Martin's Press, Incorporated.

ISBN 0-373-26235-3

...those that seek to destroy my soul...shall fall by the sword;
they shall be a portion for foxes.
—Psalm 63:9-10

ONE

THE OLD MAN STANK to high heaven, and the reek of him carved a swathe through rush-hour pedestrians who gave him a sniff, a look, and then despite a sharp veering, still had to carry a nostril-imprinted memory of sour ripeness with them as far as the corner curry house. Duffy, oblivious to everything outside his own focus of attention, scrabbled for a dropped dog-end and noticed nothing else.

The streets were freezing, the air temperature steadily dropping with the loss of daylight. Cold cut ice-pick sharp through the old man's clothing, biting into thin bones to set up a dull, maddening ache. A thought surfaced. He began to mumble and the human tide parted even faster. *Too bloody old, that's what...years an' years an' years an...* He lost the thread of it there and straightened up, weaving along the pavement, enough cheap meths and alcohol in him to blur everything in his mind, stumbling, teetering, nearly falling, but managing at the last to stay upright. Chuffed at that and feeling in a brief flash of clarity that he might still be good for something yet. Watching his feet though after that, lifting them elaborately as he headed for the old viaduct.

Manoeuvring down Mill Hill, steep and icy cobbled, took all of his concentration, then, climbing over the low stone wall at the bottom and lowering himself awkwardly on the other side, he slipped and slid down the grass bank on his bum. It took a befuddled minute, blinking up at frosty stars, to get his wits back.

A flare of red in the viaduct's bottom arch made him think of Geordie Harry who always had matches and might have a bottle of forgetfulness to share. Duffy struggled to remember if he had eaten that day and felt crab claws in his stomach when the thought came.

A rat scurried, fat and black. *Everything had to eat.* Why? Why was that? Known why once…known a lot once… Clarity slipped out of his mind as he watched his breath hang in mid-air. He breathed in and out deeply and admiringly until a coughing fit and the urge to unfreeze his fingers sent him on again.

The fire-builder stood deep in the dark arch, unidentifiable as Duffy peered past the flames with uncertainty. Swaying, trying to focus, he called thickly, 'Geordie? Tha' you, Geordie?'

There was a glint of fire on glass. 'This what you're wanting? A good drop of booze? Come on then—don't be shy—come and get it—it's your lucky day.'

Not Geordie Harry.

Duffy wavered. 'Wha' is't?'

'Made to warm old cockles. Smell it! Rum—and enough for the both of us. You coming for it?' The bottle was advanced casually, waved and withdrawn. Duffy's old bones wept and shivered. Rum…! Remembering the taste of it in his mouth, and the feel of it on his throat he licked his lips and responded like Pavlov's dog, shuffling beyond the leaping fire, already salivating.

IN LOVE for the first time and surly with misgivings, hands rammed deep into pockets, the clock showing seven-fifteen and Liz stuffing books into that damned tasselled bag she'd picked up at Oxfam. He watched her do it, a gut feeling he couldn't pin down demanding he act the heavy. Tie her down if he had to. Anything to keep her with him. His face acting as an open mirror to the thought and anger at himself building up because it was only a damned tutorial she was going to. *A bleeding tutorial—not an assignation.*

Liz picked up on the body language and came to hold him, her arms sliding around him at belt level. He lowered his head and she put her cheek next to his, chin resting on his shoulder, rubbing like a cat against his stubble, offering a compromise. 'You could come with me, love,' she said. 'Walk me over.

Drink coffee in the refectory until I'm through. How's that sound?'

He shook his head, said no, and then wished he hadn't. 'Can't,' he said. 'Got to do this bloody useless essay or I'm finished.' Sliding his arms around her, coaxing. 'Give it a miss, skip it, say you forgot. Wouldn't be the first time, would it?'

She pulled away, picked up another book, cramming it in with the rest. 'Uh-huh. Can't be done. Not this time. And anyway I can handle him; you're the one with the problem.' She squinted back at him and grinned. 'He hasn't tried to rip my clothes off yet.'

'Yeah, well, give him time. This could be your lucky night.' The words were light but Liz picked up the undercurrent just the same, and felt vexed by it.

She said tetchily, 'Look, Paul, just finish up on the essay and leave Fletch the Lech to me. Okay? Most of the stuff's rumours.'

'In a pig's ear it is!' Scowling. 'Don't know why they don't chuck the bugger out.'

Shrugging, tired with the topic, Liz said, 'He's good at his job, that's why. Besides which—if he tried anything I'd scream the bloody place down. That do? I'll bring back a pizza; think you'll be finished by then?'

'Don't know.' The scowl still on his face. Caught in a Catch-22 between heart and head he watched her shove her arms into a chunky-thick blue cardigan that belonged to him but looked a hundred times better on her. Before Liz, sex had been perfunctory fumbles and wet dreams, now he woke every morning and looked at her quiet face next to his on the pillow and couldn't believe his luck. *And if she dumped him, what would he do?* The thought frightened the hell out of him. Not looking at her he sat at the table and said gruffly, 'But if you're not back here by nine I'll break his door down.'

'Mmm-mm. Tough talk. Maybe I should warn him.' She leaned over the back of his chair, crossed her arms loosely over his chest and put on an accent. 'I'll say, hey, fat-cat, this fella of mine is going to bell you good.'

'Shit, Liz, I'd really do it if...'

She clamped a warning hand over his mouth. 'I'm not into post-feminist thought, lover, so don't get tied into this male-power thing. All right?' She kissed him, dodged his hands and was gone. A blast of cold air rushed in to take her place.

Moody, he shifted his notes and attempted some kind of concentration. *Modular teaching methods in current educational practice.* Shit! Who the hell cared? Stuff the essay! Then he started to write it anyway because he couldn't afford not to, eyes lifting repeatedly to the clock.

IF AFFAIRS WERE NEVER started there'd be no waiting for them to end. So ran Rosemary Dwyer's thoughts. She poured more wine, topped up their glasses. The more the merrier! Hah! Robert raised his to the light, turned it, drank. 'Not bad for plonk.'

'Glad you approve.' Banality of banalities, all is banality, saith the about-to-be-jilted. She put the bottle down, looking out through the second-floor window, unwilling to meet his eyes, idly watching Liz trudge up the front steps, shapeless in blue. 'I think Adrian's back to giving late tutorials again,' she said. 'Penny Cox yesterday, Liz Pardoe today.'

'I'd have thought last term's fracas would have turned even him off!'

'Except he managed to talk his way out of it again and Chrissie left...nothing proved. Maybe I should start a chaperone service.'

'They're a bit old to be clucked over.'

'Maybe, maybe not.' She was silent then, watching winter advance outside her window.

'Roz,' he said. 'I didn't mean...'

Surrogate children, replacing those she'd never had. She cut across the embarrassment of his voice. 'Of course not. I hadn't thought you did.' Both of them knew it was a lie.

He picked up her coat and said, 'If we don't go now we'll miss the curtain.' Rosemary tossed back her head, drained the wine, and put the glass down carefully.

In my end is my beginning.
'Just so long as we don't miss the final act,' she said.

IT WAS NINE-THIRTY before he gave up on it, filled with jealous unease, biting on a bitten-down thumbnail and staring out the window until, finally, unable to cork anxiety any longer, he shoved into his parka and went to meet her.

Liz wouldn't like him doing that but he'd say he needed the walk, and if she didn't believe him, so be it; the way things were going he'd be staying up half the bloody night writing as it was. He covered the distance between cottage and college at a fast lope, and when she wasn't in the refectory ran two at a time up the south stairs. Light from under the tutor's closed door gilded the corridor's brown and scuffed linoleum. He set an ear to the wood and heard nothing, burst in, saw emptiness, and went manically through the building searching every place she might be.

THE SHRUBBERY PATH clipped a corner of the lake, bypassed the tennis courts, wove a way through tangled rhododendrons, and finally reached the side gate; the whole of it unlit except by the moon. Liz normally took the long way home, down the wide drive and along the main road, but the tutorial had run late and half-afraid Paul might be strung-out enough to do as he'd threatened she took the short way, take-away pizza warm in her hands.

The darkness didn't worry her any. She'd asked herself, who'd be out on a night like this, for God's sake? Not a sex attacker that was for sure—it'd freeze his balls off. And not Fletch either after the put down he'd had tonight. Breath making dancing white ghosts she debated about telling it to Paul. Maybe not. Maybe she'd just say Fletch had been a lamb. Her mind involved with that as she rounded a twisty bend by the lake and saw a man's shape dark against darkness, shying back until she saw who it was in the thin moonlight, then walking on saying, 'Hi! Lurking isn't allowed. Had me scared there,' as she passed.

For a brief second she wondered why he didn't say something friendly too, then the pizza flew from her hands. Pinioned, kicking backwards, trying to bite she told herself this couldn't be happening, getting out half a scream before she saw the knife, staying quiet then because she didn't want to die, fear cold as the night filling her as he moved her roughly through the thick darkness.

A MIGRAINE STARTED soon after the beginning of the third act and Rosemary knew she would have to leave. The pain, coupled with blinding flashes of light, made her want to be sick. 'Feel so stupid,' she mumbled. Robert drove her home silently. With eyes closed she leaned against the headrest, thoughts moving in peaks. *Damn* headaches, *damn* being forty, *damn* endings when there wasn't any time left for beginnings.

A man at forty was coming into his prime.

The Prime of Ms Rosemary Dwyer.

Except for the fact of her biological clock running down. She held her throbbing head, thankful when the car stopped and she could get to the dark quietness of her room, sick as soon as she'd closed the door behind her. When the vomiting eased she swallowed two painkillers and stayed motionless in the bathroom until the pain lessened, then cautiously and slowly went to close the curtains in her room. A combination of pain and the drug she had taken to combat it fuzzed her mind. Images from outside the window were instantly forgotten, and he, taking care not to be seen himself, failed to notice Rosemary.

TWO

THE DOG-FOX, mateless and ravenous, was out at the first crack of light, moving at a fast mincing trot, drawn to dustbins for easy pickings, feather mouthed from a carrion dove, loping through the shrubbery and finding Liz's cold pizza, polystyrene box sprung open and pepperoni scattered around.

Eagerly hunting up bits of frozen meat, slavering over breakfast, leaving nothing but the box, the fox broke wind and gave the dustbins a miss.

FINNEY EXERCISED HIS DOG every morning in the cutting. It was a ritual for them to go down the stone linesman's steps from Piece Hall Road and along the disused and overgrown railway line towards the old arches, the dog roaming wherever it fancied. It gave Finney a chance to do some quiet thinking without having his wife ask why he was looking so glum. He watched the dog race away across white frost and told himself he'd a lot of things to be glum about, redundancy for a start, sixteen gone last week, and sheer luck it hadn't been him. As he shone his heavy torch on the hard ground he worried that next time it might be, and dwelt on that idea as he walked, seeing horizons narrow and turn grey, morose because at fifty-two he'd never get another job. Gripping the torch between his knees he blew on cold hands and wondered how much he'd get in redundancy money.

Thirty thousand? Nice, tidy sum. Finney was suddenly less gloomy as he thought on that because it would give him enough to start up on his own, be his own man.

He let the idea grow in his head so he could savour it, remembering old pipe dreams and straightening his shoulders. Something to be thought about, that. One door slams, another opens. The dog's noise stopping him there before he'd thought any further.

Fur up, the lurcher ran manic circles by the bottom arch, into it and back out again, ruff stiff, letting out a full-throated howl then settling into a steady bark, telling Finney it had found something and not coming back when he called, so he had to go lead in hand to fetch it.

He put on a little burst of speed and slid off balance, annoyed because what had been the use of obedience training when the dog took no blind notice? Pointless. Coming up to the arch Finney saw the dead fire and what lay behind it—not the full horror of it though until he was up close and staring down at the old man, flesh sliced and carved, rich, sweet putrid smell spilling out from the slit belly along with other things Finney didn't want to think about.

Sweat came, breaking out from his pores, cold and salty. He moaned and backed up, shifting his eyes from the mess— feeling them drawn back to drink in the butchery like a noxious potion, then reeled and turned away, insides churning with heat and bile that rose on a burning tide. Retching and heaving he emptied himself into the dirt, one hand braced against the brickwork for support, shuddering when he'd finished, the dog quiet now, watching. He wiped his mouth and moved away, and this time when he called the dog came whining, slinking towards him, anxious as he to get away from the place.

THE MAIN ROADS had been heavily gritted, even so Morrissey knew he'd come off the roundabout too fast, any stray black ice and he'd probably have come to grief. He headed down Middlebrook Road past the Arts Centre, speed spotted by the white police Rover on traffic patrol and followed until the driver identified the number plate and dropped back, flashing his headlights in recognition.

The chief inspector lessened his speed fractionally, weaving around two buses to swing left at the T-junction, then sharp right into a dilapidated maze of small streets etched in red on the town development map, and due for eventual demolition.

Rumour said Fortes had shown interest in siting a hotel there, but rumours are often just that and no more. He let the thought go as he was slowed to gentler progress by an ice-rink of ungritted asphalt. He turned right a second time onto Mill Hill's cobbles, telling himself it would be no bad thing when the viaduct came down, then wondering if the crime he was about to see had come out of a tin of solvent or a piece of crack.

He parked nose on to the low stone wall, climbing over it with a lot more ease than Duffy had but slipping on the frozen bank just the same. Blue and white police tape blocked his path to the bottom arch, the arch itself hidden behind canvas screens and lit by arc lights.

Ron Neilson, Scene of Crime Officer, taking samples back to the SOCO van, said simply, 'You don't want to see this one.'

'*That* bad?'

Neilson's head moved in half circles. 'Sick.'

Morrissey took note, bracing himself as he stepped behind the screens and saw DC Copeland with the dark school boy flick that wouldn't stay off his forehead, standing to one side, looking green. His bad luck to have been on call. The chief inspector ignored both colour change and Copeland's wary eye, saying briskly, 'Let's get it over with then. Put me in the picture.'

Copeland fixed on some point in space. He'd never thought of himself as a hard man but neither had he believed himself to be the opposite. Now he was having to cork himself tight just to stay on his feet, and wishing Morrissey would go and look for himself. Bad enough to have seen, without having to talk about it. He said distantly, 'It's a brisk knife job, sir. It looks bad and it smells bad. I had to come away for a bit.' He looked abject as well as ill admitting it. 'You'll know him when you see him. Older dosser with a beard. Worst thing is, uniform had him banged up in cells a couple of nights ago, drunk and disorderly. If they'd kept him a bit longer we might have missed all this.'

'It happens,' Morrissey said. 'Anything else?'

'Stripped naked and clothes dumped on the fire. Chap exercising his dog found him. Threw up over there just inside the arch—I nearly trod in it. Can't blame him either.' He stopped for a breath and tried to get back into his professional skin. 'Want me to come back inside with you, sir?' he said, and broke into a sweat at the thought of it.

Morrissey shook his head. One patch of vomit was enough without Copeland adding to it. His stomach more seasoned than the DC's he went to see for himself. The police photographer was still busy, his professional indifference under strain but doing the best he could. He moved to get a different angle and Morrissey took his place, looking down and tasting acid, appreciating Copeland's reluctance to return. The chief inspector forced himself to squat, to look and examine. Last night he would have said that no act of violence or depravity could still surprise him, but now he saw he would have been wrong to say that. This was an act of evil by someone less than human. The old man's eyes, pallid blue, had rolled back, the throat gaped open, head near-severed.

Morrissey tried to detach himself from what he saw and failed, surprised at the heat of anger that flamed inside him. The old man had been thin to the point of emaciation, too old and weak to have put up any kind of fight. The sharp smell of methylated spirits laced with alcohol overhung the sweetly putrid stench of death. Had he drunk enough to anaesthetise him? The few teeth left in the slack mouth were little more than stumps. A dentist's nightmare. Wondering why the hell he should think of that when a dentist was the last thing the old man needed, he forced his eyes to examine.

One massively deep cut from sternum to pubis had lain open the abdomen in a single sweep. Entrails drooped and stank. He pushed up off his haunches, dusting off his hands as he walked back to Copeland, thinking that if God existed he might at least get up off His backside occasionally and take a look at what the devil got up to in His absence.

LIZ HADN'T COME HOME and Paul was beside himself.

He'd roamed the college grounds until midnight, pestering

anyone he saw, making a nuisance of himself knocking on doors. Not that there were many doors to knock on. Brindley, not being a fully residential college, housed a mere twenty students and five staff; everyone else had to rent as best they could.

After his first fruitless trawl of buildings and grounds, Paul had returned to Fletcher's office and found Liz's tutor at his desk marking papers. They'd had a noisy and unpleasant confrontation, ended when Alan Salter came out of the office next door to see what all the noise was about. Paul knew that without the psychologist's intervention he would have moved on to punching Fletcher senseless. Salter had talked him down and Fletcher had locked up his own office and gone upstairs to his room.

At midnight, frozen to the bone, Paul gave up and went home, turning up the gas fire to full heat, making coffee to keep himself awake and trying to get his mind back on the essay, confused that no one shared his panic, remembering Amanda, cosy with her boyfriend and impatient. 'Hey, come on. It's hardly a first, is it? You can't say Liz hasn't floated off before, this is just a re-run. Bet she forgot all about the pizza and went down to the pub. Okay?'

Gregarious Liz, always ready to party. He stared at a half-filled sheet of paper, thinking she would have told him first.

Except if she'd gone off with Trish and Adey, out the back drive in Adey's Mini, down to the village or into Malminster, she couldn't have told him then. He wished the cottage had a telephone so she could ring, imagining her telling him, 'Love! I'm so *sorry*. I forgot all about the pizza. How's the essay? See you in the morning. Sleep tight.' Her voice so clear in his head he almost believed it.

He worked until four-thirty, then flopped out fully clothed on the bed and went to sleep until near nine, rushing out washed but unshaven to hand in his essay and sit droopy-eyed through the first lecture. Looking for Liz in the refectory at morning break, he tried to remember what her schedule was for that day as he swallowed down a bacon butty and too-hot coffee, telling himself she'd be there at one o'clock, and hurrying back upstairs for the second session, rehearsing what he would say to her before they made up.

WHEN WARMSBY GOT THERE it was after nine and the arch had emptied; the SOCOs generating gentle heat in their van, Morrissey and Copeland keeping warm in the chief inspector's car, and the photographer finished and gone back to the warmth of a processing lab. All of them glad to be out of sight of Duffy's corpse but having to face it again when the pathologist led them back in around the screens, flapping his arms, exchanging greetings with Morrissey and complaining about the toil of changing a wheel.

Duffy seemed to have shrunk while he waited but that was an illusion. Warmsby clicked his tongue, said, 'A psycho or a sicko, take your pick,' and turned on his heel, stalking back to the SOCO van to get dressed up, returning gloved and over-alled like some miniature spaceman, face impassive as he shoved a thermometer up Duffy's rectum. Copeland looked away. Indignities to the dead added insult to injury. He wondered if thinking that made him a wimp.

'He's got lice,' said Warmsby getting to his feet. 'Let's hope he passed 'em on.' Copeland edged away. 'No good doing that,' said the pathologist. 'Buggers can jump six feet, no trouble. If they fancied you they'd be there already.' *Wonderful*, thought the DC. *Just what he needed.* Warmsby grinned, finished up, and left Duffy to the SOCOs.

'I suppose you're going to ask me for a fast post-mortem,' he grumbled as Morrissey and Copeland followed him out. 'Five o'clock, if you want it done today; can't do it any earlier and it probably won't disclose anything you haven't been able to see for yourselves anyway.' Peeling out of protective clothing and dumping it in a sack. 'Otherwise it'll have to be tomorrow morning.'

'Five o'clock,' said Morrissey. 'What about time of death? Any chance of an approximation?'

Warmsby waved around, gesturing at the frost. 'Seen the weather? Might as well have had him in a fridge all night. Trouble with you is you expect miracles. If I did make a guess it would be twelve to eighteen hours, but that's all it would be—a guess.' Getting his overcoat out of the van he shrugged into it, squinting up at Morrissey and thinking he'd never known the chief inspector so silent. Dropping all banter he said, 'I know it's a bad one, John, anything that it's in my province to do…?'

Morrissey nodded. 'Type of weapon we need to look for would be a help. We haven't found it yet and it'll take some time to hunt through all this,' waving at the cutting. 'Even if it's been dumped—which I doubt.'

Warmsby read an unspoken fear, sighed and shook his head. 'I can read you like a book,' he said. 'You don't believe this is going to be a singleton. Unpleasant prospect. Chances are you'll be right of course, but that doesn't stop me wishing you wrong.' He turned away and tramped back to his car. Morrissey took a last long look at the arches then followed him, climbing the slippy grass bank stone-faced and taciturn, with Copeland half a head shorter and just as silent bringing up the rear.

FINNEY TOOK THE DOG home, his mind totally diverted from the threat of redundancy by the sour taste of vomit and a burned-in image of Duffy's unquiet death. In his absence his wife had busied herself with his breakfast, cooking black pudding with onion rings and tomatoes. Usually Finney's favourite. Not that day though. One kind of meat smells much like any other, and the warm smell of black pudding mingled in his nose with the stench of ripped flesh that he'd carried home with him. For once he was sickeningly aware of the pudding's origins. His wife took a look at Finney's sweat-drenched pallor and thought he was having a heart attack. Her own heart speeded up with fear. She took the dog lead from his hand and manoeuvred a kitchen chair for her husband to sit on. Instead he shook his head and made for the stairs—moving as fast as he could but feeling bile rise before he got to the lavatory, spewing out across the pink carpet as he flung towards the bowl and heaved.

THREE

THE NOISE SURROUNDED HIM and he pushed inside and let it buffet his ears, stretching his neck to see. The long refectory was packed solid with students, hot bodies and talking heads shoved close together, every voice trying for one decibel louder than the rest.

Normally Paul would have elbowed a way through and added to the racket—to hell with listening to opinions politely, student debate was never that prissy, instead it was butt in, shout down. Hang some weird idea up for inspection and see who blew it away—*that* was student debate. The thought passed through his mind that the whole thing was infantile, and close on its heels came another. That without Liz everything would be infantile.

Shaun Hobbs gave a thumbs up; Paul didn't respond, instead, having spotted Adey gesticulating wildly with a plastic cup as she enforced a point, he dove through the crush to reach her. She eyed him blankly and shook her head. *God,* but sex was a bind. Everybody screwing up their love life that way. Shaking her head again she shouted back at him that, no, she hadn't seen Liz since yesterday morning, then seeing something die in his eyes when she said that she reached out impulsively to put a hand on his arm. 'Don't worry. She'll be holed up somewhere with a book. You know Liz—no sense of time.'

'Not all night. Not all night with a book somewhere,' he said, jerking his arm away and shoving back into the crowd. Somebody got up from a bench and Paul stood on it. Head and shoulders higher now than anyone in the room he shuffled a slow circle. Did that three times, looking for her, something in his gut knotting hard and sinking towards his groin when she wasn't there. He stepped down like a dead man and stood

silent while his mind scrabbled for another thread of hope,
then saw Adey and the little group she ran around with still
watching him. Liz had been a part of it before she moved in
with him. Turning away he crashed into a body, near sending
the college's last Goth flying as he grabbed hold of a frail new
hope and pushed out of the place, running down the college
steps into the cold to take the path between the rhododendrons
and skirt the corner of the lake, passing only a yard away from
Liz's pizza box without seeing it. He slipped, banged his elbow hard, then picked himself up, rubbing at his funny-bone
as he ran on, telling himself Liz must have got stuck in town
at a friend's place and would by now have come home on the
bus.

Pulling out his keys as he got to the cottage door he saw
himself saying her name over and over again as he wrapped
his arms around her, holding her so close and so tightly that
she'd never want to leave him that way again.

He let himself in, full of hope, then collapsed into the arm-
chair close to tears when he found the place still empty.

ROSEMARY DWYER had scant memory of the previous night
except for her disastrously enforced departure from the theatre.
She didn't think that Robert would be back after that—hoped
he wouldn't because she didn't want to see him again. Crumbs
from the rich man's table wasn't her style. Let him go to a
new love at one swift stroke instead of by painful little cuts.
That way she could get on with mourning him in peace.

Except that of all the times in her life when she would have
chosen *not* to have fallen prey to a migraine, last night had
been paramount. Why couldn't she have been allowed that
one, last evening's grace and then said goodbye to him with
dignity? *Her* choice of time and place. Had that small thing
been too much to ask? Ask of whom? Who was she supposed
to believe was listening? A personal God in a universe of
incomprehensible size? No. The two concepts were incompat-
ible—one or other had to be a mirage.

But which?

She marvelled at the capacity people had to hold on to simple beliefs, then recognised her unusual bent of thought was due more to the pills she had taken than to any sudden interest in metaphysics. Chilled as she crossed the foyer she pulled the loose cashmere cardigan more closely around her and moved to close the outer door, skin shivering at the change in temperature. Her eyes picked up Paul's running figure and retrieved a memory of him running last night too—and herself centred in a cloud of pain looking out through her window. What time had that been? She had seen Adrian Fletcher too, crossing the drive and... She frowned, concentrating, but the more amorphous image of a third figure also seen last night vanished. Shrugging, she went back across the foyer into the staff lounge, putting her feet up and closing her eyes until the bell signalled her next lecture.

OSGODBY PACED FROM DESK to window, interlocked his fingers and palms down pushed against the joints. He fidgeted. The police yard was devoid of activity. Parked cars and parked vans neatly lined up and nothing happening. It would though. Give Morrissey fifteen minutes downstairs to organise things and there'd be all hell let loose—men pulled off other duties and nothing but complaints coming back upstairs. 'You know what I'd appreciate, John?' he said without turning. 'Six months without a psychotic killer running round loose. Think it'll ever happen?' He came back to the desk, putting a hand up and shaking his head. 'Don't bother answering that one. Say yes and I won't believe it—say no and it's too bloody depressing.' Fiddling with his fountain pen, lining it up neatly against the blotter. 'It's a drug addict's playground down there, John, you've said it yourself. Why are we looking further afield?'

Instinct, thought Morrissey, Yorkshire nous, and then had to find a way to clothe that in words that would satisfy Osgodby's need for solidity of evidence, never an easy task, but managed ultimately by him taking Osgodby back over the crime scene, pointing out the careful destruction of Duffy's clothing, the precise accuracy of two knife sweeps that had done what they were intended to do and no more. Ending,

'Too neat for an opportunist. Whoever did it knew what he was up to, he went out looking to do a job and he did it— that's my own opinion. Warmsby or Forensic might turn up something to knock that idea on its head, but until then in my book it's a planned killing, and most likely any itinerant who'd gone down there to sleep would have done just as well as Duffy. The killer picked his place and he picked his time. And from what I saw—he enjoyed what he did.'

Osgodby stared down at nothing in particular. Who'd be chief superintendent pinned behind a desk, taking all the flak? Uncharacteristically wanting to get in some hands on satisfaction again, and resenting the fact that his strength had always been in administration.

He said gruffly and begrudgingly, 'I'll authorise extra men and hope that you're wrong.'

'Wouldn't be the first time,' said Morrissey. 'Nobody's perfect.' Osgodby watched him walk out the door, cracked his knuckles, and thought about the Sheehy report. If its recommendations got nodded through it'd be the end of chief inspectors. And Morrissey wouldn't want a desk job, so what then? Always the same old story—find a system that works and mess it up. Chewing on the bloody-mindedness of bureaucracy, he picked up the phone and started doing the job he was good at instead of the job he liked.

FOUR

THE SALVATION ARMY citadel stood on the corner of Zenner Street, the Conservative Club behind it and the Saracen's Head facing from the opposite corner. It wasn't a comfortable arrangement, but the citadel had stood for fifty years while the pub had been there for only three. Saturday nights were noisy and the hostel guests were thirsty. Sometimes they strayed. Two weeks ago Devil Danny, as he liked to call himself, had staggered back to the hostel with a split lip and a black eye. It wasn't the first time one of the hostel guests had got a thumping instead of a pint, and Captain George knew it wouldn't be the last, but that didn't stop him speaking sternly to the landlord, who told him brusquely to lock the silly sods in because *he* couldn't be expected to nanny the old beggars if they got out. Then the bit of him that had once attended Methodist Sunday school and still had a superstitious bent left in it, sent to the kitchen for a catering-sized tin of baked beans as a peace offering.

Captain George bore it back across the road with gratitude and handed it to Sister Mary. 'The Lord can bring forth goodness even out of iniquity,' he said. Sister Mary wasn't too sure. She strove hard to be a good soul and follow the right path but the truth was she couldn't stand the sight, sound, or smell of the majority of vagrants who dropped in for warmth and free soup, and that surely couldn't be right in a Christian woman.

When PC Sparrow came into the citadel the day Duffy died and asked if the old man had been known there, Sister Mary couldn't block out a small joy that the evil-smelling old man would cause her no more trouble. On her way to fetch Captain George the enormity of her sinful thought grew heavy in her mind, and by the time she reached his office with the news, she was crying. That Captain George took the tears as a sign of her tender heart only added to the guilt. Patting her hand gently he led the way back to where Sparrow waited with his list of questions, and told him Duffy was very well known at the citadel, and that had he turned up on the doorstep last night he would have been taken in like any other troubled soul. But to the question of grudges and enemies he could only shake his head. Mary knew better. Nobody liked Duffy. He wet himself. He spat. Worst of all he had fleas. The tops of her arms began to itch. She scratched her shoulder delicately and stayed silent. Big, bony and plain, mousy-haired and large bosomed, it was hard to guess from looking at her that passion wasn't yet—quite—spent.

Standing in the background she listened to the list of questions, nodding in agreement with everything Captain George said, her eyes when they were on him soft as a spaniel's, and when the questions came to an end she offered Sparrow hot Bovril in a crazed white mug. Looking through the window at thick icicles pendant from the overhang, the PC accepted gratefully, loosening his greatcoat and leaning on the radiator while he added a little warmth to his innards.

MOST OF THE PROPERTIES in the Mill House area were empty and waiting for demolition, so house to house inquiries were both quick and fruitless. But on the far side of the cutting where the gas works throbbed all night Ian Copeland was luckier. One of the guard dogs had raised a rumpus around six-thirty in the evening, and the handler had gone to see what bothered him. By the time he got there the second dog had joined in. 'Wasn't anything,' the security man said. 'Not that time. Just an old wino out of sight in the arch. Nice big fire there to keep him warm. Quite envied him.'

Copeland, busy scribbling it down, said, 'Not that time, you said. What did you mean by that exactly?'

'I mean just after seven they started up again. You know. Barking. Both of them at it, so I have to have another look. The fire's died right down—only while I'm standing there the wind comes and chucks on a bit of rubbish. Blazes up like a pyre again. Must have put on a drop of meths or something.'

'Sure it was the wino?' said Copeland.

'Who else would it be?'

'What kind of rubbish? Wood? Tyre…?'

'Looked more like rags—hanging down, you know, when he put it on.'

'This he—you didn't see what he looked like?'

'Too dark.'

'You say the fire blazed up—couldn't you see him then?'

'The flames were between him an' me. I saw him a bit later though, he mustn't have had anything else to put on the fire because it was near enough to out again. I'd been doing a perimeter check, you know, with the dogs, and when I got back he was legging it towards Mill Hill. Can't blame him; it'd be bloody cold down there without a fire.'

'What was he?' asked Copeland. 'Tall, short, fat, thin?'

'Now you're asking something, aren't you? How'd you expect me to see that in the dark?'

'Not that dark,' Copeland pressed. 'Bright moonlight, white frost. Should have shown the size of him clearly enough.'

'I don't know. Average. Five-ten maybe. Looked like he had a balaclava on.'

'That's it?' Copeland said. 'You can't remember anything else?'

'Dogs probably would—given you can talk Doberman. What's it all about anyway? All the tape and stuff. Don't tell me he sneaked back and got froze to death?'

'Something like that. You've no idea what started the dogs barking?'

'Breaking glass I should think, first time. Second time…' He shifted his weight, folded his arms. 'Another dog, that's what I think it was. Or a fox—I've seen them about. Make a lot of noise sometimes. Screaming—you know?'

Copeland didn't. He'd never seen a fox, let alone heard one. 'A scream?'

'Cross between that and a howl. That's what started 'em off. Dog or fox, take your pick.'

'Thanks,' said Copeland, thinking of a third alternative and not liking it. He closed his notebook, putting it in his pocket and wondering if he looked as bad as he felt. 'I might need to talk to you again.'

'Anytime. Going to tell me what happened or do I have to wait for the evening paper?'

'It'll have to be the evening paper,' said Copeland, and left him to wonder.

DETECTIVE SERGEANT Neil Barrett, dapper with his neat moustache and a liking for three-piece suits, was busy brooding on a possible synchronicity of events. 'It's a funny thing,' he said. 'I mean, I don't see Duffy around for—must be a month, then all this week I'm practically falling over him. Has to have been a message in it.' He caught Morrissey's eye. 'What I'm saying is, if I had a superstitious mind that's what I'd think.'

'But you're not superstitious, are you?' said Morrissey. 'Pragmatist. Did you see him yesterday?'

'You could say that,' Barrett looking embarrassed. 'I almost ran him down behind the market. Walked straight in front of me without looking. I don't know what it did for his pulse rate but it got mine climbing up nicely.'

'Which way was he heading?'

'Down Zenner Street, probably heading for the Sally Ann's and a warm. I felt like dropping in for hot soup myself. Did you know I had a great aunt used to play a tambourine—bonnet and all.'

Morrissey studied the detective sergeant. For Barrett to be that forthcoming was unusual. There were other small changes too; more evidence that he was loosening up a bit. Something must be going right for him somewhere. Fixing him with an inquisitive eye, Morrissey said, 'Love life going well?'

'Hadn't really thought about it, sir.' Reaching to lift a telephone that for once had begun to ring at the right moment he listened to the fast-talking voice; interrupting just once to ask, 'Think he's a nutter?' and making little notes.

Hanging up he turned to Morrissey. 'They've got a Paul

Hanson downstairs, student at Brindley College. Apparently his girlfriend's gone missing.' He squinted down at his scratchpad. 'Liz Pardoe, twenty. Had a late tutorial, called in for a takeaway, and vanished. Says he's not budging until he talks to somebody from CID.'

'When was this?'

'Last night.' He hesitated. 'Not the official twenty-four hours yet but even so...'

'Even so young women don't usually disappear after late tutorials. Is that what you're getting at?' Thinking of his daughter Katie when he said that, knowing what would be in his own mind if he were facing the same situation, then clamping down on that train of thought because it was a road he'd already had to tread. 'No note? No telephone call?' Barrett shook his head. 'See what you think then, Neil.' Looking up and stubbing a finger at the ceiling. 'He'll go spare if it means asking for even more men.'

'Tough.'

Barrett tugged anxiously at the corners of his waistcoat, considering the diplomacy of having said that. The chief inspector's eyes noted the familiar movement of hands. That at least hadn't changed. Wondering whether that was good or bad as he went back to sifting through the paperwork on his desk, chafing because he would rather be out and doing instead of sitting like a spider in the middle of a web, joining up all the threads. Half the day gone already and he seemed to have accomplished nothing at all. He pulled out Duffy's custody record and looked at it again. Seventy-two years old and no known family. Picked up regularly for being drunk and making a nuisance of himself and given the usual treatment. Bang him in a cell for the night to sleep it off, feed him breakfast, and turn him loose until next time. Wondering darkly what malign fate had brought Duffy and a maniac to Malminster at the same time, he shoved up from the desk and went in search of food.

PAUL HANSON HAD BEEN put into the visitors' room—less formal than a stark interview room, but not exactly relaxing, even if he'd had the ability to do that. When Barrett came in the door he launched into his story without waiting to be asked. Rushing through it, then reiterating again and again that something terrible had happened, his panic communicating itself and almost infecting Barrett. 'She was wearing my cardigan,' he said. 'You know? She didn't take a coat, just that cardigan. To keep her safe, that's what she said. But it didn't, did it?' He looked ready to weep. 'She said... Oh God!... She said wearing it was like having my arms around her.' He put his head back and looked at the ceiling. Barrett watched Paul's Adam's apple move jerkily up and down and revised his intention simply to put the details on file and do nothing until the next day. The trouble was, if a child had gone missing it would be different—adults had a habit of walking off in a huff and coming back when they'd got over it.

But this?

There'd been no quarrel. Or at least—that's what Hanson said, and either way he knew he couldn't just leave it, questions needed to be asked. Then Hanson told him about Adrian Fletcher and that piece of information finally made Barrett's mind up. He'd heard about randy tutors before, the things they got up to—hadn't there been one in the *Sun* only a couple of months back? Handing out A-plusses for a quickie on his couch.

Dirty old sod.

Leaving Paul with a cup of machine tea and the promise of action, he went in search of Morrissey. It wasn't *his* fault if Osgodby hit the roof; finding extra men wasn't Barrett's problem. Let somebody else get the ulcers.

FIVE

BARRETT AND DC WOODS—and Woods with his red hair and attitude problem as cocky as ever, nothing to learn or at least not admitting it—and six uniformed PCs filched from other duties. Enough, Osgodby had said, to hunt around Brindley College for a girl who might have just gone AWOL. Barrett didn't agree. The massive four-storey building with built-on annexes and hotchpotch of outbuildings, the sprawling college grounds—including woodland—were all to search and only two and a half hours of daylight left to do it in. What did the chief super think they were, for God's sake? Equipped with infra-red night vision? Or like bats with sonic radar? If they couldn't have lights they'd need to be one or the other to make a good job of it.

Even so they made quite a splash; two squad cars and Barrett's Escort, smartly up the frosty drive to the college entrance, and Barrett unable to resist a flashy stop, back-end swinging on the ice.

To Paul's mind, standing outside the college entrance with Barrett and Woods made things seem suddenly worse, and the police presence clothed his fears with a covering of reality. Momentarily he wanted to cry a halt. Push the two men back in the car and send them away. If he did that, closed his mind, he could pretend Liz was all right. Be just like the rest of them, staff and students alike, steadfastly refusing to see what they didn't want to see. Instead he took them up to the first floor, leading them down the lino-covered corridor to the college principal's office. Three pairs of feet echoing in a measured tread until Barrett knocked hard enough on the door to put the echoes to shame.

ROSEMARY'S AFTERNOON was free. No lectures to give, no tutorials to take. And nothing to do. *Damn* the weather! Turning from the window, looking back into the room, the small college apartment seemed claustrophobic, something to escape from. That in itself was unusual, normally its very cosiness made it a welcome retreat from the pressures of college life, but today it was somewhere she didn't want to be. Staring out through the window again she rested her palms on the sill, wondering whether to take herself and her small Renault to Malminster's glassed-in shopping centre, where there was perpetual warmth. Not that there was anything she wanted to buy, it would be a window-gazing outing pure and simple, and when she tired of that particular occupation she would ride the glass and chrome escalators like the jobless teenagers.

And maybe stop at Millington's Patisserie for a cream cake.

While she thought about that, Adrian Fletcher walked from the college building to the lake path, bundled up to the ears in his dark blue Melton. Rosemary watched him enter the shrubbery and wondered where he was going. The bus shelter on the main road? Having to offer him a lift was a thought she couldn't live with—best then to take the car out the back way so she wouldn't have to. Being alone in a car with Adrian was something she would rather avoid.

Shrugging into a thick quilted jacket and zipping it up, she wondered what exactly had gone on between him and Liz Pardoe during that last tutorial. Of course he swore he'd been the soul of kindness, nothing on his part that could have been misinterpreted in any way, but for a girl like Liz to duck out like that there had to have been something.

Hadn't there?

Unless Paul Hanson was right and some even more terrible thing had happened to her.

If it had…

If it had, she thought, it wouldn't be Adrian. The most aggressive thing about *him* was his cock.

DESMOND EDWARD WILSON, unaffectionately known as Dewdrop, saw staff and students strictly by appointment. His lecture list was light—two one-hour stints each week—and kept that way so that he might deal with such complicated administrative problems as perfecting his putting. Barrett's knock threw him off his stroke. Even to his disaffected ear it signalled trouble. The bad-tempered 'Wait!' bellowed in reply was calculated to be off-putting enough to give him time to roll up the strip of green baize and stow it out of sight. For once the ploy failed. Barrett had no wish to wait.

Putter and ball in one hand, green practice strip in the other, Wilson looked caught out, and Woods grinned with a perverse joy. To his mind there wasn't much difference between a college principal and a headmaster, and he'd spent a lot of time cooling his heels outside a very similar door.

'Out! Out!' Advancing on them, sweeping with his arms, catching sight of Paul standing in the corridor and glowering even more. 'Out of my office. If you need to see me, make an appointment.' Another sweeping motion. 'Out!'

Barrett held up his warrant card, arm extended towards Wilson's face. 'Detective Sergeant Barrett, sir, and this is Detective Constable Woods. We shan't take too much of your time but we need to talk now.' His eyes drifted to the principal's hands. 'If you're not too busy?'

Wilson got rid of the putting kit, motioning them in, shutting the door in Paul's face, snapping. 'With Hanson loitering I can guess what it's about—Liz Pardoe. Right?' He moved behind the desk and eyed them. 'Lovers' quarrel—we've all had them.' Woods's eyebrows went up; some things were unimaginable. 'What's more to the point,' said Wilson, 'is that this young woman has taken herself walkabout before. Three days in her first year getting over bad exam results. A week tagged on to last year's spring bank holiday when *"The weather was too good to leave the beach."* Her words, not mine. Odd days in between when no one seems to have known where she was or what she was doing.' He settled his eyes on Barrett. 'There is nothing—and I repeat nothing—except Hanson's overwrought imagination to suggest this time is any different from the others.'

'Except that she seems to have left on a bitingly cold night wearing a cardigan but no coat, and carrying a bag full of books. That seems unlikely to me, sir. What do you think?'

'I think she is very probably staying in someone else's flat, and given time she'll come back. That's what I think.'

'Even so, sir, from a police point of view it would be better if we had a good search through the grounds. You wouldn't raise any objection to that?'

'A pointless waste of time. On top of which it is bound to disrupt college work. I suppose you want to go through the buildings too?'

'I think we'll just tackle the grounds first, sir, take advantage of the light. After that, well, we'll want to look through the rest of the place.' He leaned forward, fingertips on Wilson's desk. 'I would have thought, sir, given the circumstances, that it would be in the college's interests for us to do that?'

'If it stops Hanson making wild accusations it might be, but if it doesn't there'll be even more gossip, and that's something we can well do without.' His face became resigned. 'Do what you have to, I'll let the rest of the staff know what's happening.'

Barrett thought about that. Wilson running around like a headless chicken telling everybody to keep mum didn't seem a good option. He revised his ideas. 'I'll come with you, sir. If we make a start in the basement we can probably get right the way round before the search team finish outside. Best to do it that way then there'll only be the outbuildings to look at.'

'I thought you'd be outside directing the ground search, Sergeant?'

'DC Woods can manage that very nicely,' said Barrett. 'I don't know about you, sir, but to me it always seems best to kill two birds with one stone.'

'I'll go and get started on it then,' said Woods, shifting his feet and thinking it was just like Barrett to find a way to stay in the warm.

'Start out with the shrubbery and take Hanson. Get him to show you the short-cut path,' said Barrett. 'If anything happened to her, that's the most likely spot. Get back to me if you find anything.'

Big IF, thought Woods, doubting they'd turn up anything at all; from the way Wilson talked, they were on a right wild-goose chase. Some women needed a firm hand, and this Liz Pardoe sounded to be one of them, floating off just when she felt like it without a word to anyone. Waste of police time, that's the way it'd turn out, and frostbite with it. Walking back downstairs with Hanson to get the search started, and wondering at the same time whether to give him a homily on the sex war, he recognised Paul's obvious distress and changed his mind, thinking that maybe there might just be something in it after all.

FINNEY HAD GOT HIMSELF together and gone in to work late, feeding his card into the time clock thinking it was only the second time he'd been tardy in thirty years. The first had been when his wife gave birth at home. Only him and the two boys there, both under five and him in his overalls ready to go to work. He hadn't known it could happen that fast and he'd been scared rigid. Managed though. A daughter to complement two sons and all over before the midwife came. Standing behind the lathe, looking at his hands, he remembered the warm slipperiness of soft white fat coating newborn skin. He'd fetched a clean towel to wrap her in—hadn't dared pick her up without in case she shot through his fingers.

Funny the way things worked out. Two black marks on his time card—one for a birth and one for a death. Starting the lathe turning knowing which he preferred, and feeling sick again as he remembered the other.

THE FOX WAS FORAGING again, padding over frozen ground, memory taking him back to the place where he had breakfasted, skirting warily as he picked up the scent of humans. Trotting head down, brush down, belly low, sharp-eyed behind the density of a thorn bush as the empty box was found, the place marked.

'Don't know if it's hers,' said Woods. 'Wouldn't expect it to be empty—not if she'd been attacked. Hardly likely to share a pizza with him, was she?' Handling the container carefully just the same, patting his pockets for a bag big enough to put it in.

PC Crowther, country-boy at heart, squatted on his heels and had other ideas. 'Fox, I should think,' he said, pointing out tracks still etched in hard frost. 'Eat anything this weather—even junk food.'

Woods trod carefully. 'Could have been a dog.'

'Fox,' said Crowther.

'Don't know.'

Behind them, tired of inactivity, the fox left cover, picked a wide circle, and headed for the college dustbins.

BARRETT HAD GOT HALFWAY round the main building when Woods came looking for him, the pizza box, encased in plastic, in his hand. The place had turned out to have a maze of rooms, one running off another, so that Barrett couldn't remember where he'd been or not been. Even the cellars were labyrinthine in their extent. When Woods got there the detective sergeant was ready for a break. Wilson was less so. Left to wait six paces away he watched the two go into a huddle and tried unsuccessfully to overhear—knowing as soon as Barrett turned back to him that things were not going to be as simple as he'd expected.

Damn and blast the stupid girl, why couldn't she have said where she was going?

Believing even then that it was just another of her escapades he made light of Woods's find, pointing out that college students were not known for tidiness of habit; that the box could have been discarded by any one of them. Barrett agreed with him politely, said he'd like to go round the rest of the building later if that was convenient, and went off to see what Woods had come upon for himself. By the time he got there Crowther had found broken branches on some of the rhododendrons, scuff marks between them, and a place where there might have been a struggle. Squatting again the PC pointed to the blue fibres on a low and jagged twig. Faced with that Barrett radioed for a photographer and help from the SOCOs, sealed both ends of the short-cut, and settled down to freeze and wait, inordinately glad that he'd told Woods to send Hanson on his way as soon as the path had been pointed out.

The least useful thing he could think of having right then was a frightened lover blundering around calling for his mate.

BEHIND THE KITCHEN the fox knocked over the first dustbin, rooted inside, and came away with a chicken carcass, meat still clinging to rib-cage and back. Carrying it to his den, moving again at a fast lope, he heard a vixen bark beyond the high brick wall. Urged by a more basic instinct than feeding he dropped the chicken remains and answered, then stood, tongue lolling, waiting for a reply.

When there was nothing but silence he retrieved the carcass and feasted alone.

Over in Pel's Copse, on the far side of the fallow field, the vixen waited, biding her time. Later, when the urge to mate grew stronger, she would call again.

SIX

MORRISSEY LOATHED paperwork; hated sitting at his desk like an overtrained collator waiting for bits of paper to come in. It had always been the same; lack of activity irked him, by choice he would be out with the rest of them, asking questions instead of analysing answers. And he hated this kind of case more than any other. There was nothing to get a grip on. No witnesses, no weapon, no apparent motive except a liking for blood. Fidgeting in his chair, he played with possibilities. Make it simple. Another dosser. Burned his own clothes and stole Duffy's.

And why would he do that? Because they were better? Cleaner? Warmer?

He rocked back and heard the chair creak. Plenty of vagrants to choose from but he didn't think any of them would resort to a knife, or at least, not to use in a blood-letting done as ritualistically as slaughtering a beast. Wrong method altogether. An empty bottle and a smashed skull—that would be a dosser's way, besides which from what he'd seen none of them would be better off in Duffy's rags.

An addict then? A shooter on a bad trip? That was unlikely too. That bad a trip and he'd still have been there, climbing walls, gibbering in a corner. Straws, thought Morrissey, just straws; this was a different kind of mind with a lick of madness at the edge. Out of his chair and pacing restlessly, he looked down at the near-empty police yard, feeling a momentary empathy with Osgodby as he watched Copeland's car swing between the gate posts and park. Trying to read the DC's face he thought he saw satisfaction. Not an entirely wasted trip then? He felt his spirits rise at the thought then hoped briefly that the same wasn't true of Barrett's visit to

Brindley, because a second murder hunt could stretch them to the limit.

IT WASN'T UNUSUAL for visitors to peer into lecture and seminar rooms at Brindley, and Barrett's brief inspection had been for the most part unremarked. Wilson changed that. Quivering inside with annoyance that his afternoon had been interrupted, and intent on cutting short any police investigation, Wilson—once Barrett was out of the way—sent a porter to interrupt classes and summon staff to a meeting, telling himself that if they all stuck with the same story a lot of fuss and bother might be averted. A half-hour later, crammed into his office and listening to what he had to say, the majority agreed with him. Two did not. One was Holly Havers, the other Philip Jacques, both from Humanities, but with different reasons for not accepting that Liz had just dropped out of college for a while. Holly, closer to Liz's age than any other member of staff, had been her occasional confidante, and knew that leaving Paul had been the last thing on the girl's mind. Philip, having seen Liz leave the cafeteria carrying a pizza that night, saw no sense in supposing her intention had been to do anything but head straight home. The separation of two goats from the sheep was unwelcome.

'Which home?' demanded Wilson. 'The place she's renting or back to her family? Did she specify that? Did you ask?'

'Oh come off it! I didn't need to. Offer me one good reason why Liz Pardoe, or anybody else in their right mind, would take off at nine-thirty on a cold winter's night with nothing but a bag of books, a pizza, and no change of clothes? Think about it—it's totally illogical,' Jacques said.

'I don't need to think about it,' Wilson snapped. 'The worst possible scenario for the college would be a pointless police investigation, classes disrupted and staff and students inconvenienced, while they fruitlessly search for a student who makes a habit of taking time off when she feels like it. Better by far to stay together on this, the last thing we want is a lot of fuss.'

Someone muttered, 'Too right, not after last term,' and near the back another voice said, 'Adrian's not here.'

Wilson did a fast check and said, 'Neither is Rosemary. Anybody know where they are?' A whispered comment brought an answering snigger. Wilson's face darkened. 'Can we agree then? We all give the same answer to police questions—Miss Pardoe has done this before and we see no cause for concern.'

'No,' said Jacques. 'We can't agree, I'm not going along with it. Sorry, but that's how it is. We none of us know what happened and quite frankly, I'm worried.'

'And I can't go along with it either,' Holly chipped in firmly. 'I knew Liz well and I know she wasn't planning to drop out.'

Wilson set a cold eye on her. Perhaps this was the time to remind her she was at Brindley on a trial basis, and that such contracts were not renewed automatically. Yes. That would be the right approach, but later and without witnesses. He said frigidly, 'If the rest of us stay together two dissenters won't carry any weight.'

Alan Salter, working with Jacques on a psycho-sociological survey and between times lecturing in psychology, said succinctly, 'Sometimes the good of the whole isn't necessarily better than the good of the individual when it comes to conscience. Holly and Philip have the interests of the college in mind as much as anyone else—it might be as well to remember that.' If the comment had been meant to advise Wilson ignored it.

He said, 'Are we agreed?' More hands went up than stayed down and he looked satisfied. Everybody filed out, Holly and Philip leaving last. Walking down the corridor Philip said it might be interesting to try the new Italian place in Malminster. Holly admitted that she liked Italian food. He suggested diffidently that they might go there together and said tonight would be as good a time as any.

Holly agreed.

BARRETT TOLD the photographer and SOCOs exactly what he wanted, left Woods to oversee what was left of the search, and drove back into Malminster to bring Morrissey up to date, wondering if he'd moved too quickly, jumped to conclusions on too flimsy evidence. Having got his inspector's exam the last thing he wanted was a major mistake—not when he was looking for promotion. No point staying a detective sergeant. Putting on his car lights in the growing dusk he knew there'd not be much more useful work done at Brindley that day; come first light they'd have to start again.

If Osgodby would wear it, that was. The chief superintendent was already complaining about overspend.

Suddenly morose because he could be told to drop the whole thing, he turned into the yard and parked, trying to remember the time of the post-mortem, glad it had been Copeland on call and not him. From what he'd heard this was one autopsy he'd be glad to miss. Going in through the back door, still feeling half-frozen, he thought about grabbing a quick warm in the canteen, then gave up on the idea and took the stairs fast to get a bit of warmth going that way instead, breathing hard when he poked his head round the door and saw Morrissey sitting in the black leather chair.

All his old nervousness reasserted itself. Smoothing his moustache, pulling down his waistcoat he positioned himself in front of the chief inspector's desk a little right of centre.

Morrissey wondered what had ruffled Barrett's confidence, and speculated on that as he asked kindly, 'Problems? Or come back to tell me it's a false alarm?' Hoping for the second but guessing it was more likely to be the first.

Trying to make himself relax stiffened Barrett's back even more. He started out cautiously, watching for Morrissey's reaction. 'I don't think it's a false alarm, sir,' he said, 'although the college principal wants me to believe the opposite. It seems likely the girl took a short-cut home through the shrubbery, it's a dark little path, no lights, and if she screamed nobody would hear her. Silly for her to use it at night, but I doubt she'd expect anything to happen to her on college property. We found a pizza box there, same kind she'd bought in the refectory. Empty when we found it but that doesn't mean any-thing—looks like a fox could have had it.'

A fox? Morrissey's eyebrows went up. He wondered where Barrett had gained such esoteric knowledge. Sensing the doubt Barrett said, 'PC Crowther pointed the tracks out, sir; seems he was raised on a farm so he knows what to look for.'

'Anything else?'

'Broken branches on rhododendrons and a place where there could have been a scuffle, blue fibres that look like wool snagged on one of the bushes, and according to Hanson she was wearing a blue cardigan when she went out.'

'Taken any action?' said Morrissey.

'I got the SOCOs out—probably I should have checked but the ground's covered in hard frost out there and everything shows up nicely. If I'd waited, and there'd been a ground thaw, we'd have lost the lot.'

'It was good thinking, Neil. What next?'

Barrett relaxed, feeling like a fish let off the hook. 'We need to do a proper search with a few more than six men. The grounds are pretty extensive and there's staff and students to question.'

'Unless she turns up alive and well.'

'I hope it happens, sir, but I don't think it will.'

Not too much of a change in Barrett after all. Still cocky when he thought he could get away with it. 'I suppose you want me to go upstairs and ask for the manpower?' Morrissey said mildly. He got up and came round the desk. 'Don't worry, Neil, I'll sort something out. Better get back to Brindley and see how they're getting on without you.'

By now, thought Barrett, they'd all be frozen statues and he had to go back and join them. He took his time going downstairs, hearing Morrissey behind him going two at a time up to Osgodby's office to break the bad news.

NOT EVEN A DETTOL-SOAKED mask could hide the smell. Ian Copeland kept his eyes on the clock and refused to look down, hearing the heavy squelch of something unspeakable dropping into a stainless steel bowl and reflecting that regulations de-

manded only that he be there, not that he look. Warmsby
wielded the scalpel and grunted, searched the bowl's contents
and shook his head. 'I can't be hard and fast about time of
death,' he said. 'Whatever I say it won't be much more than
guesswork and there's nothing in the stomach but brown fluid.
If he'd had any food at all that day it had already been di-
gested.' He closed the gaping rib-cage and glanced up at Morrissey. 'Not being very helpful this time, am I? Sometime between 6 p.m. yesterday and 6 a.m. today, with a faint
possibility of Forensic coming up with something clearer after
a fluid analysis. Shouldn't think it'll help much either way.
And as to a weapon—one of these or something very like it.'
Picking up a wickedly curved postmortem knife and waving
it around. 'A single sweeping cut beginning below the left ear
and extending to the right, severing trachea, oesophagus and
carotids.' Squinting over his glasses at Morrissey. 'Probably
made by a right-handed man, but that won't help much either
given that the majority of the population are born dexter.'
Rinsing his hands and darkening the water. 'Official cause of
death, haemorrhage and shock—but you knew that all along.
Both cuts made almost simultaneously with the throat probably a *coup de grâce*.' Copeland flinched. *A cross between a
scream and a howl.* Warmsby's eyebrows lifted and he moved
away from the table, pulling off the plastic apron, peeling out
of gloves and gown. 'You can stop clock watching now, detective constable,' he said. 'It's over.'

Copeland let his eyes fall. Getting out and breathing fresh
air the only thought on his mind he trailed after Morrissey and
the pathologist, forgetting to take off the mask until they were
out of the heavy rubber doors and then discarding it with relief.

Watching Warmsby and Morrissey downing coffee in the
pathologist's office and cradling his own, he fought back nau-
sea and hoped he wouldn't disgrace himself.

SEVEN

THE GRITTERS WERE STILL working overtime trying to keep the roads free from ice. There was one a hundred yards ahead of Rosemary as she returned to Brindley, the salt and sand scattered from the back of it crunching under the Renault's tyres. As she turned off the main road and drove with more caution to the back entrance, she wondered what obstacle kept the college from investing in an automated sand-spreader. Better that than having the groundsman labour up and down both back drive and front with wheelbarrow and shovel. Debating with herself as she parked whether to blame it on cut-backs in the council budget or a lack of effort on Wilson's part, she knew both options were equally likely. Penny-pinching. Cutting corners. Intensely angered when she stepped out of the covered bay into darkness to find the two waist-high lamp standards which should have illuminated the path were both out of action, she trod blindly but firmly towards the back entrance, coat collar up around her ears to block the east wind.

Behind her an engine coughed and turned over twice before it caught. Reversing lights shone whitely but briefly with no other lights visible until the car turned out of the drive gates.

Someone cherishing his battery or someone not wanting to be seen?

Fingers on the metal door handle Rosemary hesitated. Stupid to walk back again through the darkness just to see whose parking place was empty. Better to be inside, in the warmth. Releasing the catch and pushing hard against the spring she went into the college, running up the stairs to her small apartment, still unaware when she got there that anything out of the ordinary had happened while she had been away.

WHEN MORRISSEY LEFT the mortuary he didn't go back to the office—whatever new information might have landed on his

desk could wait until tomorrow. He was quite sure that if anything urgent had turned up he wouldn't be left in ignorance
for long. Home in time for supper—happy thought, sniffing
appreciatively as he let himself into the hall and called out a
general hello. Margaret and Katie answering from the kitchen,
Mike, his son, less quickly from upstairs. Poking his head
round the kitchen door, finding there were still twenty minutes
to go before they ate and deciding to have a hot shower; he
suited thought to action, galloping up the stairs, taking off his
jacket as he went.

Mike's door stood open.

Morrissey slowed down when he saw that, because it was
usually closed against all comers and especially him. An invitation or an oversight? Tapping and walking in, seeing his
son at the desk, head bent and shoulders curved in concentration, it was easy for once to put the past year's upsets to one
side and set a hand on Mike's shoulder.

'Tough homework?'

'Not really, it's social policy stuff. Doesn't matter what I
put when there aren't any fixed answers.' Looking up at his
father. 'I'd rather have maths.'

'Analytic mind,' Morrissey said, bemused his grip on
Mike's shoulder hadn't been shaken off. 'Stand you in good
stead one day. Matches still cancelled?'

'Yeah, it's like playing on concrete.' Mike shifted, not quite
a rebuff but the hand on his shoulder removed itself. 'Hen-
derson rang the met. this morning, wanting to know when it'd
thaw. He's going absolutely spare. Says he can't fit in all the
missed matches before term end without fouling up the cur-
riculum.'

'Hard life,' said Morrissey. 'You'll not want to be a sports
master then?'

'Shouldn't think so. Train driver maybe.' Grinning just a
little, unsure how his father would take the tease. The truce—
of sorts—between them had held for almost three months with
both expecting the other to break it. Overtures like this had
been few.

'Whatever you want,' said Morrissey, 'as long as you stay away from coppering.' Awkwardness returned. Morrissey's job had started up the friction in the first place and both of them knew it.

Mike turned back to his homework. The chief inspector's hand hovered but this time didn't descend. A shower then. He withdrew but left his son's door open a few inviting inches.

It was a start.

THE MOTORWAYS WERE FREE of ice and that was a help.

He made the journey to Sheffield in under forty-five minutes, left his car in the Pay and Park behind the Crucible and walked down the hill to the tarty splendour of the Plantagenet Arms. The bar was pinkly plush, with hot-pink buttoned and pleated Chesterfields picking up the vibrancy of peony-scattered curtains. It wasn't to his taste, Chesterfields picking up echoes from peony-scattered curtains, but neither was it his first visit and he eyed the goods on offer with the discernment of an experienced shopper. If he'd gone down the Moor he'd have got better value, but value wasn't the thing he was looking for tonight. What he was looking for was a voice. A particular kind of voice. The trouble was—as he'd found out once before from a stickily close encounter with a tetchy husband—it was easy to make mistakes. None of the women looked like they were selling pussy but a lot of them were.

Easing onto a bar stool he asked for a Screwdriver, tipping generously and eyeing up a brunette in black at the end of the bar. A couple of minutes later the brunette changed stools.

He bought her a Manhattan but the voice wasn't right, and when he didn't want to do business she drifted away. Ten minutes later he saw her cosying in a corner. Five minutes after that she left with her prize.

It took five more abortively expensive drinks before his ear picked up the right sound, and when he heard the clear but slightly husky voice, vowels open instead of flat, he asked how much and didn't haggle over price.

Sitting with her in a corner of the room, sunk in pink velvet, he told her what he wanted.

ROSEMARY WAS LYING BACK in the bath with a candle burning gently at each corner, a glass of wine in her hand and a part-bottle resting on the closed lid of the loo. White wine, not red, because more often than not red would trigger a migraine, and that was not something to be sought after. The water lapped gently just below her armpits, her nipple showing through the scented foam like floating pink cherries. She touched them lightly, startling them erect, filled with vague regret that their prime purpose would never be fulfilled. Draining the wine then filling up the glass again.

To hell with Robert.

She set the glass down by the bottle and climbed out of the water to eye herself in the darkling mirror, moving her hands down across her rounded belly, smoothing them back over her hip bones, telling herself there was still time for her to get pregnant as she turned sideways and stuck her hips forward, tracing an imaginary outline with linked fingers.

Did every childless woman feel this broody when the clock neared a biological midnight? Rosemary turned again, still eyeing herself. Her body wasn't unattractive, a one-night stand with a suitable male—or a succession if that's what it took— would be easy to contrive.

Robert...

Depressed again she got back into the water, emptying the glass in long sips and reaching for the bottle again.

The telephone rang.

She counted the rings... 'four, five, six...' Silence. A second later it began again. This time she left the bath, pushed her arms through the sleeves of a pink towelling robe, and went into her living room. It was Robert. Mumbling about being worried and was she all right? A conscience call.

'Fine. I'm fine, Robert. Just fine.' Hearing a slight slurring as she said it, and looking at the wineglass she'd carried through with her. Four? Five? Tossing it back and setting the glass down with exaggerated care. 'I didn't expect you to call,

I was in the bath. Can you smell the *Amirge?* What does *she* wear, Robert? The new girl? *Poison?*'

Rosemary listened to him clumsily saying he was still fond of her. She shook the receiver in the air, began to slam it down, then thought better of it.

'What do you want me to do, Robert?' she said. 'Protest that I love you or give you absolution? Whichever it is, I shan't do it.' Pausing then to listen again. His voice trying to pour balm in her ear, talking about friendship and him being there for her if she needed him. Like hell he would! She needed him now, right here, in this room, but he wasn't there, was he? He was somewhere at the end of a telephone line with his lady-love probably listening in.

'Do for me?' she said fingering the empty glass. 'Yes, there's something you can do for me, Robert. Father me a child.' Listening then to silence stretch out along the telephone wires. She held the receiver away from her and looked at it, heard his voice come back faintly and caught the last of what he said. Told him, 'No. Robert, I'm not drunk,' and when he started to speak again put the receiver down on the little table and walked away from it.

Life was full of such small symbolisms.

EIGHT

THE VIXEN COMING INTO oestrus had called again. Three sharp barks and the wildly piercing banshee scream that made up her love-song; the sound music to the solitary dog-fox. His flat-throated staccato reply echoed across the frozen night.

This time the vixen answered.

The dog-fox, master of shadows, slipped like red moonlight over the collapsed stones of the west wall, sniffing for the markers of another male and leaving his own scent when he found none, walking the boundaries of the field that held Pel's Copse and making it his own, ranging further afield still as he extended his territory, yards turning into miles. Twice more while he shadowed the night the vixen called, and twice he answered back.

Before a grey dawn touched the sleeping ground the dog-fox stood among bare trees and smelled her perfume for the first time.

'YES. REASONABLE GROUNDS. I don't want to agree but I have to,' Osgodby had said—and then having been forced into admission sanctioned the men that Barrett needed. At first light they were crowding the drive at Brindley, with Barrett chafing that in early January that meant eight-fifteen. Lights were on in the college and early-bird students had already started snacking in the cafeteria, books spread out before them, pens speed-scratching assignments before deadline.

At eight-thirty, when the general office officially opened up for business, a strung-out line of blue-clad men were painstakingly searching the shrubbery, backs bent, fingers cold. At nine o'clock junior clerk Tessa Smith collected the night-line answerphone tape and began to play it back, typing a memo slip for each message. It was normally a boring job to which she listened with only part of her mind, the rest of it occupied with more personal things. That morning's tape promised to be no different from any other. She typed out two requests for information, sighed through three aborted calls with no message left, and wondered if a student ringing in sick really was. Then the boring routine changed. What made it different was a message from Liz Pardoe. Tessa transcribed it with some excitement. Speculation and rumour had all kinds of unpleasant things happening to the absent student, and suddenly she, Tessa, could finally put an end to it. Typing out two more messages and flinging off the headphones with a flourish, she announced loudly, 'There's a message from that missing student, Liz Pardoe, which means all that searching's been a right waste of time. I bet that boyfriend of hers'll feel a proper fool.'

Flouncing her head at questions and throwing a careless, 'Tell you later,' over her shoulder, she hip-swung her way upstairs to tap on the door of Wilson's office and give him the good news.

ROSEMARY DIDN'T KNOW the blue and white tape had been strung across the shrubbery path until she opened the curtains and saw it through the partly frosted window. After that she saw the blue police vans parked further up the drive, nearside wheels encroaching on the grass verge to leave more room for passing traffic. *When had it all happened?* Staring, puzzled, her mind automatically jumping to Liz Pardoe. Muffled in a heavy parka and knee-high boots she went out, hesitantly edging past the plastic tape, and the first policeman she saw was Barrett. Having missed yesterday's doctrinal staff meeting and with no restrictions on her freedom of speech, she answered the questions he asked, and by doing so unknowingly toppled Wilson's carefully planned solidarity of approach. Yes, she told Barrett, she had seen Liz the night she disappeared. Liz had arrived for a late tutorial with Adrian Fletcher just before Rosemary left for the theatre. Wearing? Creasing her forehead as she thought about it. A thick blue cardigan, a long black skirt and ankle boots. She peered past him through the bushes and asked questions of her own, the first one being did they know what had happened to Liz? Was that why they were there? Willing the answer to be no because the child had been so much in love. Telling that to Barrett when he stonewalled.

'We don't know where she is. A lovers' tiff perhaps,' said Barrett not believing it himself. 'Happens all the time at that age.' Feeling like an old man when he said it.

'I don't think so. No, I honestly don't believe that.' Shaking her head, she said, 'You don't believe it either or you wouldn't be doing all this.'

'We don't know where Elizabeth Pardoe is—but we're looking—that's all I can tell you,' said Barrett. Watching Rosemary turn away he thought of something else. 'Later,' he said. 'When you came back from the theatre...'

'I came back early,' she interrupted. 'After the second act.'

'Why was that?'

'A migraine.'

'Did you look out of the window again?' Barrett asked. 'You saw Liz coming, did you see anyone else that night? After the theatre.'

'I saw Paul. Running down the drive into the college, and I saw Adrian Fletcher, all bundled up in his dark blue Melton. There's a pub a hundred yards or so down the road that he frequently goes into for a nightcap. He was probably on his way back.'

'Did he use the shrubbery path?'

'Why, yes,' she said, staring at him. 'He did—and I have this vague memory of seeing someone else there too. But I'm not sure. It could have been diplopia. Double vision,' she explained apologetically when he frowned. 'I sometimes get it when I have a bad migraine. It's a bit like seeing a mirage, except that with diplopia the vision is inside my own head.'

Barrett said, 'Can't be nice. Still—if it turns out to be more than that and you remember anyone else, I'd be glad if you'd let me know.'

'Of course I will.' She folded her arms, shivering. 'I hope you don't find her in there,' Rosemary said staring again into the bushes. 'I remember thinking how vulnerable she was...how vulnerable all the female students are walking home alone after late tutorials. I've suggested so many times that they all be stopped.'

'Any special reason for that or just general concern?'

'General concern. Especially after hearing about the student rapes in Leeds—and most of those in broad daylight—it isn't the kind of thing you expect in the late afternoon.'

Barrett knew better. 'A bit silly perhaps, taking a short cut over Woodhouse Moor?'

'Why should it be?' demanded Rosemary. 'Why should it be silly for a woman and not for a man?' He couldn't answer that. He knew the reasons and so did she, but it still wasn't an answerable question. She said quietly, 'I suppose Liz would have been silly had she taken the shrubbery path home—silly in a man's eyes,' and began to walk away.

'A man has been arrested and charged with the Leeds rapes,' Barrett said. 'It isn't all bad news.'

She carried on walking and gave no sign that she had heard. The gulf in perception between men and women was as wide as it had ever been.

WILSON READ the transcribed message twice, then with an intrusive hand casually languishing on Tessa's right shoulder he walked with her back to the general office and heard the tape for himself. The feeling he had was not quite of elation but it came very close. Fuss over nothing and a waste of public money. Just as he'd pointed out yesterday. The foolish girl had walked out of her own accord and here was the physical proof—it would be a pleasure to see the nosy detective sergeant's face fall when he heard it for himself. Beaming around the office he told the expectant faces the crisis was over and the missing student safe.

At ten o'clock the porter sent to find Barrett spotted the detective sergeant staring thoughtfully at the ice-covered lake and relayed Wilson's message. A little after ten-thirty Barrett reluctantly called the police search off.

MORRISSEY'S DESK had rapidly acquired a thick sheaf of reports that he read through with increasing frustration. The last sightings of Duffy had been in the late afternoon—and a lot of people remembered seeing him then. But after that—nothing.

Two police officers exercising initiative had taken the most direct route from Duffy's last-observed stopping place on Churchgate, to the cobbled Mill Hill, knocking on doors as they went, hoping his passage might have been noted. It hadn't. House curtains had been drawn tight and business premises emptied before Duffy wove his unstraight path to the viaduct.

By mid-morning only Copeland's interview with the security guard and Sparrow's neatly recorded tit-bit from the citadel had managed to raise more than cursory interest. Such apparently motiveless murder was the most formidable to solve, and Morrissey knew from grim experience that the investigation could drag on for months and still give a negative result. He brooded at his desk, knowing that a negative result for Duffy would still be better than the alternative both he and Warmsby were afraid of. His hand hovered briefly over the telephone and withdrew. Wait and see what the investigation turned up first; time enough after that to talk to Reynolds about psychological profiles. On his feet and heading for the canteen he met Barrett coming upstairs with a face as long as his own, and a lot of wasted police man-hours needing to be explained to Osgodby.

'I suppose it was her voice?' Morrissey asked. 'Checked that, did you?'

Barrett bridled. Of course he'd checked it, what did Morrissey take him for? And he hadn't just accepted Wilson's word for it either. He'd had three tutors listen—separately—to the damn tape, with Wilson's sodding face getting smugger by the second. What more could he do, for God's sake? Tell 'em they were liars? He said most but not all of that to the chief inspector, shifting from foot to foot irritably.

'We've both had a wasted morning,' said Morrissey. 'Not your fault, Neil, you can't be telepathic.' Slapping him on the shoulder. 'Fancy a butty?' Starting to go downstairs again as he asked, then turning at the half-landing to see Barrett still indecisive. 'No point thinking about trailing upstairs, he's not in,' the chief inspector said. Relief reached Barrett's mind at the same time as the taste of a bacon butty touched his memory, and his feet turned him around without conscious command. Following Morrissey and catching up fast, he told himself that by rights he ought to tell Forensic not to bother with the Brindley stuff. *By rights.* Deciding then that with money wasted already a little bit more wouldn't hurt and it'd be interesting to see the results.

Only when he was sitting across from the chief inspector with his teeth biting into the juicy heat of bacon, did he stop to wonder what he would do if any of the results were positive.

NINE

BEMUSED AND ANGRY that police activity had come to an end so fast, it didn't enter Paul's head that the reason for it might be that Liz had reported herself alive and well. Instead his overtired mind latched onto the idea that Wilson had found some underhanded way of aborting the search. With that thought lodged at the front of his mind he was less than surprised to be called to the principal's office soon after the vans had gone. If Dewdrop's next move was to kick him out of college, he'd raise a right rumpus in the local paper—it'd go down well, the *Echo* liked raising temperatures.

Refused entry to Wilson's office when he got there and left to kick his heels in the corridor for ten minutes, his anger grew. Like being summoned before the head at school, he thought. Kept outside the study door until *Sir* thought you'd been softened up enough to take in what he said.

Legs stretched, ankles crossed, he sat on a chair and stared at a place where ceiling paper sagged. Coming apart at the seams. Like him.

When the imperative 'Come' snapped out from behind the woodwork Paul ignored it until it came again. A small measure of tit for tat that gave him perverse pleasure. When he did go in it was to find that Wilson had chosen to adopt a conciliatory line. Such attempted soothing tactics didn't help. Paul sat himself on the chair indicated and truculently crossed his arms, stiff-backed and edgy.

'It's time we cleared things up,' Wilson said with a thin smile. 'Something I expect you'd like too. Yes? This kind of rumour and innuendo unsettles the entire college. Now—Liz Pardoe. You share a house with her?'

Paul said sullenly, 'More than that.'

'Yes, so you told me—the kind of relationship that hurts if one or the other walks out. I can understand that...'

Could he? *Had the stringy bastard ever been that close to a woman?*

'...and when she returns to her studies I hope it can be sorted out amicably between you—really—you have my best wishes on that, but in the meantime I want an end to rootless insinuations against a certain member of the college staff.'

Bet he did.

'Liz called him Fletch the Lech,' Paul answered flatly. 'Everybody does. And she didn't walk out on me. She was carrying home a pizza, and somewhere between the refectory and the house she disappeared. And I'll keep on saying that until somebody sits up and takes notice.'

'Nothing happened to her. Elizabeth rang the college last night and left a message on the answerphone,' Wilson said, sifting through his in-basket with deliberate slowness before handing the typed memo to Paul. Unable to keep smugness out of his voice he added, 'As you can see the implication there is that you were part of the problem she wanted to get away from. If you'll take my advice you'll let her have some thinking time, and stop inventing gothic dramas where there are none.'

Having read the coldly typed words once, Paul's eyes slid back to the beginning and read them again. 'Is this it?' he demanded. 'Is this why the police left? You showed them this?'

'Naturally.' The starved smile back on his face. 'After that there was no reason for a search to continue, as I've been saying all along—a complete waste of time.'

Paul slammed the memo back on Wilson's desk, on his feet and leaning over it. 'I don't believe it's from Liz.'

'Sit down! Do you want to hear the tape? You're welcome to listen. I'm not the only one to authenticate it, the police insisted three people hear and comment.'

'But not me? Even though I know Liz's voice better than anybody?'

A shrug of Wilson's shoulders. 'This is the tape, do you want to hear it or not?'

Paul gave only one curt nod because he couldn't trust himself to speak. *It couldn't be Liz.* Keeping that at the front of his mind as the tape clicked into playback and a slightly husky voice filled his ears.

But it was so very like her.

'It isn't her.'

'Of course it is, man! Who else would it be?'

'From where I sit you're more likely to know the answer than I am,' Paul said getting to his feet. 'And if saying that gets me suspended—fine. I can't work. I can't sleep. Being chucked out won't make a hell of a lot of difference.' Turning on his heel without waiting for an answer and not bothering to close the door behind him. Let the smug bugger get off his arse and do it himself.

BARRETT, FRUSTRATED the Brindley business had come to nothing, and having had to play the penitent to Osgodby's long-suffering teeth sucking, had since been reading through the accumulating reports from Morrissey's desk. Like the chief inspector, he found nothing in them that might offer a lead. Copeland had got a probable sighting of the man they wanted from the security guard, but a description vague enough to fit any Tom, Dick or Harry with an overcoat wasn't going to help them any.

He said, 'Think he's right about the noise? Coming from a fox, I mean. Seems a bit unlikely unless it fancies empty glue cans. No other pickings down there.'

'Thought about the alternative?'

'Unpleasant but it'd pinpoint time of death,' Barrett said doggedly.

'Can't scream with your throat cut,' reminded Morrissey stony-faced. 'And that's a fact.' He watched Barrett take that on board and begin to hunt back through the papers for Warmsby's report. 'Two cuts inflicted almost simultaneously,' the chief inspector reminded. 'That's what he's put.' Barrett paused, he hadn't seen Duffy but he got an instant and unpleasant mind picture—then found it hard to clear the conjured image.

'Best stick with the fox, sir.'

'Any fresh ideas on approach then?' asked Morrissey. 'If it got dropped on your plate how would you handle it?'

'No different to the way you're handling it, sir,' Barrett said with new-found diplomacy. 'Trawl the dossers, find out if Duffy had a particular chum, and establish if it was his regular habit to sleep under the viaduct. It'd be useful to know if he was the only one did that—I mean we've been looking at it as being random but he might have been picked out special.'

'Personal grudge?'

'Or the weakest target.'

'Your idea we think about it being another dosser then?'

Not quite what he'd meant—not unless it was a dosser who was a raving psychopath, thought Barrett, and let political correctness fly out the window. Pussyfooting might suit trendy social workers but it didn't suit him. Two schizophrenics and a manic depressive sleeping rough in Malminster that he knew of and probably some he didn't. That's what happened when asylums got emptied. They'd be emptying jails next—cock-eyed government. Taking in a breath he communicated all that to Morrissey, glad to get it out of his system but waiting for an explosion that didn't come.

'Interesting ideas,' said the chief inspector. 'But I'll not ask which way you voted last time round. I wouldn't want to embarrass you.' Knowing full well where the detective sergeant's vote had gone, and knowing too that since it fitted in with Barrett's desired lifestyle he'd more than likely vote the same way again. True blue outside and red struggling to climb out. Morrissey himself apolitical, not seeing much difference between politicians of any ilk. 'You can check the vagrant side of it yourself, if you've nothing better to do,' he decided dourly. 'Find out what the uniforms are playing at; there's been three busy looking all morning and nothing back yet. See if Control can raise a squeak.' He finished there as another batch of papers came onto his desk, leafing through them quickly and shaking his head when he didn't find what he wanted.

Barrett went down the rubber-topped stairs at a trot; with Morrissey in that kind of mood it was best to move fast. Slow-ing down when he reached the bottom corridor, not knowing that as he pushed in through the control room doors Paul Hanson was asking for him at the front desk.

HOLLY'S THOUGHTS kept drifting back to the Italian restaurant. Funny how you could work with people and not really know what they were like. She'd quite fancied Philip Jacques in an absent-minded kind of way but she hadn't expected anything to come of it, and now—well, now, she didn't know what to think and it was hard to concentrate fully on what she was doing. She wondered if Philip was having the same problem. Probably not. For one thing he was five years older than her which meant he had to be a lot more experienced in... She stopped, acutely aware that she was standing with her back to a group of students and holding a piece of chalk aimlessly in her hand.

What was it she had been going to put up on the board?

Thomas Mann and the ideology of modernism, that was it, writing on the blackboard and finding her mind still drifting. *Would he ask her out again?* Conjuring up the text she was going to use then turning around and saying confidently, '*Lotte in Weimar.* How many have read the text?' Scanning the group she saw only three raised hands, and with a sense of relief did something totally uncharacteristic in gathering up her papers, saying she wouldn't take the seminar until the book had been read. There were shuffles and mumbles. 'Use the rest of the morning to get to grips with it,' she said blithely. 'And next time we have a new text to examine try to get conversant with it before it comes up for discussion. I'll post a new seminar time on the notice board tomorrow.' She sailed out and left them to feel sore. It would do them good. She'd been much too lenient and they took advantage of her. It was time to get tough.

Sitting with a cup of coffee in the staffroom, and going through the timetable, she heard about the telephone call from Liz Pardoe and wondered why she didn't believe it.

TEN

SITTING ACROSS the bare table from Barrett he could sense the other's impatience but was desperate. 'It wasn't Liz's voice,' he insisted for the umpteenth time. 'I don't care how many of her tutors say it was—none of them knew her that well—except Rosemary and you didn't *ask* Rosemary.' He had asked for three people, Barrett thought. How was he supposed to know there were others who knew her better? He stared at Paul but said nothing. 'Look!' went on Paul. 'We were so…close…that…damn it, I know every note in her voice! The taped message might have had the same timbre but it wasn't her.' Fishing in his pocket he brought out an audio-tape of his own. 'This is Liz's voice, this is what she sounded like, all you need do is compare the tapes—and I've been reading up on it, voice prints are easy,' holding out the cassette, eyes pleading. 'But if you let Wilson scrub the other tape there won't be any evidence.'

Barrett took the plastic case and turned it over in his hand. Enough was enough. He'd made a fool of himself already at Brindley and he didn't fancy doing it again. Telling himself one thing but thinking another as he remembered the samples he'd let go through to Forensic. What was the difference? Turning the tape between his thumb and middle finger, tapping it end on end he thought about the slim possibility of Hanson being right. If it wasn't the girl's voice and he let the college tape slip through his fingers he'd look a bigger fool then than if he faced down Wilson and collared it as evidence. Weighing the odds he made up his mind. If he ran a check and the prints matched it'd get Hanson off his back. And if they didn't…? Well, if they didn't he'd quite enjoy giving Wilson a large dose of his own medicine. He put the cassette in his pocket. 'Going back to Brindley?'

Paul spread his hands. 'Where else?'

'Give you a ride then,' said Barrett, and left him to wait while he went upstairs to talk to Morrissey.

POLICE UNIFORMS had a deterrent effect; long experience had taught Malminster's vagrants that the sight of dark blue serge and shiny boots was a sure precursor to being moved on. That being so they'd got into the habit of shuffling off before they were told, thereby saving themselves trouble. It was a habit that caused problems for the three PCs who were supposed to find and question them—since the sound of heavy footsteps coming up fast and a command to stop simply acted as a spur to speed up progress—and when the liking of disaffected and out-of-work youth to impede police pursuit was added to that, fleeing vagrants mostly gained a big enough start to find a bolt-hole. Chalky wasn't that lucky. Taking a flight of stone steps at a run, tripped by the loose sole of his shoe, then tumbling and rolling the rest of the way, the snap of his tibia breaking had the sharp sound of a fire-cracker. Chalky didn't hear it, the third step from the bottom had met his head with enough force to knock him out. PC Bell, twenty-two and no hard man, radioed in for an ambulance and felt guilty as hell.

IT HAD ALWAYS SURPRISED Rosemary that news got around so fast in a closed society, such as that within the college. It was a phenomenon she might one day devote a lecture to—not yet though—to introduce that topic at this particular time would simply add fuel to the fire. When Fletcher had quoted his ridiculous piece of verse on lost love she'd thought he meant Paul and Liz; but, oh no, his foolish little couplet had been for her. How did he…how did anybody…know about Robert? And then—the insult so obscenely hilarious that Rosemary didn't know whether to laugh or cry at it—he'd suggested she might enjoy herself more with him. *God!* If every other male on the planet disappeared and her brain became completely addled then maybe she would. Remembering his face when she told him that. Not a pleasant man. Wilson should have forced him out instead of dithering. Pushing her tray along the refectory shelf she hesitated between fish and stroganoff, then chose green pepper quiche instead, finding herself wishing that Chrissie Raines had been a stronger personality. If she had…if she'd stayed and fought…then Liz… Stopping in mid-bite, staring into space and wondering why Liz had come into her mind, the memory of Fletcher's darkly overcoated figure seen through her window plaguing her.

Liz wasn't another Chrissie; if he'd come on to Liz she would have slapped him down.

And then taken the shrubbery path back to Paul?

Suddenly sick she pushed the still-full plate away from her. It didn't matter that Liz had telephoned, or that the police were no longer searching, all that was in her mind was what might conceivably have happened on the shrubbery path.

DAVE SPARROW, near the end of his shift and with nothing much to report, used his initiative and went back to the citadel. He chose a good time. Between twelve and two the soup kitchen was open to any street person who might drop in. With a bowl of soup and a bread roll came a homily on saving souls; the homily was mostly ignored. The immortality or otherwise of an unknowable part of themselves was of no interest when compared to the chill ache of a hungry body.

When the PC took off his hat and walked into the spartan hall, he found himself looking at a fair number of vagrants who'd spent the morning keeping away from his colleagues. The surprise was mutual, and swift movement towards the back door was halted by Captain George. The courtesy of talking to PC Sparrow, he announced loudly, would earn a second bowl of soup. Bottoms shuffled unwillingly back to seats and Sparrow got busy with his questionnaires. By the time he left he'd picked up a lot of information he believed would interest Morrissey. The thought pleased him; he'd heard that where the chief inspector was concerned initiative paid off, and at that point in his career all that Sparrow could think of was getting himself into CID—where the glamour was.

BARRETT DROVE PAST the house Paul shared with Liz and dropped him off there—no sense in getting him into even further strife with Wilson. Paul didn't see it in quite the same way; to witness Wilson's discomfiture would be worth another black mark or two. He'd pointed that out to the detective sergeant but Barrett wasn't in the mood to be flexible. For one thing he was still smarting from Morrissey's condescending query about why he hadn't confiscated the tape in the first place—as if Barrett could have forseen Hanson chucking yet another spanner in the works. *Just his luck if the tape had been scrubbed already.*

By the time he'd driven the extra half-mile down the road, turned in through the drive gates and come to a halt outside the main entrance, Paul had negotiated the shrubbery path and come out the other end. Hands shoved deep into parka pockets for warmth he watched Barrett run up the stone steps into the building. Suppose Wilson told him he didn't have the tape—or that it had been scrubbed already—would Barrett accept that and come away? Shifting from foot to foot with impatience and cold until finally he gave up and crossed to the warmth of the foyer. Sitting on the second stair, hands dangling between his knees, shoulders slumped, he listened for the detective sergeant's feet. He was in the same dejected position when Holly turned out of the staffroom and stepped round him. At the first landing she overflowed with sympathy and went back.

When she came to sit beside him Paul lifted his head and waited, expecting to be told the stairs were not an ideal place to loiter. Instead Holly said perceptively, 'If it's any help, I don't think Liz would have skipped out without telling you either.'

He said, 'Thanks,' looking first at his hands and then at her. 'You know about the phone call that everybody thinks was her?'

'But you don't.'

'Does that make me soft-headed?'

'Of course it doesn't,' she said, then frowned. 'I didn't get to hear the tape—did you?'

'Yeah, I heard it all right. Courtesy of Dewdrop, up in his office with a smirk on his face. It sounded like her...you know, but...it wasn't.'

'I believe you. I mean, you'd know, wouldn't you, living in that kind of intimacy.' He looked at her with suspicion and she said quickly, 'Liz talked to me about it—you—that's how I know she wouldn't walk out.'

'Why did she? Talk to you about me, I mean.'

'Why not? For God's sake! I don't have two heads and I'm not that much older than her.' She lowered her voice and added gently, 'Liz was very much in love, that's something for you to hang on to.' He shook his head and went back to staring at his hands. The mumbled thanks when she started to get up was almost inaudible, but Holly heard it and let her hand briefly squeeze his shoulder before she went quickly back up the stairs to her office.

On the next floor Wilson was being characteristically unhelpful. For Barrett to be there at all was annoying, but to have him demand the tape as evidence was an affront to his authority. Barrett listened to an assortment of complaints about high-handed police tactics and repeated his request. 'I should think it in the college's interest to get things settled one way or another,' he said with blunt determination. 'And since we now have a tape that contains what we *know* to be Elizabeth Pardoe's voice, it'll be easy to match the two voice prints—if they belong to the same person.'

'More police time wasted!' Wilson fidgeting in his chair.

'I'm not sure if you're qualified to judge that, sir,' said Barrett. He held out a hand. 'If I can have the tape.'

Wilson skittered the cassette across his desk. 'I'll expect a full scale apology when you find the voices match, Detective Sergeant.'

'I'll bear that in mind, sir,' Barrett said flat-faced. 'Thank you for your cooperation.' That small courtesy being all the niceties Wilson was going to get, he turned on his heel and went back downstairs. Paul was on his feet before Barrett hit the last flight.

'Got it?'

'I thought I dropped you off at home?' said Barrett irritably as he pushed by.

'Did you get it?' yelled Paul following behind.

Barrett climbed in his car, started up the engine and wound down the window. Hanson could be a pain in the arse. 'I got it,' he said and showed the plastic casing. 'Now forget about it, it'll take a while, get on with your life until you hear from me.' He did a fast reverse and a swift turn, driving too fast round the bend and out of sight. Paul watched him go with emptiness building up inside him.

Get on with what life?

ELEVEN

MALE MENOPAUSE. That was the fashionable excuse for a middle-aged man to chase after a short skirt, and it didn't matter to Robert Sansom whether the wisdom was myth or truism, either way it had lost a lot of its amusement value. His life was a complicated mess, an acrimonious divorce behind him, two sons he seldom saw, and a millstone of maintenance payments round his neck. Why the hell had he shied away from Rosemary to bed a trollop like Susie whose appetites, both financially and sexually, he had great difficulty satisfying?

God only knew—unless it was the difference between a pleasant stroll and a bungy jump. Stepping off into mental space to see himself spiral in an ungainly arm-flapping fall. The folly of betrayal maybe, but not too late to turn back. If he wanted a pleasant stroll all he had to do was look contrite and Rosemary would welcome him back, he was quite sure about that, no recriminations and her salary more than making up for the shortfall in his own. Even if he married her it wouldn't put him into penury. Rosemary was—in every way—a good woman, and he still cared about her; enough so that last night's telephone conversation continued to push his worry button. The plaintive *'Father me a child'*, bounced in his head like a hard rubber ball. Something else nagged too.

He could tell she'd had too much to drink and that wasn't like her. He'd done more damage than he'd thought. As soon as he'd put the phone down the swiftly lethal outcome of alcohol and migraine tablets came into his mind and wouldn't go away. He told himself that Rosemary was too level-headed to do anything stupid, but even so... Last night with Susie had turned into a shambles because of it. A cross between nightmare and farce, Susie unaccustomed to failure and himself humiliated.

Or maybe the failure was because he was coming down with something. Picked up a stray bug. This morning when he'd dropped Susie at the secretarial agency where she worked, exchanging a long, deep and lingering kiss that would normally have set his loins on fire, he hadn't felt a thing.

Normally.

She'd patted his inactive crotch and said if he *did* have a bug she'd minister to him just as good as any nurse. Remembering that as he leaned moodily on the steering wheel, mind drifting on to the forms such ministering might take. For a few seconds everything else faded out and he swelled uncomfortably. Relief rocked his brain.

Nothing much wrong with the honourable member then.

God, but it was cold!

Stationary on the road outside Brindley College wall he gave the place a final glance, slipped into gear and drove home. No sense relighting candles—not yet anyway—better to keep in touch from a distance, leave the door ajar ready for when and if he felt like commitment. He eased his position in the driving seat secure in the thought that Rosemary would be there if he did.

DC Smythe was driving carefully. Last week, when the freeze-up began, his back wheels had slid sideways and sideswiped a new Renault. He'd been in a police car, on police business, but that didn't make the Renault owner any happier. Smythe had been raked over the coals for fast driving and waste of police funds. Today the car he drove was his own and he was being circumspect. No need to be anything else, there was no rush, the vagrant PC Bell had hospitalised wouldn't be going anywhere except a sanitised bed. Pity the poor sods who'd had to bath him. Taking two lefts and then a right before he pulled into the hospital car park. Chances were he'd learn nothing interesting anyway; nothing a uniform couldn't have found out. As he swung into the slot next to a green Fiesta its door flew open and spoiled his paint as he parked. He sat for a second thinking about justice then went to inspect the damage.

A woman, thirties, fake fur-collared black nylon parka, heavy boots and a pom-pommed tea-cosy yelled at him. 'That's bloody stupid, isn't it? Why'd you drive in when I'm getting out? I mean, you *could* see I was getting out, couldn't you?' Smythe fingered the scrape and dent in his side panel. 'Could have killed me. You know that? Bloody careless.' Slamming her door and starting to walk away.

Smythe said, 'Just hold a minute. Driver's licence and insurance, if you please. I'd like to see them.'

She turned. 'You what? Get stuffed!' He showed his warrant card. 'Jeez!' The woman began hunting in her handbag, balancing it awkwardly on one lifted knee. 'Could have said,' she complained. 'Didn't have to stand there like a dummy.' Amazed by a self-restraint he hadn't known he possessed, Smythe noted her name and address and held out his hand again.

'Haven't got insurance with me,' she said.

'You've got three days to present it then. That and an MOT certificate, at Malminster police station.' He touched the side of his Escort. 'You'll get the bill for panel work and respray.'

'Hey! Wait on a minute...'

'Your fault,' he cut across curtly. 'Next time look what you're doing.' She snatched her licence back and stalked off.

Smythe followed her into the hospital, watched her flounce away down the corridor and took the stairs up to the orthopaedic wards. PC Bell was having a cup of tea, cosy in the sister's office, only the sister wasn't there, instead a pretty staff-nurse was giving him the glad eye. When Smythe walked in she tested the teapot and offered to get a fresh brew. Bell, not out-ranked, heard Smythe refuse and took his time over finishing. The warm looks exchanged when he put the cup and saucer back on the tin tray suggested that his waiting time had been neither onerous nor wasted.

'Depends what you'd say to a Friday night date,' said Bell when they were out of earshot and Smythe brought it up. 'Want me to find out if she's got a friend available?'

'No thanks,' said Smythe shortly, slicking back an expen-

sive haircut and wondering why it couldn't have been him.
'Where's this broken-legged dosser?'

'In theater having it pinned.'

Smythe brought up short. 'What?'

'It isn't him I thought you'd be interested in,' said Bell.
'It's the one came in three days back. Geordie Harry. Claims
he was shoved under a bus but likely drunk too much and fell.
From what he says, he and Duffy were drinking mates, and if
he hadn't been in there that night...'

'He'd have been under the viaduct with Duffy.' Smythe
finishing it off. Maybe the sun was shining on him after all.
'Thanks,' he said. 'I owe you one.'

'Don't fret,' said Bell, 'I shan't forget it. Fifth bed on the
right. Wait here, shall I?' Grinning happily as he went back
into the sister's office to pick up where he'd left off.

PATRICK HOBAN, known as Tesco, twenty-five and society's
reject, wasn't an alcoholic but he never refused a drink; alcohol meant calories, calories meant warmth, and his body was
in dire need of both. Having fallen for the worn-out message
that the nation's jobless should get on their bikes, Tesco had
done just that, but it hadn't done him any good. He'd cycled
down the A1 from Sunderland with two Tesco carrier bags
full of underpants, socks and food, stopping at every town he
came to looking for work. A week here, a week there, and a
lot of disappointment. The odyssey had lasted until he got to
Malminster where someone stole his bike, and because the
Tesco bag with his underwear and socks had been in the sad-
dlebag he lost that too. He wasn't sure why but the theft had
knocked the stuffing out of him. Since then he'd slept rough
and spent his days haunting the pedestrian precinct holding a
piece of corrugated cardboard with the words *Homeless and
Hungry* written in large letters.

The pickings were poor.

Last week he'd gone to the Oxfam shop looking for a
thicker coat and the woman had taken pity on him, and deliberately misread the five-pound tag as fifty pence. The dark
blue ex-yuppy Melton didn't help all that much against the

cold but it was better than nothing. Every day he looked for
his bike, telling himself that if he found it his luck would
change and he'd move on. It was the only piece of optimism
he had left.

When PC Sparrow paid his second visit to the citadel, Tesco
had been there savouring the warmth, staying firmly on his
chair instead of joining the pushing rush to the back door. He
didn't see the sense of it; as far as Tesco was concerned the
sooner Duffy's killer was caught the better. Somehow or other
gory details of Duffy's death had spread through the vagrants'
sub-culture, and he for one hadn't slept well since. Better tonight though, his hand in the pocket touching the knife he'd
picked up at the secondhand stall for twenty pence; blunt when
he got it but sharp now. Duffy had been a soft touch, an easy
kill—poor old sod. Anybody coming after *him* would find it
different, blade against blade, all to win and nothing to lose.
Squatting cross-legged outside BHS's back door, saying thank
you to the woman who gave him a pound coin, he watched
the cold grey sky darken. His mother would have food on the
table, he could go home if he wanted to. Admit defeat. Make
the long trek back and join the wasted weekly trail down the
Job-Centre. All he had to do to be fed and warm was swallow
his pride and go north.

Except that with pride the only thing not yet taken away
from him he preferred to freeze.

TWELVE

SPARROW'S REPORT and Smythe's were both of them useful enough for Morrissey to think a small crack might be opening up in what had seemed to be a solid wall. He'd praised Sparrow's common sense and the PC had gone out of the office light-footed, telling himself initiative paid off, no doubt about it, and grinning like a Cheshire cat as he went off watch. One day, he told himself, one day.

Smythe too, having come up with something positive, felt pleased with himself, but not so much so that he forgot to give due credit to Bell. If he'd overlooked that part of it and Morrissey found out, he'd have been in deep dog dirt. Cooperation between uniform and CID—that was the current name of the game. It wouldn't work of course. A couple of months and everybody'd be one-uping each other just like always.

'So what's your opinion?' Morrissey asked. 'Fact or fiction? Do we put it down to imagination and bad booze or did he get a push?'

'I don't know, sir, but nobody's going to convince Geordie Harry it happened different to what he said, and if a stalker had been looking to get Duffy on his own that would have been a good way to do it. I've pulled the accident report, but nobody seems to have noticed a thing until Geordie was laid flat.'

'Lucky escape.'

'Wouldn't have had except the 190 had slowed right down for the stop. If it had been the one after, the 201, he'd have had his lot. Keeps going fast until Queen Street.'

'Too many coincidences,' said Morrissey. 'We need a better witness. Ask uniform if everything's here,' tapping the report sheet. 'Notebooks are good places to lose bits of information. Know that, don't you?' He watched Smythe grow uncomfortable. 'If they picked up any addresses that haven't had a visit, go yourself.'

'Tonight, sir?' Surreptitiously checking his watch and wondering if he could do that and be back outside the Odeon at eight.

'Of course tonight,' said Morrissey. 'Take a long-term view. If the girlfriend doesn't understand there's no point in her going out with a policeman.'

'No, sir,' said Smythe, thinking that if Morrissey still remembered what it was like he'd know that with a body like Zoe's there was a queue waiting. Going downstairs in his Armani-type suit and bright tie he thought that maybe if Copeland had nothing better to do he could farm a couple of addresses out on him—share the load—then he discovered that uniform had been as economical with information as Morrissey had suspected, and came away with half a dozen addresses miles apart. It was insult added to injury having to watch Copeland grin and say sorry, not tonight, but he'd stand in with the girlfriend if that would help? *Like hell it would!*

Left with a straight choice between Morrissey's displeasure and Zoe's he picked up the phone and got busy with his excuses.

MORRISSEY GOT HOME at seven, forgetting that his wife had a meeting at half-past, and found her rushing round trying to get ready and complaining that it felt like she was running a cafeteria and not a home. First it had been Mike bringing Gareth to be fed before they went off to the cinema, then Katie coming in wheedling, 'Something quick, Mum, I've got to meet Ian.' Now it was her husband, tired and depressed and looking sorrowful at the thought of getting his own dinner out of the oven. Enough was enough. It wasn't as if she even *wanted* to turn out on a night like this. If it were any of her other committees instead of the NSPCC she would have rung up and made excuses. But tonight was important; they needed to raise more money and they needed good ideas.

Bending red-faced to get the casserole out of the oven and put it on a plate while Morrissey washed his hands at the sink,

she wondered if maybe feminists had it right after all. Wife
and mother seemed increasingly interchangeable with slave
and skivvy. Putting the plate on the table, she cut a wedge of
apple pie and thought *damn it*—she'd made a special point of
reminding him about the meeting this morning and he'd forgotten all about it—again. Shrugging into her coat she grabbed
her loaded bag, to be stopped in her tracks when he planted a
contrite kiss and said he was sorry. She crunched out over
iced gravel to unlock the Fiat, and refused to acknowledge an
itch of guilt.

There were other things in life as important as police work.

SMYTHE'S FRUSTRATION increased in correlation to wasted
time. It peeved him that those who had witnessed Geordie
Harry's mishap should live so far apart. You'd think a knot
of people converging near a bus stop would come from the
same end of town, but oh, no, it was out of one estate, across
town to the next, up diagonally to the third then out to the
northern suburbs where nobody would answer a door bell after
dark. He seethed as each successive journey drew an information blank, because instead of trying to read house numbers
in the dark he could have been snug with Zoe on the back
row—his mind drifting to Sunday night when with her eyes
and mind on Harrison Ford he'd managed to get his hand up
her skirt. Smythe's thoughts were still occupied with that when
his back wheels started to slide. He straightened out, cut his
speed, and asked himself if it was worth going all the way out
to Hazleton on a wild-goose chase.

Chances were if nobody else had seen Geordie get a push,
this Jameson woman wouldn't have either. *If* she opened the
door to him. *If* she was in. Thinking how by giving her a miss
he could get back into town, ring Zoe, and still salvage something. A late meal, a couple of hours at Pimms night-spot and
he might still be in with a chance.

Driving down the Middlebrook Road he gave up on the
idea, taking the road south over the river bridge. Best to learn
from past mistakes. It wasn't that long since he'd held back
on what he thought was useless information and near enough

come to grief: if he slipped up a second time he might not be so lucky. He kept that at the front of his mind, feeling relieved to have made the right choice when he got to Hazleton and spoke to Ida Jameson.

Seventy-four, cuddly-plump, and seemingly sharper-eyed than anybody else Ida said, yes, she'd seen Geordie Harry get a push all right—although of course she hadn't known that was his name—and how was the poor man?

The poor man was eating his fill and driving the nurses mad but Smythe didn't tell her that; instead he said that given his broken bones Geordie was doing fine and could Ida describe the man who'd pushed him? Not really, said Ida, it had all happened so fast. One minute she'd been standing to the side and a little behind Geordie who'd been dithering at the pavement edge, and the next—well!

'Such a lot of traffic at that time. A crossing would be a big help, dear,' she said. 'All I saw was this hand come out and give him a push right in the middle of the back. Then he went flying into the road and the bus hit him.'

'So you didn't get a good look at the pusher?' Smythe said, feeling disappointed.

'No, I wish I had, but you know what it's like, I just didn't think. He had a dark blue overcoat but that isn't much help, is it?' she said brightly. 'If I were more like Miss Marple of course I'd have noticed more.' When he looked confused he lifted the book she'd been reading to show the cover. 'Agatha Christie. I've read every one of her books and now I'm reading them again. Do you read her too? No? Well, perhaps you should, you might find her quite a help, she knows so many odd ways for people to die.' Smythe blinked a couple of times and thought how he'd better things to do than read about crime, swallowed down a sharp answer and politically said he'd heard she was very good but could Ida think of anything else about the man who'd pushed Geordie?

'Well,' she measured Smythe with her eyes. 'He wasn't as tall as you and...' Frowning, she struggled with a reluctant memory then clapped her hands together. 'I do know,' she crowed, excitement pinking her face. 'I remember where he

went...when the traffic stopped he walked right across the
road and went into the gents by Harper's Funeral Parlour.'
She looked up at him expectantly. 'Does that help?' she said.
'Does it really help?'

Smythe told her it was the best information they'd had from
anybody, and to prove he meant it stayed to have a cup of tea
with her, pushing thoughts of any further progress with Zoe
from his mind.

Driving towards Malminster down the narrow and twisting
Hazleton Road that passed the back entrance to Brindley College, his headlights sweeping the grass verge picked out two
foxes locked in post-coital ecstasy, rump to rump, tongues
lolling. The red depths of the dog-fox's eyes reflected eerily
as the car swept by, potently reminding Smythe of lost possibilities. Negotiating the right-hand sweep out onto the main
road he hoped Morrissey's libido stayed as unsatisfied as his
own.

Coming back over the river bridge the first shards of freezing rain hit his windshield. Pessimistically he knew that Traffic
would be in for a busy night.

THIRTEEN

HOLLY SET HER RADIO alarm early, climbing out of bed to put the light on as soon as Radio One began pulsing out an old Blondie number. She hadn't yet worked out what it was about Philip Jacques that she found so attractive but it was a new experience that she intended to explore. There was something about him—not shyness exactly, more a holding back—that she found intriguing. She told herself it was maybe that he behaved differently from the men she had dated before, and didn't feel the same need to rush things; if so, that was something else Holly liked. Males with one-track minds could be a pain. Yawning and shivering simultaneously, she shrugged into an ancient and woolly blue dressing-gown that wasn't in the least glamorous but who cared about that?

Although if things progressed with Philip...

Dozily day-dreaming, padding barefoot to part the curtains, looking out into a darkness that orange street lights and white frost made even less inviting, the sudden image of Liz Pardoe and the wretched shrubbery path startled her by its intensity. Letting go the drapes and turning back into the well-lit room didn't help; apprehension rising on a flood tide wasn't something Radio One's brittle cheerfulness could disperse. She cursed softly, the pleasure of her waking mood already destroyed.

THE TWO FOXES RAN together, the vixen head and neck in front of the dog, angling her head to look back in adoration. By the time pale grey edged across the black sky and touched Pel's Copse they had gone to earth, the dog wakeful, scenting a human rancidity that sent its ears back. Thirty yards south and upwind where lightning had split and toppled a tall beech the squatting figure had no sense of being observed, and the roughly put-together tramp's lean-to hid a secret more awful than the roll of blood-stained clothing that had excited the fox's nose.

Less than a foot beneath the damp surface of earth lay the gently rotting body of the lean-to's maker, despatched in much the same way as Duffy and without guilt because the world would be cleaner without its kind. The squatting man knew that. The voices said so. They were there now in his head, whispering in the background, too quiet to demand all his attention. When they grew raucous again he would take the knife and do as they bid—but with more caution. Yes, definitely with more caution.

He should have gagged the old man, down in the viaduct. Not doing so was a mistake, one his father never made: If he had, the neighbours would have heard. The taste and the feel of thickly wadded towelling suppressing tongue and straining teeth came back to him. Given time pain became a pleasure. Father had said so. No more mistakes then, no more being carried away by the moment. Sweat came freely, along with a memory of the security guard up behind the wire fence, the dogs restively pawing the mesh, and him hoping all the while that the man would be less intelligent than the animals.

And he had been. Either that or less courageous.

It was a matter of psychology. Uniforms didn't make brave men; given a choice between trouble and looking the other way a simple and primitive reflex arc turned heads sideways. Not so with a dog. If a Doberman had got through the fence only his knife would have quietened it.

Dog was God backwards.

What to do with the clothes...? Should have buried them before the freeze. Leave them—who'd come looking? Six weeks already and nobody had. England's green and pleasant land was full of rotting corpses that nobody missed. Back on his feet and walking away as the chanting inside his skull grew stronger. Ruff up, teeth bared, memory imprinted with the man's scent, the dog-fox watched him go.

BARRETT HAD OVERSLEPT, not a habit of his but it made him last in. Smythe had his head down busy on a report, tapping away, two fingers on each hand and a thumb, cursing when he hit the wrong key and had to use Tipp-Ex. Woods was in his own corner, a pile of files in front of him and his pug-nosed face looking like he'd been fitted up. Barrett said, 'Where's Copeland?' and had to ask twice before Smythe lifted his head long enough to say, 'Canteen.'

Already? Glowering at Smythe's bent head and about to snap a sharp answer when he remembered Copeland had to give evidence on a mugging case. Waste of a morning hanging around in court waiting to be called. Only thing magistrates'd do to a fourteen-year-old'd be slap his wrist and send him on holiday. Somewhere warm and sunny most like—pocket-money on the rates. He helped himself to a couple of Bics and headed for his own desk in Morrissey's office, hearing the chief inspector talking on the telephone as he opened the door and hesitating until he saw the waved hand.

When he made inspector would he get his own space?

Who was he kidding?

As likely to increase establishment to two inspectors as pigs were to fly.

He filled in a request sheet and dropped it, the recording Paul had handed him, and Brindley's answerphone tape, into Forensic's collection box as Morrissey hung up.

'Something new?'

Barrett shrugged. 'Possibility. Bit of a long shot though.' He recapitulated the sequence of events from Hanson coming in to his third visit to Brindley, ending, 'Thought I might as well send it—settle things once and for all. No point in us looking idiots if she is still missing.'

'Think she is?'

'Wish I knew. Doesn't feel right but that's not much to go on.'

'A good copper develops an instinct for such things,' Morrissey said. 'No reason why you should be any different.'

Barrett's eyelids flapped; he stared down at his shoes. It *sounded* like a compliment but experience made him wary.

'No sense chasing duff hares,' he said obliquely and shifted the conversation. 'Anything new on Duffy?'

Morrissey picked up the fattening file. 'Best read it for yourself. That way if anything strikes you I'll not have put it in your head.'

Nice one, thought Barrett, slow-pacing back to his desk. And if nothing struck him, what then? On a hiding to nothing as usual. Page turning until Smythe came in with his typing exercise. 'Forgave you then, did she?' asked the chief inspector.

'A bit iffy.'

'Not true love then.'

True lust, thought Smythe. Love didn't have anything to do with it. 'I found a witness,' he said. 'Claims Geordie Harry got a helping hand.'

'Prepared to make a statement?'

'Yep.'

'Description?'

Smythe's shrug said it all. 'Dark blue overcoat and that's it.'

Barrett leafed back, found the forensic report he wanted but stayed silent until Smythe was gone. Designer clothes and body-building brought out a jealousy streak.

'That witness statement could tie in with this, sir. Dark blue wool fibres under Duffy's finger nails that could come from a rug or from clothing. Shouldn't think a rug'd be likely but a dark blue overcoat might fit the bill.' He set the pen file in front of Morrissey. 'It's not the best lead we've ever had but it's something.'

'Pity Smythe's witness didn't get a face to go with it.'

Barrett's finger moved. 'Lavatory attendant might. Worth a try?'

Definitely worth a try, thought Morrissey, annoyed that Barrett's eyes had picked out the relevant line before his own and that Smythe hadn't had the sense to think of it for himself. He revised that view when he crossed the corridor and found Smythe zipped up in his parka and ready to go out.

'Somewhere interesting?'

'Gents' lavatory on Monk Street. Thought there might be an attendant.'

'Let me know what you come up with.'

'Sir.' Smythe grinned a little as he went down the stairs, pleased the penny had dropped before he'd had to be told.

THE FIRST HOLLY HAD SEEN of Philip that day he'd been coming in from the cold and blowing on his hands, face preoccupied and eyes distant, taking the stairs at a fast lope and not seeing her through the open staffroom door. The pleased smile had faded from her face. She couldn't just go and ask him, the invitation had to be casual, spur of the moment, not something she'd been planning since early morning. Drat it! Suppose they missed each other for the rest of the day?

At lunchtime, queuing with her tray in the refectory, she saw him sitting with his back to her at a table in the corner and carried over her soup and salad. 'Hi,' she said, taking the seat opposite and unloading her tray.

He smiled like he was pleased to see her. 'I've been thinking about you,' he said.

'What about?' Delighted that she'd been in his mind.

'That we ought to go out again sometime.'

'That'd be nice.' Gathering courage and jumping in. 'I could cook a meal and we could eat at my place. Tonight if you like, the larder's well stocked for once.' Holding her breath then thinking, *God!* what if he thought she was propositioning him? 'Just for a meal,' she added quickly. His eyes smiled.

'What else?'

She broke her bread roll, buttered and bit.

He said, 'Tonight's difficult. I'll be tied up until late.'

'Oh?' Looking at him.

'A stack of papers to mark.' Not quite meeting her gaze.

Let it go or not? Diffidently, as if it wasn't the most important thing on her mind, she said, 'You'll be hungry when you're finished then? I don't mind eating late—say ten o'clock?'

'If the car starts.'

She bent her head, concentrating on a piece of mushroom, chasing it around the bowl. 'I'll make enough for two and if you don't get there I'll freeze what's left. It's no big deal.'

He looked at his watch. 'Got to go. Might see you later.' Watching him stack his tray and pots on the self-clear trolley she thought what a waste if he didn't come. And then she wondered if the papers were just an excuse, because tomorrow was Saturday and he could easily have marked them then instead.

Unless he was doing something else like going home for the weekend? Stabbing hard into the cheese and onion quiche she wondered why life threw up so many complications.

FOURTEEN

SMYTHE'S LIBIDO still smarted from disappointment, a state of affairs he was unaccustomed to. To soothe it he used the last units on his phonecard and called up Zoe, who told him with bored indifference that she wasn't supposed to take calls at work. He overrode that by outlining his idea of how they should spend Friday night. She listened to his thoughts on a Chinese meal at the Silver Dragon, some flashy dancing at Casanovas, and a curry at throwing out time to eat back at his place, and told him being stood up once was enough. Besides which she was going out with the marketing manager who drove a H reg Jag and was buying her a proper meal at the country club. Smythe's phonecard ran out before he could come up with a sufficiently biting reply.

By the time he got to Monk Street he was ready to take out his frustration on anybody, even the lavatory attendant, but that didn't work out either. When he got there the place was dark, its wrought-iron gate closed and padlocked. Rattling the bars brought no response. He backed off, tried the brightly lit undertakers next door and found them closed too. It was always the same, let one sodding thing go wrong and everything else followed. He looked darkly at a tobacconist and sweet shop on the other side of the gents, lights spilling out over the pavement. Not likely they'd be shut too, was it?

The girl inside, dark hair, pretty face, cushiony plump, dimpled at him nicely, one hand pushing back a stray strand of hair. Smythe, preferring the top-heavy model look, noted the wedding ring without much regret. He took out his warrant card and the smile on her face faded. 'It isn't Donny, is it?' she said. 'There isn't nothing happened to him?'

'Nothing I know about, I just want some information about the gents next door. How long has it been closed?'

'Closed?' she said doubtfully. 'I don't know. Well, I wouldn't, would I? Not the sort of place I look at.' Frowning and then pinking up. 'If you're took short I suppose you could...'

'No,' he said hastily. 'I'm not. It's the attendant I need to talk to. Don't suppose you know where he lives?'

'No.' She leaned on the counter, breasts flopping forward heavily. 'Eddie,' she said confidentially. 'That's his name. Little bloke, getting on and smokes Players? That who you mean? Comes in on a morning and buys a twenty pack. Now I come to think of it, I haven't seen him for a couple of days. Must have flu or something. Not surprising this sort of weather, is it? Everybody what comes in seems to have a sniffle. What's he done?'

Smythe scribbled down his name on a card and gave it her. 'If you see him let me know, all right?'

'I don't know,' she said doubtfully looking at the slip of pasteboard as the shop door opened again.

'It's nothing to worry about, he's only a witness,' Smythe told her hastily as she eased up off the counter.

'That right?' she said, and turned her smile on a real customer.

WHEN MORRISSEY'S phone rang and the man's non-local voice introduced itself as George Webber from the Salvation Army citadel, Morrissey's interest perked up. 'Captain George?' he said, and got a chuckle.

'Sounds like something out of Gilbert and Sullivan, doesn't it? There's a bit of information I don't believe anybody mentioned to that intelligent young policeman you sent around.'

'Oh? What would that be?'

'The psychiatric department at the local hospital and the social-studies department at Brindley College are involved in a joint study into vagrancy. Causes and cures, ideas for the future, that sort of thing. They hold a talk clinic here two afternoons a week, invite vagrants to drop in and help them in exchange for goodies. Not something I entirely approve of, but we also get a donation to funds, which means we can offer more help with soup kitchens and shelter. Uneasy bedfellows you might say, since there's nothing particularly Christian in the psycho-social approach.'

'I'm glad you thought to tell me about it. Which afternoons would it be?'

'Wednesday and Friday.' He sounded regretful. 'I—um… Today's session just ended. If I'd thought to mention it this morning it might have been more help.'

'Don't fret about it, I'm glad to be put in the picture.' Morrissey paused, then asked, 'Anything else you can tell me that might help?'

'Nothing that comes immediately to mind, but I'll let you know if anything does. I wouldn't want it to happen again.'

'You think it might?'

'I'm *afraid* it might,' corrected Webber.

And so was he, thought Morrissey as he hung up, and that was the worry of it.

LEN TOLD HIMSELF—and anyone else who would listen—that it was force of circumstance that made him sleep rough and not any fault of his own. Unfortunately his almost perpetual state of inebriation made that difficult to believe. Twice Captain George had dried him out, found him lodgings, a decent set of clothes and a job, and twice he'd bounced right back. This time, partly at Sister Mary's instigation, he was being left to fend for himself. Captain George wasn't altogether happy about that, but when Sister Mary set herself against something her disapproval was tangible enough to make things hard for everybody else. 'If he doesn't want to be saved, let him find out the devil makes a careless master,' she said primly.

Len had given them both a V sign and walked out.

This afternoon he'd come back and told his story to the trick-cyclist and the social meddler in exchange for warmth and food. He'd called them that to their faces and his knowledge and intelligence had, he thought, surprised them. 'I am,' he said, not hearing the words blur, 'a good and virtuous man fallen among thieves.' When he left Captain George had set a hand on his shoulder and asked how he was doing. Len had swung a wildly circling arm, snarled, 'What do you bloody care?' and woven unsteadily away. A different reply might have saved his life.

FOUR-THIRTY WHEN SMYTHE got back to the station and made a bee-line for the phone. It didn't do him any good. Getting action out of council employees was difficult at the best of times, late on a Friday afternoon it was downright impossible. And no, they hadn't known the gents on Monk Street was closed, nobody had told them. That last said aggrievedly as if it was his fault. He suggested someone might go down there with a spare key and got told that somebody would—on Monday morning. Restraining his impatience and asking for the lavatory attendant's address didn't get him anywhere either. It wasn't, said the female voice on the other end of the line, the kind of information they gave out over the telephone. After all, he might *say* that he was a policeman but how did she know that? Couldn't see his warrant card down the phone, could she? Best thing for him to do was come down to the office.

Wearily he said he was on his way.

No point, not now, the voice told him chirpily. Everybody was going home and so was she. 'By-ee.' He dropped the receiver from a height and hoped she was still plugged in.

LEN HAD SOON PICKED UP the jargon; skippering was sleeping rough, and a skipper was the place where you did it. If you found a good one you kept it to yourself because if you didn't, every dosser in town came in, shit and piss all over the place and no privacy. Len still liked privacy. The skipper he'd found was a boarded-up garage on Manor Road, petrol pumps ripped out but still a water supply that was a lot better than begging for a wash at the gents. He'd pried a few boards loose around the back and once he was in fastened them up again from the other side. He'd been there four weeks—ever since Captain George threw him out—and up to now nobody had bothered him. Not the police, not vandal kids, not nobody. Hadn't breathed a word, not until today, and then he'd done it quiet so he was safe from prying ears. Lot of them down the Sally would have liked to hear what he said. Snuggled down early, a hand-out cheese sandwich and two bottles of cheap wine for company, he was halfway between sleep and mindlessness when he found himself with company. Thick-voiced and hazy-brained he called, 'Who-a-as that? Go way, haven't got nothing.' He struggled to get himself upright and find his middle-drawer voice. 'These are my premises, you're trespassing. Out with you. Out or...or...I'll call the plorice.'

Taking his coat off, hanging it on a handy nail, the newcomer walked towards Len. One push sending him off balance.

Staggering, sitting down heavily, cracking his coccyx on the concrete floor, Len wavered, 'Got no money. Got nothing.'

'Wouldn't want it from a piss-pot like you. Want to see what I've got?' Letting a seepage of orange from the street lights reflect on the knife's blade. 'Take off your clothes.'

'Too cold.' The knife flicked. A warm trickle ran from below Len's right eye.

'Clothes.'

Awkwardly, overbalancing, Len stripped. 'Sex?' he said. 'Sex you want? Not a pooftah, you know. Not a pooftah. No disri...no disri... No offence.'

'On your back.'

'What...?' The knife flicked again, this time nicking Len's left breast. Flat on his back, the concrete cold and rough on his nakedness, Len waited for unspeakable humilities and instead got unbearable pain.

TEN O'CLOCK and Holly had almost given up on him, the oven turned down to low, the cling-film-covered salad bowl in the fridge along with a bottle of M&S Lambrusco, and the chocolate cake tempting her to spoil its wholeness instead of waiting any longer. Like a kid, she thought, pudding first, dinner last, and had the knife poised ready to cut when the doorbell announced that he was coming after all. A muscle at the back of her throat tightened with nervousness. She smoothed her hair, ran a quick check in the mirror and opened the door.

Hands deep in pockets, Philip blinked in the flood of yellow light. They could have been strangers, she thought, the way he looked at her, standing there almost as if he didn't know why he'd come. Maybe it had been a mistake after all, asking him. She pasted on a smile and held the door wide. 'Good timing,' she said, watching as he appeared to gather himself from some faraway place and step inside her door. 'I was just about to start without you.' Surrounded by warmth and light he became the Philip she knew, smiling as he took off his coat, telling her that whatever she'd been cooking it certainly smelled nice.

'It isn't anything much,' she said. 'Just a cassoulet and salad.'

'Nothing near as good as a refectory butty,' he mocked and she laughed. Perhaps it wasn't going to be a disaster after all.

FIFTEEN

SOFT SNOW FALLING on hard ice and the gritters not coping with anything except bus routes. Shopkeepers with customerless shops and long faces, and Smythe and Woods on weekend call-out. Both of them expecting a quiet time. Local criminals tended to be real softies when it came to bad weather. Saturday lunchtime, ever hopeful, Smythe telephoned Zoe again. Her mother said she hadn't got in until three and wasn't up yet. Smythe's mind moved to steamed-up windows and reclining seats. 'Tell her I'm pleased she had a good time then,' he said and hung up. At five he rang her again.

'Should have gone out with you instead,' she told him without preamble. 'Jag or no Jag. That Mick Shaw's a waste of time.'

'Why's that then?'

'Thinks a meal and half a dozen drinks gets a night's shag, that's why.'

Wasn't the only one, thought Smythe, thinking he'd have to wage a longer campaign than he'd planned. 'How about Monday night then?' he offered. '*Philadelphia* at the Cannon and a late pizza.'

'Sounds nice. Outside at half-past then?' Adding with a rush. 'Thought I might watch a video tonight. Mum and Dad'll be out 'til late if you want to come round.'

'Working,' lied Smythe, home to meet the parents not being in his plans, then fitted in a quick goodbye and hung up.

A couple of hours later, looking out at the weather, he decided on the corner pub and a stress-free night.

PAUL HAULED OUT OF BED late, pulling on a T-shirt, sweatshirt on top, putting the kettle on to boil while he shaved, staring at his reflection in the mirror and wondering why he bothered.

What did it matter? Could look like a tramp and nobody would care. Liz would've. So would his mother if she could see him but she was too far away to worry. He nicked himself and stuck a piece of loo-roll over the cut.

His father used styptic pencil, swearing while he did it.

His father.

Maybe they were more alike than he'd thought, running round like headless chickens when things went wrong. Like when Davy broke his leg—his dad trying to lift him up and Davy shrieking out. Then his mother coming. 'Leave him where he is, you daft lump, can't you tell it's broken? It's an ambulance we want, not a strongman.' She'd knelt under the big tree and looked up at splintered wood.

His father had stood, uncomfortable, wanting to avoid a fuss, afraid of getting to hospital and being told there was nothing wrong and him being diminished in other people's eyes. Brusque because of that, telling his wife not to panic, it was only a sprain. Shifting, foot to foot, not recognising the panic was in him and not his wife.

No, they weren't that much alike after all—him and his father. Paul didn't give a shit what anybody thought about him.

He dropped two teaspoons of instant in a mug and got near-black coffee, found mould on the bread and skipped toast in favour of muesli that without milk tasted like sawdust.

What if the police were humouring him? Suppose they did nothing with the tape, didn't look at it, just brought it back and said it was a match?

Shit!

Staring out of the window, nothing to do and nowhere to go, his hands itching to take somebody apart, he watched the snow fall like white death on the ground.

Liz!

SITTING ALONE in the office Sunday morning, nothing new in the incident room because Duffy's death wasn't apparently disturbing any Malminster citizen's sleep, Smythe waited for Woods to come back upstairs with coffee and butties, and caught up on paperwork. When Communications put the call through to him he didn't recognise either the name or the voice until it said, 'It's about the gents—you know—the one on Monk Street?' Then he realised it was the overfed girl from the tobacconist and his interest perked up.

'Is Eddie back?'

'No. I wish he was, then he could do something about it. You'd have to smell it to believe it.'

'Smell what?'

'I don't know what. From the gents. Dead meat or something.'

It'd have to be dead if it was meat, thought Smythe. 'I can't do anything about smells, love, it's the council you want for that.'

'Except they're shut Sundays. Can't you come down and see?'

'Wouldn't do any good if it's a burst drain.'

'Doesn't smell like a burst drain, they had one last year and it wasn't nothing like this.'

'Sorry, love, wish I could help.' Saying goodbye and putting the phone down as Woods came back. He flicked through emergency numbers looking for the council's, his butty half-eaten, as he thought how Eddie was the only person who might put a face on the man Ida Jameson said had pushed Geordie Harry—and here was he, stuck with his hands tied until Monday. He'd found the number he wanted and started to dial before it hit him that the man in the dark blue coat might have had the same idea.

SUNDAY, SWEET SUNDAY. Morrissey blissful in his easy chair, re-reading Priestley's *Angel Pavement* and half-dozing because he'd eaten more than he should. Not enough to make him uncomfortable but enough to make his eyelids droop. Half-dreaming when the phone rang, the distant *ping* and Mike's voice making echoes in his head. Keeping his eyes shut, willing it not to be for him. Useless exercise. 'For you, Dad.' Mike hung his head through the door until Morrissey moved, then ducked upstairs to whatever it was he'd been doing.

Morrissey took his time, marked his place and went to the hall where the telephone receiver hung vertically between its rests. As soon as he heard the tone of Smythe's voice he knew that was Sunday finished. He listened to the details and didn't say much himself except to ask if Warmsby had been informed—telling Smythe not to bother he'd do it himself, when the answer was no.

Margaret lifted her head when he went back, said, 'Work?' and getting a nod let her eyes fall back to her stitching. Twenty years married to a policeman had given her a certain resignation about such things. A minute later, hearing Morrissey moving about upstairs, she laid aside the patchwork and went to heat a thermos of soup in the kitchen. Wherever he was going it would be unpleasant and too cold for comfort. She was screwing on the top as her husband came downstairs, his face pleased when she went out with the flask. He bent his head and kissed her cheek, awkward as a teenager. 'Don't know why you bother,' he said gruffly. Neither did she, thought Margaret. Not after this last six months.

Driving down Monk Street where police tape fluttered, Morrissey noted the number of spectators with something like wonder. Did nothing keep them away? Catch him freezing his sodding toes off if he had the choice. Parking his dark blue Senator behind a police Rover he was about to be sent packing until his face was recognised and he got nodded through, getting the first whiff of something nasty as he went in the white-tiled entrance to the gents where a forced padlock hung loosely on its chain.

Smythe was on his way out, face like yellowed marble, pulling up short when he saw the chief inspector coming in. 'Just going to take a couple of breaths outside, sir,' he said. 'Gets a bit overpowering after a while,' turning in his tracks and starting back regardless, Morrissey close behind. 'Heating's been turned up all weekend—mightn't be so bad if it hadn't.'

'SOCO arrived?'

'Shouldn't be long. Police surgeon's been and gone. Shame to bother him.'

'Forms in triplicate,' said Morrissey.

'Not much else for him to do though, is there, except certify death?'

'He gets paid for it,' reminded Morrissey urgently. 'It isn't a job done out of goodness of heart, so don't waste time feeling sorry for him. I doubt he'll be wasting many tears over you.'

'Sir.' Wondering what had bitten the DCI, he speculated on whether the old man had been tucked up in bed with his missus when the phone rang. Thinking that'd get anybody annoyed. He passed six cubicles on the left, ten urinals on the right and then got out his handkerchief and covered his nose as he turned into the washroom with four handbasins and a drier, and a lavatory attendant who'd spilled out his guts on the floor.

MORRISSEY HAD NEVER had more than an uneasy tolerance for the press, and from choice passed on as little information as he could get away with. It wasn't his choice that news got out so fast about the lavatory attendant's death. Had he been able to do so he would have kept it quiet at least until Monday, and even then issued no details. Sometimes it seemed that Providence worked directly against him. Graham Diggs took an opposite view; he'd worked on the *Malminster Echo* for just over a year and knew that when Morrissey was on the other side of police tape a good story wasn't far behind. He also knew better than to ask the chief inspector what the story might be. That day his wife had sent him out to the supermarket—not an uncommon occurrence now there was Sunday opening—and it had been sheer luck that he'd been driving back along Monk Street when the blue and white police tape went up. He'd cruised by, circled, come back, and parked on the other side of the street where he could watch comings and goings. Morrissey had been an unexpected bonus. So had nipping into the tobacconist for a packet of Benson's.

The girl had been spilling over with information after she found out who he was, and been only too eager to take him out to the back and show off the offending window that let

out the noxious smell. After a fiver had persuaded her to go
back in the shop and leave him to it, he set about finding out
what was going on. She'd been right about the smell, even in
the ice-sharp snow it was sickeningly ripe. An upturned dustbin topped by a tomato box filched from behind the greengro-
cer's next door provided him with unstable access, the slatted
wood creaking and threatening to give way under his weight.
Gripping the brick sill, easing onto his toes, heat came out to
meet him. *God!* He swung his head sideways, gulped less
tainted air, and held it in his lungs as he twisted his head,
squinting one-eyed through black metal vents and seeing
enough of Eddie to know where the smell was coming from.

He was grateful enough to the plumply helpful girl to pile
spilled rubbish back into the bin, but didn't go into the shop
again, walking instead down the rear alleyway and taking the
long route to his car, arriving just as Morrissey came out of
the gents. Useless effort or not Diggs couldn't resist walking
briskly over to ask for a press statement, not one whit disappointed when all he got was a grunt.

SIXTEEN

THE FIRST TIME ROSEMARY met Robert she wanted him. No point in denying that. Not that she had told him so. Not then.

One walk in the park, two candlelit dinners, and they had been in bed.

How silly of her to take him home to Penrith to watch him charm her parents and feel happy. Except that he hadn't quite managed to charm her mother. 'Rosie, I'm worried about you. How do you know he won't leave *you* for somebody else?' she had said in the quiet privacy of the garden. 'If he's done it to one woman he can do it again, and I don't want you to get hurt.'

It's inbuilt, Rosemary thought, the way girls never listen to their mothers.

She cleared the remains of dinner for one, then came back to the window and stared out at the night, wineglass in hand, wondering what Robert was doing now—what *they* were doing now—tormented by images into opening a second bottle. Thinking if she kept on drinking like this she'd be an alcoholic in no time.

MONDAY MORNING the *Sun* and *Express* vied for the most lurid heading. Malminster Maniac Claims Second Victim lining up against Psycho-killer Strikes Terror—the *Post*'s Lavatory Attendant Killed in Mystery Slaying, civilised in comparison.

Morrissey took the morning briefing out of sorts. Osgodby had seen the headlines too and wanted to know which bright little mother's son had run off at the mouth. Nobody had. Diggs had been in the wrong place at the wrong time—or the right place at the right time, depending on point of view—but Osgodby couldn't seem to get his mind round that. 'How in hell did he get the lurid details then, eh? Explain that.' Morrissey couldn't, it was something he wanted to know too. He made that a priority as he looked round the assembled faces, his eyes staying with Smythe long enough to suggest that was where he expected the answer to come from. How the shit was he supposed to know? Smythe thought, sidling out with the rest of them, Eddie's looming post-mortem taking up most of his mind. Funny though the way Diggs had known about fiddling little things like Eddie's Puma trainers. Black and white and red all over like sodding newspapers. Almost as if he'd had a bird's eye view of things. Couldn't have had though, could he? Running his mind around the washroom walls and remembering the vented window high up on the west wall. Couldn't see in through that—not without a ladder. Except that the gents was three steps down from the pavement. He saw a glimmer of light.

'Going somewhere?' asked Woods.

Shrugging into a chunky car-coat with its 'Warehouse' label Smythe muttered under his breath and left him in the dark. Asked the same question a few minutes later by Barrett, Smythe said shortly, 'Monk Street,' and carried on downstairs. Behind him Barrett grinned, recognising the effect of Morrissey's flint eye in the DC's rush of activity.

MIDDLE-AGED WOMEN liked Sparrow—younger ones too but for a different reason, then giving him the glad-eye as they went by swinging head and hips, although mostly so bundled up in winter clothes it didn't show. Older women got lucky, something about him stirring memories, sons grown and gone, or young lovers with downy skins and soft promises never to be heard again rising like gold dust and turning them soft-headed. Like Jeanie Hawkes. She watched him stamping his feet, intercepting men but rarely women, showing a photo and scribbling with frozen fingers on his clipboard, and thought how a pot of tea to warm him up wouldn't go amiss, tipping in a good measure of brandy to make sure it circulated properly. Out through the side door and across the pavement, the wind biting through skirt, cardigan and sensible thick-knit tights making her wish she'd stopped to put on a coat. 'Thought you needed a warm,' she said, handing him the pot and taking a squint at the photo. 'Who'd do a thing like that? I ask you. Quiet little man like him—don't know what things are coming to.' She rubbed her upper arms and shivered.

'Knew him then?'

'Saw him every day or just about, coming in and going out. No harm to a soul.'

'What's your name then, love?' Sparrow, sipping, tasted the brandy and feeling a warm surge thought he'd got a double gift, his eyes looking past her through the open door and up a flight of stairs, registering the Jeanie Hawkes in his brain as he said, 'Thanks for this,' and raised the mug. 'Bring it back up in a bit, if that's all right?'

'No rush about it,' she said comfortably. 'I'll leave the latch off and keep the kettle hot.' Half-running back to her warm room and thankful when she got there. Sparrow, behind her, gulped fast, changing his stance to take in the door because he didn't want anybody else slipping in there while it was an open invitation. He wondered why it was that plums seemed to be dropping into his lap lately.

'I DON'T SUPPOSE there's much chance it's somebody else,' Barrett said, making it a statement and not a question. 'Two nutters with knives wouldn't bear thinking about, and I suppose if we're looking for a reason this is it,' reading a typed-up copy of Ida Jameson's statement and wondering if there was any way it could leak out that she'd seen something she shouldn't have.

'Depends how many people she's told already,' Morrissey said, thought-reading again. 'And whether she's bright enough to put two and two together when she reads the paper. Be useful to have another word with her.'

'Smythe?'

'Since she confided in him before.' Looking at his watch he said, 'Where is he?'

'Gone whizzing off to Monk Street in search of that leak.' Barrett flicked through papers in his in-tray, saying off-handedly, 'Any more news of Inspector Beckett? Close on three months now and we could do with him back.'

'When he comes it'll only be light duties for a bit. Minimum stress was the last I heard, but don't quote me on that and don't spread it around.' Watching Barrett's face and rightly reading the reaction. 'Looks like you'll be doing the job without the title for a while yet.'

'Sir.' The sergeant liked independent action but fancied the money to go with it. If Beckett ended up with a desk job…? Cut off there in his musings by Morrissey preparing to go out; the DCI putting on a police-issue car-coat, past worrying about trendy labels when all that mattered was it kept him warm.

'Anybody wants me I'm at the psychiatric unit.' He was half out the door before he swung his head round. 'Brief Smythe on the Jameson woman, Neil—when he comes back.'

'Pleasure,' said Barrett, getting down to some paperwork, then breaking off to scribble 'See me' and his initials on a piece of scrap paper and line it up neatly on Smythe's desk. Be a close run thing when he got his pips, Smythe and Copeland both after sergeant's shoes.

He walked blithely back across the landing and wished he got the casting vote.

THE SAME GIRL was there, filling up shelves, standing on tiptoe and still not quite reaching the top. Smythe flashed his warrant card at her and said he wanted to see out the back. She stopped what she was doing and put the cigarettes down fast, pinking up enough to show she knew why he wanted to do that, and unfastened the counter flap.

'Better come through,' she said turning and heading for the back door.

'What about the shop?'

'What?' swivelling to look at him.

'The shop door. Wouldn't want to lose half your stock, would you?'

'Shan't be gone half a tic,' she pushed the rear door and walked through with a flounce of her head. Brainless, he thought. 'This what you wanted to see? Stockroom?'

'The backyard. That's where you took Diggs, isn't it?'

'Who?'

'The reporter. The one who slipped you something to let him look around outside. Don't suppose you thought it might impede police inquiries doing that?'

'Don't see how it could have.' She folded her arms. 'Anyway, I rung up and you didn't want to know.'

'What did you think we'd come there for?'

'How do I know? Didn't come and tell me, did you? If you'd said I shouldn't have let him in I wouldn't have, would I?'

Gritting his teeth because females of her type were never logical, he barged past to find that the vented window didn't need a ladder when the dustbin would do nicely. Busily occupied in upturning that receptacle when he heard a faint *ping* from the shop and sent her back, because he didn't want to end up chasing a petty thief and looking a right prat with all the uniforms about.

Taller than Diggs, and not in need of a tomato box, Smythe squinted down into the washroom and got the same bird's eye view. Now all he had to do was go back and confess that the window had been left unsecured. Another black mark against him. But nobody else had thought about it either—not Woods, and not Morrissey when he came down. Not that that'd make any difference. He dusted off his hands and was nowhere near as careful tidying up after himself as Diggs had been.

Back inside the shop he waited while she weighed out two ounces of dark shag and rang in the money, then he handed out a snappy warning about talking to Diggs again should the reporter come back. Luckily he didn't see her stiff finger him as he walked away.

SPARROW SAW SMYTHE coming and going, speculated on the whys and wherefores of it and slowly froze until close on eleven, when he picked up his pot and went looking for its owner. Chances were she'd add nothing that he didn't already know, but at least he'd get a warm out of it. A couple of minutes later, perched awkwardly on a chintz-covered chair

letting the gas fire thaw ice from his fingers while his bene-
factor fixed a new brew in the kitchen, he tried out a few
questions in his mind beginning with, had she seen the road
accident?

'Couldn't help but have, not with all the noise,' she said
when she came back. 'Sounded like a live parliamentary debate on TV. You know what I mean?' Laughing at him. 'Baa-
ing and moo-ing like a farmer's field.' Pouring tea and settling
comfortably. 'Makes no wonder the country's in a mess the
way they carry on. Drop of brandy? Might as well, if you're
going back out there.' She tipped the bottle before he could
stop her. If the sergeant came round and smelled his breath
he'd be in right bother; nothing for it but to nip over to the
tobacconist himself for a packet of Polo's before he got back
to his clipboard again.

'So you saw it after it had happened?' he said. 'You didn't
see the bus hit him?'

'Not what you wanted to hear, is it, love?'

'Depends. Did you notice Eddie?'

'He came out for a look like everybody else, didn't stop
there long though, too cold for him. Arthritis.'

'Did you see anybody go into the gents after that?'

'Well, there's men going in and out all the time, love; it
gets a lot of traffic.' Hesitating. 'If I knew what you wanted
me to say...?'

He didn't *want* her to say anything, didn't want to put words
in her mouth that'd do neither of them any good.

She fidgeted then sat forward, elbows on knees, cup in both
hands, staring at him as if she was remembering something he
ought to know. Sparrow kept quiet and waited. 'Chocolate
biscuits,' she said abruptly. 'That's what we want. Chocolate
biscuits. Like them, don't you?' Up on her feet and away to
the kitchen without hearing the denial. Sparrow looked at
framed photographs on television and mantel, blue knitting on
the floor at the side of her chair, everything in the room neat
and tidy, no one to disturb it. How old was she? Fifty? Sixty?
He was hopeless at telling ages. His gran was seventy but
didn't look it to him. Putting his cup and saucer down square

at the side of his chair he waited for her to come back, only to have to take a biscuit and speak through the crumbs.

'After the accident?' she said. 'After?' Screwing up her forehead. 'There was one chap ran over to the gents nearly straightaway—I remember me thinking it must have properly upset him to want to get there that fast. It was right after that Eddie came out to have a look. Is that what you want to know?'

'Part of it,' said Sparrow. 'Do you remember what he looked like?'

'Youngish from the way he ran, and a blue coat like solicitors wear, but he didn't do Eddie any harm, I saw him Friday morning and he waved to me. Eddie I mean, not the other chap.'

Scribbling fast, Sparrow let her refill his cup and felt lucky.

SEVENTEEN

THE GARAGE on Manor Road had been a Texaco station and Texaco were reluctant to lose all of their investment. Ralph Spivey was there to look it over with a view to opening it up again, with upgraded forecourt and new management. He sat with the car heater going on the cracked forecourt for half an hour watching traffic flow and decided there was no shortage of passing trade. If Texaco reopened with a better deal than the Shell station two hundred yards further up trade should slow. He looked critically at the old cement building and thought it would have to come down, everything start up again from scratch, courtesy rooms and hot drinks, a tidy forecourt and a few flowers to get the women drivers in. Yes, it could be pulled back into profit given time.

It was when Spivey left the car and took the padlock off the side door that he knew something was wrong. He entered the building gingerly. A dog or cat not able to get out? Recent thought—it wouldn't still be that ripe after six months. He left the door open behind him, fetched the torch from his car and swung the beam wide, picking out first the workbench then the makeshift brazier before he pin-pointed the source of the smell and backed out fast, glad the firm provided him with a mobile phone. Sitting in his car, waiting for the police, he put two strong mints in his mouth, started up the heater and turned on the radio to distract his mind—then asked himself if it were a plus or a minus, the thing that he'd found.

Murder drew people like honey drew flies. Look at that Michael Winner series on TV. If they got started building fast enough... Still working on that when the first Panda arrived.

THE PSYCHIATRIC UNIT had been given a face lift. Tiled walls and echoing floors replaced by heavy-duty carpet tiles and cream walls. Multi-hued paintings cheered the formerly depressive atmosphere. 'Looks better,' Morrissey told Reynolds. 'If you don't watch it they'll be queuing to get in.'

'They already are,' Reynolds said. 'A penalty of success or a measure of the state of society. Take your pick.' He reassembled a file he'd been leafing through. 'Right—what are you going to dun me for?'

'Information, what else? Specifically to know what's going on at the citadel—some sort of psychological study?'

'General interest or something else?'

'Both. There could be things picked up there that I'd like to know.'

'Thinking of last week's murder?'

'Among other things.'

'None of which fringe on confidentiality or we could run into problems?' Reynolds looking at Morrissey and getting a resigned head movement, friendship could stretch only so far and both knew it. Morrissey also knew that he'd walk all over the ground rules if he had to. So did Reynolds.

'Anything you can tell me?' invited the chief inspector.

'The citadel project has been set up to examine causes of vagrancy, the idea behind it being to find a point of intervention—and it's a participatory exercise—meaning that it's up to the vagrants themselves to decide whether or not to give life histories. We don't try to force them and they're promised confidentiality,' he emphasised. 'More to the point, John—it isn't my project.'

'Whose then?'

'Alan Salter.'

'Someone I should know?'

'No reason why you should. He came here on a research project from Durham University three months ago, and teamed up with a social science lecturer from Brindley College.'

'Brindley?' Morrissey asked sharply.

The psychiatrist looked at him. 'That causes a problem?'

'No. Something I wasn't expecting, that's all. Carry on.' He told himself that coincidences abounded.

Reynolds shrugged. 'Not much else to know. It's a jointly

funded survey, Social Services and the Health Authority pick up half the tab each. The aim, as I already told you, is to talk with and counsel vagrants, and its main preoccupation is the gathering of life histories. Enough of them and an improved intervention policy might come out of it.'

'Improved? I never knew there was one,' said Morrissey dryly.

'Apart from police cells.'

'Something like that.'

'If they come up with a common trigger, primary intervention should be possible.'

'How primary?'

'God knows. Before secondary school probably; once they hit the streets it's nearly always too late.'

'And you aren't involved?'

'Not directly.' Reynolds doodled question marks. 'I've been asked to oversee this side of things by the Health Authority—mainly because Alan is newly qualified—them covering their backs again, but up to now there's been no need for input from me, he's doing well enough on his own; seems to be asking the right questions and getting useful answers.'

'Any I might find interesting?'

'None that would help in a murder hunt.'

'Still being diplomatic.'

'Goes with the job.'

'If Salter is based here, in the hospital, I'd like to speak with him.'

'He isn't. He has room and board at Brindley, in exchange for which he lectures final-year sociology students. It's a fair arrangement, helps him, helps the college, and gives him a chance to compare notes. Most times that's where you'd find him, but today you've dropped lucky—he's here. We were going through his last batch of interviews when you turned up. I'll call him in but, as his minder, I'd like to sit in with you.'

'He isn't a suspect,' reminded Morrissey.

'If you want a tête-à-tête you could always see him at Brindley when I'm not around. Up to you. That way it wouldn't be on hospital property and would be out of my jurisdiction. The problem is that while he's here my head shares the block.'

'And I owe you a few favours.'

'Not something I planned to remind you of.'

'Fetch him in,' said Morrissey. 'If he gets it wrong you can put him right.'

'Don't expect callow and beardless, John. Alan is a late starter, and what he lacks in experience is made up for in acumen.'

A warning to mind his p's and q's or just for information, wondered Morrissey as he waited. Then Salter came and he got down to asking questions, easing out answers, and finding that Duffy had not only been known by Salter but had contributed a rambling and disjointed history. Morrissey asked for access. Salter refused. Morrissey pointed out acerbically that being neither priest nor doctor, Salter had no grounds for refusal. Salter snapped back that the files were confidential.

Reynolds put in mildly, 'The man is dead, Alan, and not very pleasantly, I don't think you should worry too much about confidentiality. In this case Duffy's interests would best be served by giving access.'

Salter shrugged. 'You're the boss I suppose, but I don't think there's much in there that will help. It's mostly reminiscences.'

'Nothing about friends?' asked Morrissey.

'Vagrants don't have friends, if they had they wouldn't be out on the streets. That's one thing they all have in common— no support network to fall back on.'

'They don't make friends among themselves?'

'Of a sort. They organise into pecking order like the rest of us. Duffy was bottom rung, a jack drinker, the closest he got to having a friend was Geordie Harry, who shared a drop of rum with him sometimes. The rest of the street people avoided him. It's all in here.' He began to release pages from the fat folder in front of him. 'I'd appreciate having them back fairly soon.'

'No reason for me to keep them once they're read,' said

Morrissey. 'But it's very possible I'll turn up at the Wednesday session. Won't put you out much, will it?'

'It won't be welcome; it's hard enough to establish a relationship with men who spend their lives in shop doorways at the best of times. They have no trust left. When we first started up the project it took three weeks of bribery and cajoling to get the first one in with us. A police presence could wind it up.'

Just like that—blunt and be damned, thought Morrissey. Reynolds would have been more diplomatic but Reynolds had experience. He said just as bluntly, 'A murder inquiry takes precedence over everything else. I'd appreciate having cooperation but if I can't have it I'll tread on whatever toes I need to.'

'Alan's thinking about the project,' said Reynolds.

'Won't be one anyway if he runs out of candidates. Any more deaths and they'll start moving on.'

'You think you'll find Duffy's killer at the citadel?' asked Salter. 'Unlikely.'

'I'm not writing it off as a possibility. Any reason why I should?'

'No.'

Morrissey studied Salter's expressionless face. 'We'll find him,' he said. 'Wherever he is. One thing you can be certain of.'

Salter smiled. 'The first fact of life I learned in psychology was that we can never be certain of anything.'

'Have to wait and see who's right then, won't we?'

Reynolds said quickly, 'Alan, ask Celia to photocopy the file sheets—then the chief inspector won't have any worries about sending them back.' Salter didn't argue, simply got up and walked out of the office. Alone with Morrissey, Reynolds looked apologetic. 'He's a bit edgy, he wants to get it right.'

'And I wouldn't try to stop him,' said Morrissey. 'If we need a presence at the citadel we'll step carefully.'

'I know that, John. Anything more you need?'

Overstayed his welcome, thought Morrissey, about to say yes, there was something else when his pager bleeped and he learned what was waiting for him in the old Texaco station on Manor Road.

SMYTHE STOOD passively through the lavatory attendant's postmortem, forcing his eyes to the table when Warmsby spoke and for the rest of the time occupying them elsewhere, counting rows of tiles, watching the second hand move on the wall clock, wondering what made a man trained to save lives want to specialise in pathology. He grappled with that, going back to school biology lessons and the thin-faced kid who'd delighted in cutting up rats. Maybe it was part of the same thing.

'Throat first this time,' Warmsby said gruffly. 'Tell Morrissey that. A single cut from behind, left to right, the body exsanguinated before the abdomen was opened up, probably a matter of minutes separating the two.' Squinting up at Smythe. 'Can you think of a reason for that?'

Smythe's mind moved from school lab to gents washroom.

'Keys,' he said. 'He'd have had to take the keys and lock up before anybody else came in.' His mind racing. Where were the damn keys? *Shit!* Morrissey might not have queried that yet but he would before the day was out. Something else Smythe had slipped up on—unless SOCO had turned them up. Bagged them and said nothing. If they had he was safe; if not he'd have to get them back to poke in the drains. They'd love him for that.

'Not going to be much else to interest you here,' Warmsby said. 'Shame you need stay to the bitter end.'

Wasn't it though? He mumbled something about it being interesting, both of them recognising a lie for a lie.

TWICE THE DOG-FOX had led the vixen out of Pel's Copse and across the field to Brindley, instinct drawing him back to the safer earth. Both times she'd returned to the copse and he, besotted still, had trotted after her, the instinct to mate over-

riding that of perceived danger. At noon with the beginnings
of a slow thaw softening frost, he sniffed the bundle of old
clothes for the umpteenth time and screamed into the quiet air.

EIGHTEEN

BARRETT'S MESSAGE reached Smythe just before the post-mortem ended, relayed to him by the mortuary attendant. Not the whole thing—but part of it. Like contact Barrett before he left the hospital, and when Smythe did that he heard himself directed to go and talk with Ida Jameson again. The idea didn't please him. For one thing he wanted to settle down in the canteen with strong tea and something neutrally filling—like a chip butty. Something to convince his stomach that creating gas wasn't the only thing left in life. Besides which—regardless of Barrett's own worries—he didn't see how Ida could be in any danger. From where he stood it was bee-in-a-bonnet time. Even if she gossiped a bit to her friends it wasn't likely to get back to the man they were looking for.

And in any case—this time men were targets, not women.

In his experience that meant Ida was safe.

Had to.

Striding down the outer corridor he was satisfied with that deduction, until a small and less self-assured part of his brain questioned where the experience he was drawing on had come from. Nothing local, that was for sure. Something read in a true crime book then? Couldn't believe much of anything in those. Facts tarted up to read like fiction and from what he'd heard and seen difficult to separate one from the other.

Well then…

Nothing for it but to go, and he'd best do it straight off because he wouldn't want a wrong decision loaded on his conscience with everything else.

Sniffing the air as he stepped out of the mortuary building he found it not so cold. Either that or being closeted with dead bodies had made him notice it less. Getting inside the car and starting it up he looked out the windscreen and saw patchy green showing up among frosted grass.

Not imagination after all.

Better for brass monkeys.

Driving out of the car park faster than he should and taking the Brindley road again, he got to Ida's just as her dinner finished cooking, near overwhelmed by the warm brown-gravy smell of it.

'Sit down and I'll get another plate,' she said when she saw it was him. 'I never did get out of the habit of making for two and it'll be a real pleasure sharing a table again. Hot-pot that's all it is, always seemed the right thing for this kind of weather.'

Smythe sat himself and waited, salivary glands working overtime in anticipation. Why he'd thought about wasting time on a chip butty he couldn't for the life of him think.

SPARROW'S RELIEF turned up at twelve-thirty, and not happy about it either because he should have been day off and taking his two kids to the panto, not freezing to death asking bloody silly questions while his wife went with her mother. Not that the kids would mind; wouldn't matter to them who got them there as long as they went. Four years and six years and already accustomed to an absent dad.

Maybe his wife was right. Maybe he should look for something else. Join Group Four and get a laugh out of it.

'Give the canteen mince a miss,' he warned. 'Tipped the sodding salt cellar in.'

'Thanks,' said Sparrow. 'If you hadn't said that I'd likely have found out the hard way, tending to go for bolognaise like I do. Makes a change off sausage and chips.'

'Anything happening?'

'Not a lot.' Sparrow straightened his hat and strode off, eager to get to the canteen and have a proper warm up before he passed his report along the chain of command—knowing it would get to Morrissey's desk eventually but wishing he could hand it over himself just the same. Get his face known. That's what it was all about for footers like him when you came right down to it, being noticed, separated out as brighter than the average plod. And if it wasn't him angling for a move up or sideways it would be somebody else.

And never once in his career plan to stay a constable.

HATCHED IN SOME unseasonably warm place the fly settled on the edge of his plate, lowered its probiscus and began to feed from leavings. Arms folded he watched, at ease with himself until memory of another fly surfaced from his subconscious. Then he was six, with the salt taste of semen in his mouth and his anus on fire, watching his father pull the legs off a bluebottle, its fat body pinned grotesquely to the kitchen table. When both wings were gone his father had dropped the useless body into his unwilling hand. 'See it? Tell anybody, and I mean anybody, and this happens to you.'

It would have suited his father to have him legless and arm-less, a mouth and an anus. And nothing more.

NO MORE LATE TUTORIALS. Wilson had made that clear at the staff meeting, and Adrian Fletcher knew it had been aimed primarily at him. Not second-hand this time but straight from the horse's mouth. He also knew what they were thinking, this sex-bound group of pseudo-puritans he worked with. Colleagues? Back-stabbers every one. Some blame lay on him, couldn't deny that, but not all his fault. He thought of Christine Raines, flashing her thighs. Giving him that wide-eyed come-on and no virgin, whatever anybody else might say. All right—in the end he'd gone too far, taken no for yes, but she'd provoked him. Blood alcohol too high and that had tipped the scales, but nothing to say the embryo she'd dropped in some Huddersfield clinic was his. Could have been anybody's, and her acting like little Miss Purity.

It had taught him a lesson.

One he hadn't forgotten.

But Liz Pardoe was different.

Not like Christine Raines at all.

BARRETT HAD GOT THERE before him, distance making the difference. Not much of a head start though and when he got there wishing like everybody else that he'd been busy else-where. Not saying that to the chief inspector, and not needing to with his face letting the cat out of the bag.

Morrissey stood in silence and took in the kind of horror that was becoming familiar to him. No misplaced cuts. Some-body who knew his work; somebody who'd had practice. Where? The army? Previous kills on somebody else's patch? Possible but not probable, else the nationally linked police computer would have picked it up and spewed out reports, suspects, forensic findings. That it hadn't done so still puzzled him, he wouldn't expect that kind of knife work to come right first time. His eyes picked out the two bottles near the body, one empty of cheap wine, the other holding a third of its vol-ume in industrial spirit. Close up by the brick wall an old oil drum made a brazier, hole-punched sides near burnt through.

Some enterprising mechanic keeping warm before the place closed.

Now there were new ashes, underneath and around.

And a body naked as Duffy's.

He went back to his first thought and pursued it again. Somebody trained to kill or who'd trained himself?

Which?

Commandos were taught to slit throats. So were the SAS. A likely solution? A good man gone bad? Or an edge of the pit-dwelling psycho who'd watched too many horror movies? Either way there had to have been a trigger. Something to precipitate lambent hate into mordant activity.

Barrett said telepathically, 'I'm thinking Duffy mightn't have been the first, that the man we want could have been doing this for a long time. On the quiet, where bodies weren't likely to be found, instant graves in woods and ditches. Trou-ble is finding them. Did he start round here or just drift in and us unlucky, getting him when he's ripe?'

'God knows.' Morrissey sounding as morose as he felt.

'I haven't told Warmsby yet. Thought you'd probably want to do it yourself.'

'Who found him?' Nodding at the body.

'Site inspector from Texaco. Chap called Ralph Spivey, fifty-one, comes from Eastwick.'

'Talked to him?'

'Briefly. Told him he'd need to come in and give a statement.'

'Be useful if you organised that now.'

'Be a pleasure, sir.' He left on the trot with a grateful nose to tell Spivey to follow him into Malminster, the both of them glad to be away, and Barrett tied up with that and other odd-jobbing for Morrissey until early evening. Not getting to read the report on his own desk until Brindley College had closed down for the day, by which time there was nothing to be done about it until morning.

NINETEEN

BARRETT WAS IN EARLY, had made an effort to get there first and succeeded, winding himself up for the question-and-answer session he'd have to face before he could get what he wanted. He put Liz Pardoe's file on his desk, the audio technician's report practically burned into his memory, then read it again half-hoping he could find some let-out.

Luck of the draw he supposed, sending the tapes through at a quiet time—although for once he could wish the technicians had been busy. Better by far if he could have put off all the decision-making until other things quietened down.

He set Liz's photograph in front of him. Reddish hair and a spattering of freckles, direct eyes looking right through the camera and out the other side.

Examining him in return.

Or at least that's what it felt like.

Not the type to mess somebody about—he'd accept Hanson's word for that. So where was she? Not gone running home that was for sure, he'd already checked that out. And now they knew she was missing her parents had joined in the clamour.

Not surprising.

Only person acting like they expected her back any minute was Wilson.

And none of it helped much in deciding what should be done next—not that the final decision was his. First it had to go through Morrissey and after that climb upstairs. Dangle in front of the chief superintendent and likely as not get thrown right back at him. As far as he could see there was only the one option anyway—go back to Brindley and finish the search this time. No more pulling back because of some telephone call. He puzzled over that for the umpteenth time, because whatever the origin of it, somebody had believed the voice a good enough imitation to pass for Liz's.

He slammed the file closed. The whole thing was a sodding contradiction, and that being so, how was he supposed to convince Osgodby it wouldn't be another wild-goose chase he was setting off on? That this time if he had the men they wouldn't be wasted?

Last thing the chief superintendent would fancy was to pull men off a triple murder hunt—especially to look for a missing girl who could turn up alive and well.

Like being caught between a rock and a hard place. Story of his life.

SMYTHE HAD CHECKED—as far as he could see—every possibility, but he hadn't tracked down the keys to the gents on Monk Street, and Copeland and Woods were giving him fishy looks that said they knew something was up.

Psychic.

Edgy as a bitch on heat, he hung back after morning briefing. Barrett, with problems of his own, walked on by, an action that Smythe viewed as a small mercy. A pity everybody higher up than him didn't go off sick then he could get it sorted on his own. Mentally girding his loins as he advanced on the chief inspector.

Morrissey said, 'Something to tell me?'

'Sir.' Smythe dithered, then started out with Diggs and the vented window, plunging straight into the missing keys, then standing firm and waiting for the sky to fall.

'Read her the riot act then?'

'Yes, sir. I don't think she'll talk to him again.'

'Wouldn't have anything left to tell him, would she?'

'Nothing that I know about. Sir—about the keys. I thought it might be an idea to get SOCO back to look at the drains.'

'Better do it then.' Morrissey leaned back, played a small tattoo on the chair arm. 'Did you talk to Mrs Jameson?'

'Yes, sir. She knows now not to talk about what she saw. I told her we might need her for a line-up sometime and she seemed pretty relaxed about it.'

Anticipation or wishful thinking, wondered Morrissey.
'Anybody in mind?'

'Not yet, sir. Matter of time though, isn't it?'

'You'll let me have it all in writing,' Morrissey recognising
butter when he saw it. 'Shouldn't take long—let's say on my
desk in an hour.' Grinning inside himself as he read Smythe's
face, worse at typing than Copeland and more to learn. And
what made either one of them think Barrett's shoes coming
empty would mean promotion—hadn't they ever heard of new
blood?

ROSEMARY HAD SEEN the ad in the local paper. Had dithered
about it over the weekend because it wasn't something she'd
even thought about doing until now. But now she had to think
about it because Robert had gone and there was a hole in her
life she had to fill.

Lonely hearts.

The kind of thing that got laughed about in the staffroom,
a bit sad and silly. She'd done it herself—read out something
juicy and then asked, *'What kind of people are these?'*

Well, now she knew. They were people like her, put back
on the shelf, dumped on the reject pile and sorely in need of
another warm body.

And it was nobody's business but her own.

She ran her finger down the third column until she found
him, unsure why that one announcement had caught her eye.

'Intelligent but lonely male (43) seeks companionable
woman to share conversation, music, and life. Must enjoy Mo-
zart. Box 7057.'

Somebody with tastes and needs like her own.

She tore the ad out raggedly and dumped the rest of the
paper in the waste-bin before writing her reply, sealing it in a
self-seal envelope and taking it to the post box on the main
road before classes started.

It couldn't do any harm and it might even be fun.

BARRETT HAD TAKEN the plunge, stated his views, watched
Morrissey's eyes flick through the audio report, and then he

had waited stiff-backed.

'I don't see an alternative,' said Morrissey. 'There's a missing person and a hoax tape, and it can't be left to gather dust. I imagine the chief superintendent will see things the same way.'

'Be hard finding the men.'

'His problem. Goes with having a desk upstairs.'

Something he planned to avoid, but implementation of the Sheehy report on police staffing and structure would take away the choice. Annoyed that his mind kept going down the same tunnel, until the thought came into his head that it still wasn't too late to set up a market garden. Something he'd talked about years back when he'd gone through a sticky patch. Margaret had liked the sound of it then—*would she now?*

He gathered the slim file together and paused at the photograph. Some other man's daughter and no doubt as cherished as his own. Finding an echo of old anger as he said stonily, 'I'll take it up to him. He won't like it but he won't have an out either.' Stamping out of the room in a frame of mind that made Barrett glad not to be on the receiving end.

PHILIP WAS MOODY, sitting by the staffroom window, coffee on the sill. Holly picked up two wrapped chocolate biscuits and took her coffee over there too, proffering a chocolate crunch and sitting opposite him on the wooden settle. He stared at her hand blankly then shook his head.

'Penny for them.'

His head twitched sideways and his eyes moved away from her. Unwilling to give up on him Holly sat where she was.

'It's beginning to thaw—look at the dirty green patches coming through on the lawn. You know, I haven't seen any birds for ages; it always worries me when we get this kind of weather in case they all die and I never get to see one again. Silly, isn't it? I mean, I know they sit it out in barns and towns but I still worry.' *Damn it* she was prattling, acting like a schoolgirl with a crush, and he was staring at her as if she'd gone out of her mind. Then she saw the shade of a smile.

'I'm not good company,' he said, 'but thanks for trying.'

'You'd rather I went away?'

'Not forever,' he said. 'But just for now, yes.' Watching her cross the room, pick up a magazine, and sit half-turned away from him flicking its pages.

He drank down his coffee, knowing caffeine was the last thing he needed with a head full of hammers, and a minute later walked out of the room in search of aspirin. Salter, at the other side of the room with his feet up, watched him go, then catching Holly's eye said, 'He thinks too much, he needs to loosen up instead of trying to solve the world's problems.'

'That's what I like about him,' said Holly. 'He cares.'

'Don't we all?' said Salter, and went back to his book.

PAUL OPENED THE DOOR, saw Barrett, and read bad news in his face. Hope sank through his insides like jagged granite. 'The tapes,' he said woodenly as Barrett came past him into the room. 'I was right about them, wasn't I?'

Barrett's hands moved to tug his waistcoat and unzipped his parka instead—like thumb-sucking, he thought, something to leave behind—then seeing the lines and hollows of a sleepless night etched on Hanson's face he cleared his throat and fished for words, because giving out bad news was the worst part of the job.

'Yes,' he said. 'You were right. The voice prints were close but didn't match. I have to work on the assumption that whoever made the call knew Miss Pardoe well enough to imitate her voice.'

'Or was chosen for the job,' Paul said, watching Barrett's face but this time reading nothing.

'Either way makes it someone who knew her, had to, to get that close in timbre and inflection. Any ideas?' Getting only a shake of the head for reply. 'What about the ex-boyfriend?' Barrett pressed. 'Did she talk about him? Was he all right about the break up?' Eyeing the slumped shoulders and hands in pockets as he wondered which way depression would take Hanson, and whether he, Barrett, knew the whole cause of it.

'It ended,' said Paul tersely. 'She said he was all right about it.'

'Do you have his name and address?'

'I know his first name was Darryl, I never bothered to ask the rest, it wasn't something I needed to know.'

'No jealousy about it then?'

'What did I have to be jealous about? She chose me, that was enough.'

'Common enough to be jealous, easy to worry about what went on before, get possessive, let things eat away at you.'

'Not me,' said Paul firmly. 'I didn't need to. Once Liz closed a door that was it, finish. And like I told you—what we had was special.'

It always was, thought Barrett, until something went wrong, then all kinds of things happened. Like last year when Dr Gilmour came in and reported his wife missing, and nearly silver-wedding time. Weeping buckets and convincing them all he was gutted until they found out about the affair she'd been having. That had altered viewpoints. A week later they dug her out from under a young lilac in her own back garden.

'This hers?' Picking a pink sweater off the back of a chair.

'I didn't feel like moving it.'

'Comforting?'

'Like she might come back.'

Barrett dropped it back in place. Careful with it. Hanson didn't know yet but if Liz Pardoe turned up dead he would be top of the list of suspects—it was always the same—lovers and husbands first, ex's and family next.

And nine times out of ten one of them fitted the picture.

Chances were this time would be no different.

'Anybody else you can think of then? A girlfriend who'd cover up for her? Somebody with the same kind of voice?'

'No. Cover up what, for God's sake?'

'She might have needed some space.'

'No.' Definite about that, close to anger.

'Anybody with a grudge to settle?'

Paul shook his head. Liz didn't make enemies. He told Barrett that, still half-believing that wherever Liz was Fletcher had a hand in it. He said that too and watched Barrett's face grow noncommittal. Up to him what he wanted to believe. Barrett didn't know anything about Fletcher yet, and when he did he'd change his mind. Convinced of that Paul began to recount the tale of Christine Raines and the abortion she'd had last term.

TWENTY

AT MIDDAY IT BEGAN to snow. Large, soft flakes that clung to everything. By then they'd been searching an hour, a long line of men strung out at arm's stretch, prodding hard ground, scattering leaf mould, crawling around and under bushes that hadn't been cut back for a generation. Curious faces appeared at college windows, stared out and withdrew, speculation grew wildfire fast. Wilson was incensed.

'Utter rubbish!' His voice in anger more highly pitched, grating on Barrett's ears. 'Who's your chief officer? I want his name. Something's wrong when a detective sergeant can disrupt a college for an ill-thought-out whim. Nothing wrong with the girl. Nothing!' Glaring at Barrett.

Barrett enlightened him on Osgodby's name and rank then added, 'The search is under his authority, sir; he isn't likely to call it off.' He stared hard back at a man for whom dislike grew with acquaintance. 'I'm sure he'll be more than happy to confirm that for you.' A hundred per cent more confidence in his voice than he felt. Drop a name like the chief constable's in front of Osgodby and he wavered on the spot. He wondered if Wilson knew the chief constable.

Wilson's eyes hooded and shifted. The bluster dropped, he waved a hand. 'Get on with it! Waste your time! That's all you'll be doing, and after this, when Miss Pardoe does come back she'll be sent packing.'

'I don't believe we'll be wasting time, but I wish I did think that. Tell me, sir, do you know of a girl named Christine Raines?' Watchful eyes seeing the principal's face turn darker still.

'A student, no longer at the college.'

'Why is that, sir?'

'Because she left.'

'Any particular circumstances?'

'None that have a bearing on Elizabeth Pardoe.'

'I'd like to hear them just the same.'

'The circumstances are confidential.'

'I've already been given one version.'

'Gossip.'

'Possibly,' Barrett acknowledged with smooth politeness. 'Adrian Fletcher, one of your lecturers,'—Hanson had said 'lecherer', almost spitting it out—'I believe he knew Christine Raines quite well—intimately well, if I believe what I'm told. I take it you're happy with Mr Fletcher's work and general conduct?'

'Obviously.'

'Well liked, is he?'

Wilson stared back silently.

'I'm trying to think why Hanson would go bursting into his room the night Liz Pardoe vanished.'

'Manic jealousy, completely uncalled for. The girl attended a tutorial and then left. You established that last time you were here.'

'That's true, sir, but I didn't know about Christine Raines then.'

'I really can't see a connection.'

'Can't you, sir?'

Silence again.

'Thing is,' pursued Barrett, 'wouldn't it be better for me to hear the truthful version from you than pick up gossip secondhand? Better for the college too, I would have thought, than having rumours fly round.'

'What rumours?' Wilson snapped edgily.

'About a connection between the two girls. Things build up, get out of hand. I've heard of tarring and feathering for less than he's supposed to have done.'

'That's all there is to it,' said Wilson. 'Rumours. Hard for any man to defend himself.'

'Fletcher needed to then?'

'Needed to what?'

'Defend himself.'

'I didn't say that.'

'Best if I discuss it with him then.'

Silence.

'Christine Raines—was she anything like Liz Pardoe?'

'No.' Definite about that.

'Wouldn't make the same mistakes then. A good student?'

'Patchy—good when she put her mind to it.'

'Meaning she didn't do that often? What about Liz, how did she do academically?'

'She'd be heading for a first if she kept her mind on it. I find the girl annoying, intensely so, but she has a fine brain.'

'Sociology student?'

'Combined course, sociology, psychology, and political science. Academically she's streets ahead of Hanson. If he breaks his back he might get a two-two.'

'You're saying he was jealous of her?'

'I'm saying there was friction.'

'You know that for a fact?'

'I have no reason to doubt it.'

'Gossip getting around?'

Silence again.

Barrett flipped back through his notes. 'You work on a tutor system?'

'Of course. As a university extension college our degrees have to be validated by the parent university. That being so we keep to the same system of tutelage.'

'And Liz Pardoe's tutors would have been...?'

'*Are*, Alan Salter, Philip Jacques, Holly...'

'Were they also Christine Raines's tutors?'

'Christine was a humanities student, combined history and English, so of course she wouldn't have the same tutors,' Wilson said on a pettish note.

'But they both had Adrian Fletcher—why was that?'

'Elizabeth chose to do a one-year supplementary option in English history—Fletcher's subject. It isn't a compulsory part of her course and doesn't count towards a degree, but she felt it would help her understand the roots of sociology and political science.'

A workaholic, thought Barrett. That's what she sounded like. And workaholics sometimes had breakdowns. Feeling uneasy again.

'And Christine Raines?'

'Lacking in concentration, not a good student, but adequate when she wanted to be which, as you already suggested, wasn't often. The plain truth is that Christine looked on her time here as three years' fun and not three years' hard work. Not an attitude I encourage.'

'Skipped lectures?'

'She had adjustment problems—yes.'

'What kind? Flirting with the tutors?'

'Drinking too much.'

'Not easy to do anything about.'

'No.'

'And when she left it was of her own free will?'

'I had already given her three warnings of increasing severity but I didn't request her to withdraw from the course. She left for personal reasons three weeks before the end of term.'

And if Hanson was right had an abortion a week after that.

And Adrian Fletcher the putative father.

'Pregnant?' Barrett said, and watched Wilson's face suffuse again.

ACCORDING TO A well-known pathologist whom Morrissey had never met but whose reputation was great, it was impossible for a murderer to exit a crime scene without both leaving something of himself behind, and taking something—hairs, fingerprints, blood of the victim—with him. It was a comforting theory and one that had held good in Morrissey's books until now. Not anymore though, not where physical evidence was concerned—not unless SOCO or Forensic had lost both eyesight and skill and he didn't believe in that idea either. No; whoever he was hunting had put some thought into it, which gave him a sort of lead in itself. More than average IQ then. Someone who knew that given the right circumstances fingerprints could be lifted from cloth? Was that why he made a bonfire of dead men's clothes? He should have been covered in blood, soaked in the stuff, unless he'd come around behind them like an assassin, grabbed a handful of hair and pulled back making the stretched throat ripe for his knife. That way blood would have gushed forward, little if any back. Except that Warmsby had said that only happened with Eddie, not the other two.

And he hadn't burned the lavatory attendant's clothes. Hadn't left anything of himself on them either.

Gloves of some kind but what about the rest of him?

Coveralls? The disposable kind supermarkets sell to amateur handymen? Easy to burn. Coming back to the fact nothing had been burned in the gents, which meant Eddie's killer would have had to walk out of there wearing the clothes he'd killed in, and since he was intelligent he wouldn't have wanted to go far. Leaning back in the black leather chair, Morrissey closed his eyes, and visualised that area of town and the absence of any punitive parking restrictions. No, the man he had to catch would have had a car on the street or in the narrow alley at the back—the street quicker, the alley darker.

Eddie the unlucky, wrong place at the wrong time. Morrissey had known that for certain since he'd read Sparrow's report and made the connections. A man in a dark blue coat pushing Geordie Harry under a bus. The same man—had to be—running across the road and into the gents. And Eddie unsuspectingly seeing a face that didn't want to be remembered.

Could he have put a name to it?

Worth digging deep into Eddie's affairs on the off-chance. He gave that job to Copeland and made it his responsibility, telling the detective constable he wanted to know everything, doctor, dentist, butcher, baker, who Eddie saw—and what he did down to changing his socks and underwear.

Then he sat back and watched Copeland blink at the thought of it.

THE RENEWED SEARCH surprised him, he hadn't expected it, not yet at any rate, and this time they meant business. It worried him, looking out of the window between classrooms, wondering if there was anything he'd overlooked, then seeing the copse out of the corner of his eye and knowing there was. Somebody would be bound to think of looking in there; a bright spark out to make an impression. Not until they'd finished with the grounds proper though. If he went out at lunchtime, turned up the farm lane, he could cut across the field from the other side without being seen, pick up the clothes and be away again. Nothing for them to find then but a makeshift shelter not used for months and no sign of what lay buried nearby. Ironing out his face, he walked into the next room and faced his class, telling them, 'Today we're going to look at man in society, glancing at the Freudian approach to violence and examining its social causes.' Watching them all become busy with their books as he said it.

FLETCHER HAD a free period, unlucky for him but lucky for Barrett, catching him on the hop as it were, still in the seminar room but quite alone. Barrett noted the rubric nose and decided it wasn't only Christine Raines who'd had problems with a bottle. Had it been that colour last time he talked to him?

Didn't matter either way, except that the nose didn't pale down like the rest of his face when Barrett talked about Christine Raines's abortion and the gossip about Fletcher's part in it. 'I'll be getting a statement from Miss Raines,' he said. 'That doesn't necessarily mean I'll need to talk to you again but it's a possibility, depends on what she says.' Staring at Fletcher as if he'd already got him tried and convicted. 'So. If there's anything else you have to tell me about Liz Pardoe, it'd be best doing it now and not later. Best for you, that is. Did anything happen at the tutorial that night that would have upset her?'

'No!'

'You made no suggestions of a sexual nature? I'm sorry, sir, but in the light of Christine Raines that question has to be asked.'

'No!' Colour came back to Fletcher's face in a quick rush. He paced to the window and saw Jacques trot briskly to his

Fiat, the second of his back-stabbing colleagues to make a fast exit in twenty minutes, wishing he'd beaten them to it.

'If anything should come to mind…' said Barrett, scribbling his extension on a card, '…you'll find me on that number. Better sooner than later.'

Fletcher looked at the card as if it might catch fire in his hand, saying heavily, 'It's a mess.' Barrett's ears pricked up.

'What is, sir?'

'Bloody life.' Getting to the door and exiting fast before the sodding little plod thought of anything else.

THE DOG-FOX HAD BEEN out to forage, keeping low, heading for the college dustbins again before he saw all the activity and flattened himself among the gorse, nose fast-scenting, sensing that others were hunting too, turning tail to come luckily on a grounded pheasant disorientated by the weather. Later, lying fed under the thicket in Pel's Copse he scented man again, this one particularised in his mind as enemy. Edging forward, lips tightly back, he watched the rank bundle of clothes carried away.

A LITTLE AFTER TWO the softening snow became sleet and a westerly wind picked up strength, forcing the mix of rain and snow into eyes and ears and down the necks of waterproofs. By then the search had swept through the shrubbery and the immediate vicinity of the college buildings, and passed beyond into the formal gardens which led down to the back wall and gate. To the east were vegetable garden and nursery, with three glasshouses, two large sheds and one small, before a croquet lawn and clock-golf gave way to scrubby grass and low gorse between the wall and path on the far side of the lake, the gorse in turn giving way first to rough thicket and then bare and arching larches before swinging south again to the shrubbery and tennis courts.

When light began to fade the line of men picked up speed, looking to finish by the end of the day, and with nothing to show but miscellaneous litter, scratches, and one twisted ankle got from a grass-covered rabbit hole. To all intents and purposes the search was over—would have been if one conscientious soul stretching his back hadn't looked east across the field to Pel's Copse and wondered if they'd been looking in the wrong place.

Passing that thought on to the man in charge got him a wounded look. Maybe he'd have done better keeping his mouth shut. He mulled over that until the uniformed sergeant—co-opted unwillingly from Manor Road—told him grudgingly it was good thinking and he didn't know why he hadn't thought of it himself. Everybody else knew though. Nothing like a new baby and sleepless nights for numbing heads.

And not one man among them looking forward to another trawl the next morning.

TWENTY-ONE

WEDNESDAY MORNING and no frost, just a curling wind and grey sky, Morrissey preoccupied as usual at breakfast, and only half hearing what went on around him, until he saw they were all looking at him expectantly. He paused with a forked mushroom midway between plate and mouth. 'Sorry, I don't know what I've been asked.'

Mike said, 'If you can give me a lift home, Dad. Thing is, I'll have a stack of homework and there's bound to be rugby practice right after class.' He looked at his father with only half a hope. Morrissey temporised.

'I thought your mother picked you up on rugby days.'

'I do,' said Margaret. 'When he wants me to. But today I can't; there's a special meeting I have to be at. NSPCC business.'

'I'd do it, Dad,' said Katie, 'but I've got drama rehearsal. I'm sorry, Mike,' looking at him as she said it. 'Honestly, if we weren't doing my part tonight I'd skip it.'

'Doesn't matter,' Mike said. 'Pity it had to thaw.'

Morrissey chewed on the mushroom with Margaret's eyes still on him. 'I will if I can,' he said trying not to sound grudging. 'But don't take it as a promise—don't get upset if I'm not there,' meeting Mike's eyes and hoping for understanding. 'Depends what comes up. You know that.'

Didn't he though, thought Mike. Plenty of experience at fatherless growth, missed outings, Mum at home-matches shouting him on, lost among all the dads. Given a choice who'd have a policeman for a father? Guilty at that thought because when he was small he'd believed his dad invincible and wanted to feel like that again. Aching with the loss of it. He dropped his eyes and said stoically, 'It's all right, Dad, I'll manage.'

'Bottom gate at six-thirty if I can,' Morrissey said gruffly, well aware of his own shortcomings. 'And five minutes leeway.' Gulping down his tea he pushed away from the table, a market garden more attractive than ever but more affordable, if he put in all his time. And then what? Too old to tackle it? Life making promises and taking them away? Morose when he got in his car and in no mood for nonsense when he got out of it in the police yard.

IF THEY'D HAD HEAVY SNOW as well as a fortnight's frost, then with such a rapid thaw they'd have had flooding down the beck and out on the low road to Manorfield—and that would have meant more man-hours to be covered, with nobody left to pull in extra except the sick list. Something to be grateful for if not much, Barrett thought, dispirited that yesterday's search had drawn a blank, and feeling a thread of guilt about that because if it had been anything else the girl would be dead. He tried to tell himself a negative result was good news—it meant she might still be alive—but the same kind of gut-feeling he'd often doubted in Morrissey told him she wasn't as he looked at the copse.

If there was nothing in there, what next?

A headache, that's what.

Impossible to search every field, wood and hedgerow, pessimistically thinking she could be laid in a ditch and there forever, unless some sniffing dog found her out. Plenty of perfect murders around except no one admitted it. Only the careless ones got caught.

Them and the ones who wanted to be.

When he talked to Holly Havers again he wondered why there'd been no teachers as good looking as her when he went to school. Probably just as well; it hadn't exactly been a school for gentlemen. He asked about Adrian Fletcher and the girl students and watched her clam up, workplace loyalty taking precedence over his questions. When he brought up Christine Raines he got told prettily that Holly hadn't been at Brindley last summer. Blanks all round. Looking out the corridor window while he waited for the next one to come he guessed he'd get the same answers he'd been given last week, almost as if they'd put their heads together. He had started to turn away when he saw a male student running, coming pell-mell across the drive and into the building, feet heavy on the stairs.

Barrett reached the stairwell at the same time as the student, who stopped, out of breath and hesitant, holding something that dripped rhythmically.

'One of Liz's books,' he said. 'I thought you'd want to see it, it was in the lake.' Shifting from one foot to the other, nervous and trying not to show it.

Barrett, stretching out a hand to take the sodden article, cursed himself that all this time she'd been under the ice.

COPELAND WAS THOROUGH, more so than Smythe, and although his eyes also were fixed on making sergeant he had a head start on that, with both parts of the sergeant's exam under his belt to Smythe's one, and two years extra in the force because he'd been a cadet. Copeland also planned on marrying soon and didn't mean to wait around for Barrett to move up. Could be tomorrow, could be years, could be never before that happened. Which was why he'd got into the habit of running his eyes down national vacancies every time he got the chance, because moving from Malminster wouldn't be all that much of a hardship, and his future mother-in-law could be better tolerated from a distance. It also gave him all the more reason to turn in a good job for Morrissey when he got the chance, pluses on his sheet being better than minuses, and the chief inspector being respected enough for a recommendation from him to go a long way. Thinking of his fattening dossier on Eddie with a sense of satisfaction. Everything Morrissey had asked for and a bit more.

He came out of Eddie's local chuffed, expecting to add to what he'd already got by talking to a girlfriend the landlord had pointed him to, marvelling that a man of Eddie's age and health still had the stamina. Or maybe all he did was lie back and think of England. Or look. Either way better than nothing and a long way from what he had, thank God. He found the block of council flats two streets away from Eddie's place and climbed to the seventh floor because the lift wasn't working. Not even thinking she might not be home until he rang the doorbell and heard it echo emptily, then he remembered the long walk down and grudged having nothing to show for it. His thumb went on the bell again. Counting slow to twenty he tried one last time, jamming his ear to the wood as the bell stopped and about to give up when he heard something. Thumb still on the pusher when the door swung in and he recognised her face.

Mutual.

'If you're after a quickie you've had it,' she said and started to shove the door shut. His right hand and foot moved together.

'Never thought of you as an Amanda,' he said.

'Never thought of you as a john.' Pulling a pink satin wrap a bit tighter and tugging the sash. 'I'm off duty, love, catch me down Carter Street tonight.'

The other end of town from her regular pitch and both of them knowing it. 'It's not about that, Mandy, it's about Eddie. You used to drink with him sometimes in the Red Lion. Customer was he?'

'No.' Her face sagging and wetness in her eyes. 'Nothing like that; he didn't even know I was on the game. A nice man, Eddie, a gentleman, not many of them about.' Her eyes told him he was included in that.

'About as many left as there are ladies,' said Copeland. 'Do I come in and talk or do we do it at the station?'

'No need to be like that, not if it's Eddie you've come about.' Mandy let go of the door and turned back inside, Copeland behind her. 'Not that I know nothing, so it's no use you hoping. If I knew who'd done it I'd have shopped him. Wanta cuppa?' Veering off she went into the kitchen, Copeland startled to find it that clean. 'I'm having one, so you suit yourself. Won't catch nothing.' Seeing a doubtful look she reached down a box with a mug inside, dancing cats on it. 'Use that if you like, untouched by human lips, Eddie gave it me, Christmas. If you're looking for his killer I reckon he wouldn't mind having you use it.' Busily putting on the kettle as she spoke.

'So how did you know him?'

'Took a tumble outside his place, carrying shopping home. He come out and helped me.'

'Then what?'

'Then he carried it back here. Wouldn't let me. I gave him a cup of tea and we got chatting. Wife gone, kids not bothering with him.'

'Kids?'

'Two. Not round here though, hadn't had sight of them in years. Glad I don't have any sometimes. Why'n't you sit down?'

Only sometimes? Pulling out a chair. 'Any idea where they are?'

A shake of her head as she stirred the pot. 'Don't think he knew.'

'And you saw him again?'

'Bobbed out of his place a week after and asked how I was. Said did I ever go round the Lion. I told him no, I never had,' she squinted at him sideways. 'I keep what I do away from here, wasn't any way he'd have known.' She put a part-bottle of milk on the table and poured tea.

'And he asked you out for a drink?'

'S'right. And that's all there ever was to it. A drink in the pub, fish and chips, the pictures sometimes. He was nice, I'd have liked him for a dad.' Her eyes wetted again and she grabbed a kitchen towel. 'I mean it,' she said. 'He was all right. Only thing in trousers I ever knew what was.'

Copeland picked the silver top off the milk, topped up the dancing cats, hovered it over Mandy's mug, pouring when she nodded, seeing a side of her he hadn't thought about. He wanted to ask why she did it if men were that bad but kept his mind on Eddie instead.

'Was he worried about anything—anyone bothering him?'

'Got the other sort down the lavatories, looking for company—you know? That bothered him a bit, he didn't like that kind of thing but they didn't give him any trouble.'

'He talked about work then?'

''Course he did, what men do, isn't it? Work and cock and

not much else with most of them.' Scornful, then softer when
she said. 'Not Eddie.'

'When did you see him last?'

'Thursday night. Seemed all right, we had a drink in the
pub, called in the chippy and took them back to his place.
He'd borrowed this video, *Call Me Madam*. I hadn't seen it
before. It was good Eddie said him and his wife watched it
when they were courting. At the pictures of course, wasn't any
videos then.'

'What happened to her?'

She shrugged. 'Died five, six years ago. Got the big one.
You think there's anything in this afterlife thing?' Uncom-
fortable, Copeland shook his head. 'He missed her,' she said,
'Be nice if…' shrugging again, 'Con like everything else.'

'Lot of people think it's right.'

'Yeah, one born every minute.' Grabbing another paper
towel to blow her nose. Wet-eyed in this setting she didn't
look like a tom. Getting his mind back to Eddie again he asked
about the traffic accident. Had Eddie mentioned it?

'About a week since? That one? He didn't see it, said he
went to look, after it happened, but he couldn't see for people.'

'Is that all he said?'

'Told me somebody ran in down the cubicles, jumping up
and shouting *yes*, loud like. Then when he sees Eddie he ducks
out of sight. That's when Eddie went out to have a look.'

'He didn't see the man leave?'

'I don't think so.'

But he'd got a good look at the man's face, thought Copeland.

'Did he say if he was young, old, fat, thin?'

'I didn't ask.' Startled as she saw the connection. 'You think
he's the one who…?'

'Anything's possible, Mandy, we don't know.' He went
back through the names he had written down, the places Eddie
visited, her face blank as he read out most of them, although
there weren't that many.

'There's one place you haven't got down,' she said when

he'd finished. 'The hospital. Didn't his doctor tell you about that?' The doctor hadn't.

'Why was he there?'

'He got really depressed when his wife died, had to keep going back to see somebody but I don't know who.'

Copeland wrote that down as another string to follow, but not much else to go with it. No enemies and not many friends either come to that, or at least—not close. Unless you counted Mandy, *have* to count her considering how upset she was. He got to his feet and awkwardly thanked her for the tea.

''S' all right,' she said. 'Won't make any difference next time you pick me up.'

'You could try a different job,' he said.

'Yeah,' she said. 'I could be a sodding policewoman.'

TWENTY-TWO

MORRISSEY HAD GONE downstairs and asked a favour off uniform. Could he borrow Sparrow? No, not anybody else, Sparrow or nothing. And Morrissey being Morrissey got what he wanted. Sparrow, back to foot-soldiering again, couldn't believe his luck, into mufti faster than he'd ever moved in his life. Expecting to be teamed up with somebody in CID he found no one there except the chief inspector, and got a minute's panic at the thought of being teamed up with *him*.

Morrissey said, 'Know why I wanted you?'

'Not exactly, sir,' said Sparrow.

'Because you've already been to the citadel and managed to get some answers without frightening the customers. Is that right?'

'Yes, sir.'

'How would you fancy going back again?'

'I don't mind doing that, sir. What is it you want me to find out?' Confident on the surface but panicking underneath because what if he blew it?

'I want you to listen in. Talk to anyone who'll let you. Two vagrants gone in a week means some at least will be starting to worry, and I don't doubt a few already thinking about moving on. Find out if anybody's been noticed taking an interest in their comings and going; anybody chatting them up, offering goodies. Especially in a dark blue coat.'

'Yes, sir.'

'Off you go then. So far you've done well at collecting information, and I'll be expecting better still today. Bring what you get directly to me. Understood?'

'Understood, sir. Thank you, sir.' Turning smartly he made good time back downstairs, the station sergeant looking at him with open curiosity and wanting to know what was going on.

Sparrow tapped his nose, said something special for Morrissey and sorry, Sarge, but he was in a hurry, a cherubic grin as he went down the front steps instead of out the back door, pleased with himself, then thinking that when he got out of uniform for good, one thing he wouldn't miss was the boots.

BARRETT, STANDING AT THE lakeside, most of the ice gone but still some semi-mushy stuff at the edges, felt less sure now of what he would find in the lake. Nothing to be seen except water, murky and dark. No way of knowing how long the book had been in there either. He tried to remember something about lakes and ice formation. Thinner in the middle than at the sides, everybody knew that, but if she'd gone in the water the night she went missing would it have frozen over again by next morning? He wondered just how deep the lake was and how many weeds were at the bottom. Not enough to hold her down, he wouldn't have thought, but if she was in there something had to be. His brow furrowed. There were decisions to be made, and he wanted to make them himself before going to Morrissey. Nothing worse than dithering without clear purpose. Sighing, he walked over the arched wooden bridge and stood in the middle of it looking down.

If she were a jumper…?

Had to be considered.

Could she swim? Something else he didn't know. But if she had gone in deliberately she'd have weighted herself down, wouldn't she, most jumpers did, swimmers or not. Arguing with himself in his mind about the likelihood of it, he decided suddenly that there was no choice to make, and moved away from the lake and back to his car. There he raised Morrissey on the police radio and recounted developments, relieved when the chief inspector agreed with him on police divers.

Nothing to do after that but wait.

SPARROW OUT OF UNIFORM, beardless and soft-skinned, looked nothing like a policeman, and that being so he didn't see why he should make things difficult for himself by admitting to anyone except Captain George that he was one. 'Look,' he said. 'I can just hand soup out can't I? Extra pair of hands.' Sister Mary, topping up the tea urn, pursed her lips and said nothing, disapproving all the same. Lost souls all of them, every man-jack, and getting further away from their maker with every day that passed. Sooner they left their mortal remains behind the better as far as salvation went. Two of them in the far corner already and one of them hawking and turning her stomach over. She eyed Sparrow and wondered which side of the great eternal fight he was really on.

Tell a lie and get a lie, didn't he know that?

Captain George said, 'Probably get a rush today, a better menu on offer Wednesdays and Fridays, courtesy of the inquisitors.' That he'd let his dislike of the survey show caused him to flush a bit, because from what he'd seen there was no harm being done and he was grateful for whatever corner help came from. He was quick to explain that to Sparrow and got a sympathetic look in return, something Sparrow was good at and nobody knowing how often it was only skin deep.

'Don't suppose you ever get to know what goes on in there?' The salvationist shook his head. 'So the men never come out and sound off about it?' Sparrow pressed.

'They'll have a bit of grumble but that's about it.'

'What sort of a grumble?'

'Being made to go from thread to needle.'

'Life stories?'

'They don't always like looking back.'

'Not much different from you and me once, I suppose,' said Sparrow with an unwelcome flash of insight. 'You've heard Geordie Harry's in hospital?'

'I visited. Surprising what a difference clean pyjamas and a shaved face can make to a man, he looked almost godly.'

'Being sober would help I suppose.'

Webber's eyes smiled. 'They let him have a pint of Guinness after supper—medicinal—highlight of his day.' The smile fading. 'He said he hadn't fallen under the bus, somebody pushed him?'

'It's something we're looking at,' admitted Sparrow.

'I offered to provide a bed here, when he's discharged. Geordie said he wouldn't come near the place again—a little more colourfully than that, but it worries me.'

'Turning over a new leaf? Doesn't want to mix with this lot again and backslide?'

'The simplest explanation perhaps, but I don't think the right one. I had two constables here yesterday asking about Leonard Lawson.' Checking his watch Captain George took a step away, then stopped again. 'The men are starting to get nervous, two of their number gone and another in hospital. I don't think it will be long before Malminster sees an exodus.'

'I don't think many people would mind that.'

'Sad reflection on human nature,' said Webber, and this time when he moved away he didn't stop.

THE COPSE SEARCH was over and nothing of interest to anybody except PC Crowther but an old tramp's shelter, dropping to bits and looking like it hadn't been used in months. Crowther, country boy and hunt follower, had found something else. A fox's earth deep in thicket and tracks that showed Charlie in residence. Old rabbit warren probably, dug out and enlarged; fox's faeces on the spoil heap. Hunting round he decided there were two of them, and most likely dog and vixen. Standing at the copse edge he looked round, wondering who the land belonged to, something to find out before he had a word with the hunt master, pleased with himself that it hadn't all been wasted time.

HE DIDN'T KNOW what to do with the tramp's clothes but they couldn't sit forever in the boot of his car, whether in a bin-liner or not. He tried to assess the chances of a car search. Remote, had to be, without a body. Even so... Call at the council tip on the way back and get rid of them for good. Yes! Relieved he'd come up with such an easy answer and hurrying downstairs, where Rosemary, on her way up, stopped him to say with troubled unease, 'Did you know they're going to drag the lake? One of Liz's books has been found, floating near the bank—the police think she might be in there too.'

Eyes blank, mind working overtime at this new threat, he said. 'That she drowned herself, you mean? Jumped in?'

Rosemary's eyes widened. 'You think that's possible?'

'Or she fell in. What else could it be?' Surprised at his own calm ease.

Rosemary frowned, staring past him. 'It was so cold that night—and slippery—she *might* have fallen. I certainly can't believe she killed herself, but why would Liz be by the lake?' Low-voiced and half to herself, not really expecting an answer, or surprised by the brevity of the one she got.

'I really don't know that and I'm sorry, Rosemary, but I don't have time to talk right now.'

'Of course not,' she gave him a quick and meaningless smile and moved on up the stairs. Turning at the half-landing to look back, an image building in her mind.

MID-AFTERNOON, almost three o'clock, when Morrissey thought he'd given Sparrow enough time on his own. What he hadn't coaxed out by now probably wasn't worth having. He pushed up from his chair gratified to have an excuse to get out of the building, knowing Salter wouldn't be any too pleased to have him disrupt his vagrancy project. Driving more sedately than usual, the streets black with salted grit and dirt, and Morrissey not keen to help increase his car's corrosion. Nosing down Zenner Street he turned into the Salvation Army car park, and wondered idly why they would need that much space. More like a school playground than anything. He parked neatly beside a Fiat, and wished as he went through the front entrance that he was a head shorter and thinner to boot, so he could slip in unnoticed. Easing through the door still trying to do that and succeeding for less than five seconds. His eyes searched out Sparrow and found him behind a trestle-table handing out tea, a bonily angular woman watching every move.

Sister Mary. Every bit as formidable as he'd been told.

Morrissey advanced on them. Sparrow said cheerfully,

'Good afternoon, sir, can I get you a cup of tea or were you wanting to see the captain?' Leaning on the table nonchalantly, stance telling the chief inspector that as far as the vagrants were concerned Sparrow had never set eyes on him before. Morrissey played along.

'Both,' he said gruffly. 'Cup of tea *and* the captain.' Sister Mary bustled away before Sparrow could move. 'Helping out?' said Morrissey loudly. 'Or a permanent fixture?'

'Extra pair of hands. Got to do something to pass time on and it's this or rob a bank.' Grinning at Morrissey and wondering if he'd gone too far.

'You're telling that to the wrong man,' Morrissey flashing his CID card at him so everybody could see, and Sparrow relieved the chief inspector had caught on, handing him a hot mug and watching him turn away to talk to Captain George, everybody in the place nervy and ready to move out fast if he said the wrong name, and sinking back into near-apathy when they found out it was Salter he'd come to see.

'In my office,' said Captain George. 'You could be lucky, I don't think there's anyone in with them right now.' Leading the way, surprised Sparrow hadn't warned him, unaware that Morrissey's coming had been as big a surprise to the young constable as it had to him.

TWENTY-THREE

AT THREE-THIRTY, when the grappling hook caught in Liz's clothing, Paul Hanson was by the lake watching, white-faced and shivering. Barrett standing with him suddenly wished they'd drawn a blank there too, that it had been only a book in the lake and nothing more. Sending one of the constables back to his car for a blanket and insisting Paul either put it round him or go home. A frogman padding down to the lake like the creature from the black lagoon and slipping under the water, and everybody, or so it seemed, holding onto their breath until the goggled head surfaced again. A confab with the men waiting silent in their boat and another dive. The grappling hook hauled back and put away. Paul saying, 'What's happening?' and Barrett shaking his head, knowing but not saying. An age later, but only seconds in real time, the body was lifted over the gunwale and brought to shore. Paul seeing the drowned and ravaged face threw up into the grass, wishing he'd waited at home.

Wishing that like her he was dead.

Then anger flashed through him, hot as redemption.

But not until the bastard who did this to her was!

SALTER AND JACQUES were talking shop. Both looked up when Morrissey walked in and Salter's annoyance showed. It wasn't something that worried Morrissey. 'Mr Salter,' he said. 'Or is it doctor? No? Got it right then.' Turning to Jacques and raising his eyebrows. 'And I don't know you at all, but I expect you're the sociologist.' Shaking hands and filing Jacques's name away for future reference. 'Did Mr Salter tell you I'd be dropping by? No? Must have slipped his mind then,' giving Jacques an enigmatic smile and settling on a straight wooden chair, looking at them both expectantly.

'Well, then, which of you is going to explain the system? Vagrants come in and you ask them questions. Let's pretend I'm a vagrant, and you put me through the mill.'

'You don't think role playing might be a bit childish?'

'Not at all, Mr Salter. Not when I'm looking for a murderer. Which reminds me, I haven't had that copy of Duffy's case file yet, you know which one—you were off to photocopy it when we got interrupted. Do you have it here?'

'No,' Salter said shortly. 'It slipped my mind, there is no photocopy—yet.'

'I see. Tell me then, was Len Lawson one of your interviewees too? I'm asking that because on Monday we found him dead. Killed in much the same way as Duffy. Makes me wonder who'll be next.'

Jacques said, 'He was one of ours, not all that cooperative though, a lot in his life he didn't want us to know about.'

'Such as?'

'Come on,' said Salter. 'If he didn't tell us how are we supposed to know?'

'Insight, teasing it out, whatever way you like. Wouldn't have thought you'd get stuck.'

Jacques said, 'It's a voluntary exercise, we don't force things.'

'I've explained that already,' said Salter. 'The chief inspector thinks we go in for brainwashing.'

'Not at all, but what I don't understand,' Morrissey remarked, 'is an apparent reluctance to help in a murder case. That's difficult to comprehend when the victims are the very men you're supposed to be helping.' He watched an exchange of glances.

'To achieve that we need their confidence,' Salter said. 'We have to look as if we're on their side.'

'Hm. Only look?' said Morrissey.

'Figure of speech. Look, Chief Inspector, we neither of us have a wish to obstruct the law, but we come up against professional ethics when you ask for information.'

'Pity the killer doesn't know that. Two dead already and probably more to come. Now the killer might pick them at random, or then again the ones he chooses might have something in common. I don't know what. Anybody's guess. But I'd say the best thing for you to do is keep them alive now and sort out social problems later.'

Jacques said, 'That's how you see the men—as a social problem?'

'What else?'

'All sorts.' Rubbing his hands through his hair and the action making it stand up. 'Spiritually lost, meths drinkers, victims of a monetary system. *You*, I should have thought, would see them as offenders and not much else—probably dislike them for smelling out the cells. Am I right?'

'If you mean that, as a policeman, I look at law and order first then, yes, you're right,' Morrissey said sternly. 'That doesn't also mean I'm without compassion, or that I don't see another side to it.'

'Yes, well, everybody sees another side to it. Alan here sees psychological problems and I see social inadequates. Truth is, they're a bit of everything.'

'And sorting them out isn't my problem. Your job, that. I've got worries enough trying to track down a killer, and a little help in that direction would suit me better than a lecture on cause and effect.'

He glowered at them both until Salter said stiffly, 'I'll let you see the files.'

Bet you will, thought Morrissey. One way or the other.

BARRETT COOLED HIS HEELS in Morrissey's office until the chief inspector came back looking satisfied with himself, then briefed him on developments at Brindley. Morrissey dropped into the black leather chair, gloomy again.

Barrett said, 'Not suicide,' firm enough to show his intent to convince. 'I can't see it that way at all—not without some good evidence of depression and there is none.'

'Then what do you say we're looking at?' said Morrissey shortly as he watched time getting on and another broken promise to his son loom up. Half a promise anyway. 'Are we ruling out the possibility of accident too?'

'Unless something changes.' Fingers tugging waistcoat, unable to control hands and logic at the same time. 'No reason for her to have gone anywhere near the lake. She was carrying a pizza. She was going home. The pizza box ended up in the shrubbery—which must mean she got that far before someone stopped her.'

'If it was her box. What about fingerprints?'

'Forensic have taken them from the box, the next thing we need is to get a match from the cottage, from her belongings.'

'Not from the body?'

'No, sir. Too much fingertip damage.'

'Fish?'

'Perch, some bream. There's facial damage too.'

'Lay it out then, but be quick. We've got a suspicious death, possibly another murder inquiry. That's what you're suggesting?'

'Yes, sir.'

'Someone who laid in wait, do you think, or an arbitrary killing—with her in the wrong place at the wrong time?'

'I think I'd go for someone she knew, but not someone she expected to meet. It might be rape. We don't know that yet. But if it was, then without it being somebody known to her, he'd have no reason to kill.'

'You can't know that,' Morrissey reminded sharply. 'Not with any degree of certainty. It happens. It's happened before now in Malminster.'

'But as the result of an escalating violence,' Barrett argued, 'and there's been none in this case.'

'That we know of.'

Drawing himself up a bit straighter because Morrissey seemed to be picking holes in everything, he said, 'We've had no violent rapes reported. I'm going for someone she knew. A stranger at that time of night just happening on her in the shrubbery doesn't seem much of a possibility. It'd be too early for a drinker with a bellyful of beer, and I doubt the path is familiar to anybody outside of the college.'

'Should make it easier for us then, knowing where to look.' Saying it bullishly. 'Remember, though, she wouldn't be the

first young woman to leap off a bridge—and only Hanson's
word for there being nothing wrong between them. Safer to
wait on a post-mortem?'

Morrissey playing devil's advocate again, and Barrett knowing it and refusing to be discountenanced. Ticking off on his
fingers.

'Blue wool fibres, scuff marks, somebody playing silly buggers on the answerphone. It might be circumstantial but we've
set up murder hunts on less.'

'And had to drop them.'

'With respect, sir, not many,' said Barrett holding his corner. 'The sooner we set up an incident room at Brindley the
better.'

'And you want me to tell that to Osgodby?'

'Yes, sir.'

'It'll make his day.' He looked at Barrett stone-faced, then
relented and gave credit. 'It's what I'd be pushing for myself,
given the same circumstances, Neil. Organise it for tomorrow.
Take Copeland and Woods and let me know as and when
anything turns up. It'd be nice to get something solved.' He
said that on a sour note and caught Barrett's aggrieved look,
reflecting that although it hadn't been meant as such, a spur
might be no bad thing. Nice if he knew where to apply one
in the other business.

Envious of Barrett doing something straightforward.

SIX FORTY-FIVE when Morrissey went down the back steps in
a long leap, the car being good for once and picking up at the
first turn of his key. He swung fast out of the yard and through
the back streets to the rear gates of Fisher Comp, looking at
his watch when he got there and seeing six-fifty on the face.

And no Mike.

How long since he left?

How long would *he* have waited, given the same circumstances? Moving away slowly, headlights at full-beam, telling
himself it was a waste of time, his son would be long gone,
having waited the required five minutes and no more for an
unreliable father. Better to turn around and drive directly

home. But he didn't do that, instead he cruised around the corner of the sports field and up the narrow Close, seeing a laden figure leave the road and edge into the railings. When he drew level and opened the nearside door, Morrissey saw a slow grin of pleasure spread over Mike's face.

THE TIP HAD BEEN CLOSED when he got there, which meant he hadn't dumped the sack of clothes, instead he'd kicked the iron gates and rattled them in annoyance until a security light came on, spotlighting him in its glare. And then he'd seen the video camera on its metal pole, black head swivelling to suck him in through its lens. He'd ducked his face then, pulled up the collar of his coat and scuttled back to the car, taking his rubbish with him, cursing the fact that a public amenity should be restricted to such limited hours.

Driving back along the dual-carriageway, past the spot where a dozen 1930s semis had had their gardens cropped to make way for the road, he noticed a skip, and braked. Peering out through the side window he saw the house behind it empty and in the middle of renovation, the houses on either side private behind drawn curtains.

It took less than twenty seconds to dump the plastic sack among the plasterboard and rubble and drive away.

TWENTY-FOUR

PAUL HAD DROPPED onto his bed after midnight, still fully clothed, and lain there with closed eyes watching morbid pictures display themselves in his mind until he could stand them no longer. And then he tried to get drunk. Except that when he'd downed the last four cans of Newcastle Brown, finished off stale-tasting dregs of loosely corked red wine, and scavenged every cupboard in the place to find nothing better than two miniature whiskies, he was still nowhere near the point of inebriation and the soul-haunting visions were still there even with his eyes open.

He thought this must be the way suicides felt before they took the final step; sliced into a deep vein, popped the pills or slid beneath the water. He pushed that last image away fast but unsuccessfully, Liz in the water rigid in his mind. He'd read somewhere that a plastic bag over the head was quick and painless. His eyes settled on a Tesco carrier behind the door, and he nursed the thought of that for a long time, until the old clock Liz had picked up in a junk shop struck four. For a second he saw her with it in her hands and for some reason he couldn't fathom he got up and took four aspirins. Four pills for four pips. He didn't understand why that made him laugh, but it did. This time when he dropped onto the bed he slept deeply until Adey banged on the front door at seven-thirty, setting the old dog two doors away barking hoarsely, banging again and again without pause until he dragged himself to open it.

He'd expected it to be the police again.

Barrett or someone like him.

Adey was a surprise.

Blinking at her, memory shards floated in his mind. When her pounding broke his sleep he'd been dreaming, something dark and struggle-filled whose form and content slithered away when he opened his eyes.

Just as well perhaps.

Staring at her.

He looked and smelled a mess—he knew that—waking up bathed in sweat and disgusted by his own rancidity. Impossible to sleep in clothes worn all day and wake up smelling like a lily. He let Adey in without speaking, then went back into the bedroom and closed the door, tearing off the sheets, bundling them together ready for the washer; stripping off himself and squatting in the bath-tub, the rubber hair-spray a make-shift shower.

When he went back out to find her, Adey had boiled the kettle to make instant coffee, black enough to clear his head. Except he wasn't sure about wanting a clear head.

He said, 'Thanks,' and avoided her eyes.

'Look—I'd have come last night but I didn't know what to say. None of us did—it's just too awful.'

'Yes.'

Paul went and stood by the window. Words were words and meant nothing. Adey's chair scraped and he didn't want her to come near him. He flinched before she touched his arm, already moving away to grab up the coffee and take a too-hot gulp. It seared his throat and stung his eyes and when the shaking began he couldn't stop himself. Coffee slopped over. He slammed down the mug and swore. Adey reached for his hands and held on tight, not letting go even when he tried to pull away.

He didn't know how long they sat like that, but when the shaking stopped she threw away the cold coffee and put the kettle on again.

NOBODY AT LOGGERHEADS with him. A minor miracle. Mike coming downstairs to breakfast with a grin on his face like old times, and saying, 'Good morning, Dad,' as if he meant it. Margaret giving them both a look of pleasure. The whole of it making Morrissey enjoy breakfast more than he had in a long time. All because guilt had sent him looking for his son instead of turning around and driving straight home. He reflected on that as he chewed. It ought not to have taken guilt to make him do it, being a father should have been enough. He poured a second cup of coffee, a reinstated patriarch wondering how long it would last. Savouring it and putting off the moment when he had to go to his office and sift through another batch of dead-ends, half-minded to elbow Barrett aside and get some hands-on experience where there was something solid to go at—the thought coming into his head that it might be a good idea to get that fake tape broadcast and see if anybody recognised the voice. After the post-mortem, though, not before. Something he'd suggest if Barrett didn't come up with it on his own.

He pushed up from the table with a bellows sigh, his mind already busy with the morning briefing.

ADEY CAME OUT of Paul's cottage with a clutch of books. Barrett, halfway up the short path and his mind putting two and two together, came up with five. Standing himself square in front of her he asked if Paul was home—Adey shrugged her shoulders and said, where else? Then saw in his eyes what he really meant and didn't know whether to throw her head back and laugh or feel sorry for him.

'I've been here an hour and a half,' she said. 'Not all night.' She said it aggressively, brassed-off with the way people like him jumped to conclusions, adding, 'And nothing to do with you if I had.'

'I wouldn't go that far,' said Barrett. 'Until I find out exactly what happened to Elizabeth Pardoe everything is my business. You're a student?'

'And I'm late.' She tried to move past him but Barrett moved with her. Adey snapped, 'What!'

'There must be a good reason for making that early a visit.'

'There was. He's shattered. I'd have come yesterday, right after they pulled her out of the lake, but I didn't know what to say—I mean… *God!* If you'd known her… They were like that.' Wrapping two fingers around each other. 'That close. We were best friends, Liz and I, until she met Paul—but once they'd seen each other it was…' shrugging '…I don't know… Magic.'

'That's why you came?'

'Liz would have wanted it.' She said that so simply he had to believe her—until the hardened policeman in him reasserted itself and said it could still be true but how about jealousy?

'How did you feel about it, losing your best friend?'

'Hey, come on, she wasn't my *only* friend.' Dislike showed. 'I was glad for her like she'd have been glad for me. Okay?' She made another attempt to get past but was blocked again. Squinting at her watch Adey said, 'Look, I'm late.'

'I won't keep you much longer, I promise, but you'll want to help us discover what happened to your friend.'

Adey shivered. 'Can we go back inside then? It's not exactly warm out here.' Looking at the thin dress, boots and denim jacket Barrett could see why.

'We can sit in the car,' he said. 'More private.'

'Don't think I'm going to say anything I wouldn't want Paul to hear,' she said, 'because I'm not.' She followed him across the pavement and climbed in when he opened the door, waiting until he got in the driver's seat to say, 'It wasn't an accident, was it? Somebody killed her.'

'What makes you say that?'

'The telephone call. It couldn't have been Liz, could it? Not if she was in the lake.'

'Unless someone made it to keep her out of trouble thinking she'd sneaked some time off again.'

'Like who?'

'One of her friends.'

'Meaning me? I wouldn't do that, it'd be stupid.' She scrubbed her hands over her face. 'I can't get used to it. I can't believe Liz is dead. I can't even work out what I should feel. I mean, I saw it all yesterday from the attic, and I couldn't think it was her, I still think I'll see her in the refectory. But I won't, will I?''

'No,' Barrett said, letting her talk.

'I want to mourn her. I cried—in there,' nodding at the

cottage. 'But that was for Paul. I can't do it for Liz, and I don't know why.'

Barrett said, 'I need your name.'

'Adele Hutton, Adey for short. I live at number five, Warren View. I suppose that's the next question.'

'That's where you shared a flat with Liz?' She nodded. 'How long since she moved out?'

'Four months.'

'Did she have any men friends before Paul?'

'Of course she did, you never knew her so you wouldn't understand. Liz was fun to be around, like a magnet drawing people in. Liked partying, liked to dance—liked living. And it brushed off on other people, male *and* female. That doesn't mean she bed-hopped.'

'Who was the one before Paul?'

'Darryl Kenning, I guess; they were pretty close.'

'You don't sound sure.'

'I'm sure.'

'How did Kenning take it when she took up with Paul?'

'He got drunk. After that he was philosophical. Anyway he's an item with Charlie Derwent now.'

'Charlie?'

Adey picked up the inflection and giggled. 'Charlotte to you. They've been together since Guy Fawkes' night and from what I hear it's steaming hot. So if you're looking for suspects cross off Darryl.'

'Where would I find him?' Barrett asked, busily making notes.

'If you mean where does he sleep, it's at Charlie's place on Cricketers Road.' She screwed her eyes up, thinking. 'Fifteen, I think. Not sure.'

'Was there anybody else special, besides Darryl?'

'Not special-special. Men liked her, she was good at listening. I'm not,' she said honestly, and added gravely, 'I mean I get by, but I'm Sagittarian, and Sagittarians would rather talk than listen. What are you?' Eyeing him up. 'Libra, scales of justice, I'm right, aren't I?' She crowed triumphantly when he said yes, and Barrett felt annoyed that she'd got it out of him.

'These late tutorials,' he said. 'Are there a lot of them?'

'Bet you've already asked Dewdrop that.' Catching his look she said, 'Dewdrop. Desmond Edward Wilson. Our revered principal,' and wrinkled her nose. 'No. Not many. Sometimes if they think a student's having problems the tutors fit in extras, but not often.'

'What about Adrian Fletcher?'

'Oh, Fletch! Everybody knows about Fletch. Ye-ah, he gives late tutorials but Liz had his number, you know? If he started talking dirty she slapped him down. Anyway, it wouldn't be him.' She frowned. 'It wouldn't be his style, lurking in bushes, he'd have been more likely to jump her in his office. Try to anyway. But he wouldn't have got anywhere, he's a joke.'

'What about Christine Raines?'

'Ye-ah—the gossip—but, you know, Chrissie wasn't exactly an angel, she wanted a good time and that's what she had. I mean, if Fletch went past a feel-up I doubt he had to try hard.' She squinted at him. 'Sounds bitchy? Can't help it; if all the men were laid end to end bet your boots it'd be Chrissie doing it.'

Barrett felt a grin start and looked away. Not exactly the way Paul had put it. Thinking back to his conversation with the college principal he looked at it from a different perspective.

'Did you see Liz, talk to her, that last night?'

'I wish I had. I mean, if I'd been heading home myself I could have given her a lift, couldn't I?' Adey fiddled with the twisted wool strap on her tote bag.

'Where did you get that?'

'What? This? Oxfam. Liz got one at the same time—beginning of last summer. Why?'

Because Liz's, wound twice around her neck, overweighted with books and a lump of stone, had held her down.

But still not proof of murder.

'Paul Hanson,' he said. 'Would you say he was jealous?'

'No!' The word came out fast and loud. 'Look, Liz thought he was the love-god, he didn't have any need to be jealous.'

Except that as a young male walking round on three legs Hanson might have seen it differently, Barrett thought, about to frame another question when she looked at him wide-eyed and said, 'And if you're going to ask me I think Paul could have killed her, forget about it. He couldn't—not in a million years!' Vehement. She and Barrett staring at each other until she opened the passenger door and fled, leaving Barrett wondering just how long it was she'd been in love with Paul.

Sure of the signs because he'd been there himself.

A love-god. Was that how Liz had met him, through Adey? And might that be why Adey found it so hard to mourn? He climbed out of the car and trod back up the path to the cottage, saw Paul's red-rimmed sleepless eyes but still asked the things he had to ask, taking Paul through Liz's final night minute by minute until he had the details straight in his head. Then he asked about Adey and heard Paul say, yes, he'd been out with her a couple of times before he'd met Liz.

A couple of times?

Well, maybe half a dozen. But nothing in it.

Unaware that there had been for Adey. And all kinds of things done in the name of unrequited love.

'There's one other thing,' said Barrett. 'How long is it since you cleaned the cottage—dusted furniture. This week? Last week?' Paul looking at him as if he'd gone out of his mind. 'It is important or I wouldn't ask.'

Paul shook his head, looked around and saw a layer of dust, thinking who the hell cared? *Christ!* If the place burned down he wouldn't care. He told that to Barrett, amazed when the detective sergeant nodded and looked pleased—but then he had to listen to the unavoidable reason why someone had to come and take fingerprints—and having listened, he longed, wretchedly, to bang his head, hard, against the wall.

TWENTY-FIVE

WHEN THE MORNING briefing ended Sparrow was waiting outside Morrissey's door, boots polished until they could near enough reflect light. He snapped smartly to attention when the chief inspector came into view.

Morrissey said, 'Did you get anything?' exercising hope more than belief, the same kind of hope he'd had when he sent Sparrow down there, the PC having a knack of encouraging confidences.

'It's possible, sir.' Sparrow saw Morrissey's eyebrows lift, and followed him into his office. 'About the tea business, sir. I thought they might talk more openly if they didn't catch on I normally wore a uniform. If I'd known you were coming down, sir, I might have thought twice about it.'

'And hidden all that initiative? That's not the way to get noticed. Let's hear what you found out then? A bit more than that the tea's strong enough to melt a spoon, is it?'

'A homeless man called Tesco, sir. Not a vagrant proper. I'd been asking if they knew anybody with a dark blue coat, and one of them said it sounded like Tesco. I think I know who they mean. I moved him on about a month ago, but he had an anorak then, and not a thick one either. Carries a Tesco carrier bag round with him all the time, that's how he got his name—he's not a wino—could be one that got let out when they sacked the keepers though. Never stops going on about his bike.'

'What bike?'

'One he had stolen. Says he cycled down from Sunderland looking for work, first day here somebody took the bike. Middle of summer. He's still looking for it—or at least—that's what he says. Dark hair, five-nine, about twenty-five. I checked him out, sir, we haven't had him through the cells.'

'Didn't pick up any hints on where he sleeps?'

'No, sir. If he's found somewhere good he keeps quiet about it.' He fidgeted, looking like he'd just remembered something he should have said first.

'What else?' said Morrissey.

'He carries a knife, sir. I picked that up from three different people. They were a bit vague on what sort of knife, and they didn't seem all that bothered about it.'

'Worth us having a look at him though. You've done well again.'

'Thank you, sir.' He hesitated, then turned for the door, hand out to open it when Morrissey said, 'I might co-opt you again before long.'

Swallowing a grin of satisfaction Sparrow said, 'I'll look forward to it, sir.' Walking on air when he went to pass on the chief inspector's message.

ROSEMARY HADN'T EXPECTED that swift reply when she answered the lonely hearts ad. It took her aback. Pinkly flushed when she put the telephone down, she thought how things done on the spur of the moment sometimes rebounded too fast, and half-panicked at what she'd got herself into.

Had it been unwise to give the college telephone number? Probably.

A letter would certainly have been less hard to say no to, but she'd heard his voice now—and liked it. And it wasn't as if he'd suggested meeting in some quiet place. Planning what she would do as she sat at the desk, chin cupped in one palm. The important thing was that she arrive in her own car, establish an independent position right from the start. Apart from that it was just a friendly dinner to look each other over and share some conversation—nothing else. Her mind flipped onto what she would wear, and regretted that everything she had in her wardrobe had been seen and touched by Robert. Remembering that made her sigh. Far better to wear something new than trail clouds of disappointment, but to do that she would have to rearrange things—cut short her eleven o'clock seminar and pack the little darlings off early which they wouldn't mind at all, then she could fit in a swift trip to Malminster, pick out something smart, and still be back in time for the two-thirty tutorial. Easy! If she didn't dither and the car started.

Rosemary hurried into the lecture theatre still pink-cheeked, with speculation over the cause of it running through the students in a surprised ripple.

MORRISSEY HAD SOMETHING to work on at last, a vague stirring of sixth sense telling him there was more if he could tease it out, but satisfied for the moment in that the man he hunted had made one mistake. Half a bloodied thumbprint. Not much, but better than nothing. What they needed now was a thumb to match it with. He expected pessimism to rush in there and felt gratified when it didn't. He wondered how long it would take to bring in Tesco, and then, his mind swinging to Sparrow, thought if any more junior vacancies cropped up he'd know in which direction to look.

Arms above his head he stretched—yawned too because he spent too much time drowning under paperwork—then went downstairs two at a time, briefcase in hand, a prisoner fresh out of jail, told the desk sergeant he could be found at the psychiatric unit if anybody wanted him, and went out to his car with the thought that maybe he could get three birds with one stone. Halfway to the hospital he began to wonder what Reynolds's reaction would be when he heard his unit was the only common link they had between three dead men.

BARRETT'S TOLERANCE for unpleasant things had grown without his noticing. He stood stoically through Liz Pardoe's postmortem, shutting out as much of the bloated, putrefying body as he was able, watching friable skin peel away at a touch, while his stomach did nothing more than murmur unhappily. A year ago the detective sergeant would have been pale and sweating. Warmsby noted the change with approval, squinting at Barrett owl-like through metal-framed spectacles.

'You'll want to see this,' he said, handling lung tissue with dark-stained gloves. 'Waterlogged—so that settles one question, death by drowning. As to did she slip or was she pushed...?' The pathologist shrugged. 'With this amount of skin desquamation, finding any superficial bruising is near enough to impossible—which means that without other good evidence what you're looking to get from a coroner is an open verdict—and that's not what you want to hear.'

Too right it wasn't, thought Barrett.

'I need more than that,' he said doggedly, seeing his case slide into a declared suicide and not liking it.

'I can't give it to you,' Warmsby said . 'Not without some evidence of violence and there is none. I could almost wish there was—settle it one way or the other. Undamaged larynx, no head injury, no stab wounds, and as far as rape goes...' he shrugged. 'If it happened then somebody was clever enough to get her clothes back on the right way round—and all without using undue force.' Rinsing his hands in clean water. 'Doesn't sound probable, does it?'

'Possible though, with a knife, if he made her do it.' Barrett grasped at straws.

'You might like to have a look at this,' Warmsby said quietly, voice flat, his head bent over the table again. Barrett forced his eyes to look. 'A gravid uterus, eight weeks—possibly ten,' the pathologist cut deftly, lifting uterus and embryo together, handling them more gently than Barrett had ever known him to handle anything, and the detective sergeant filled up with new anger, feeling it rise on a quick hot tide of emotion, still convinced this wasn't a suicide and wanting to the last cell of his body to see whoever was responsible as dead as the girl on the table.

TESCO WAS ON the pavement outsides Marks & Spencer, hunkered down with his piece of cardboard, its legend saying *Homeless and Hungry* not eliciting much response, a whole morning and all he had was two pounds and a cold arse. Busily thinking it'd buy him tea and a scuffler at the market caff when he saw the two uniforms bearing down on him, nothing better to do than harass. Up on his feet fast and into the store, down to the basement and out the other end, glad they'd built the shopping centre, down another floor on the escalator and into the supermarket, picking up four breadcakes in a cellophane packet and a tin of sild on the way through and paying for them at the Church Street exit; across the road then and through the old churchyard, eating his ragged sandwiches at the other end of town long before the police stopped cruising round the shopping centre looking for him, Tesco still unaware that every policeman in Malminster was waiting for him to show his face.

TWENTY-SIX

REYNOLDS WAS OUT on the wards, which meant Morrissey cooling his heels and cramping his backside on a corridor chair, with nondescript coin-machine coffee doing nothing to cheer him up. When told he couldn't get straight to Reynolds he'd asked for Salter, only to learn that Salter wasn't in that day. That surprised him, he'd expected the opposite to be true—that Thursday would have been one of Salter's prime days for discussing new recruits. Or was it that yesterday he'd drawn a blank? Hit on a bad day for life stories? Well aware that he, at least, had put a damper on things, whether Sparrow had or not, he felt not one whit disturbed by the thought.

When Reynolds came and saw Morrissey hunched on the chair, legs stretched, he speeded up, not overly enthusiastic about being tied up with police business on his main clinic day. The one word greeting, 'John,' as they shook hands conveying that before he pointed out his time shortage and opened his office door.

'That why Salter isn't in?' Morrissey asked settling onto a more comfortable chair. 'Clinic day.'

'Space problems. He gets to use an office three days a week, the rest of the time it becomes a consulting room.'

'But the vagrancy files will still be there?'

'In locked cabinets.'

'Doesn't matter about that,' said Morrissey mildly, 'provided there's a key. Duffy's file is what I've come for. If you remember, I got called away before I got a copy.'

'Another vagrant. I heard about it.' Reynolds mentally tossed the coin of confidentiality and decided death exonerated him. 'This one was known to me. He came in as a voluntary patient...um...five years ago. Well respected in business before that.'

'In which case,' said Morrissey, 'I should know him too, but it isn't a name I can place. What firm was he with?'

'Lawson Dyers and Finishers, Mill End.'

'His firm?'

'Family business. Still there and operating efficiently without him. I don't expect you'd agree to me breaking news of his death?'

'No I wouldn't,' said Morrissey. 'Something for us to do. Now we know where his family is, we'll need to talk with them. Let's hope there's enough good will among them to deal with his funeral.' He looked at Reynolds speculatively. 'Was there a quarrel?'

'Nice try, Chief Inspector, but that kind of thing is still confidential.'

'I appreciate the information I've got,' said Morrissey gruffly. 'What gave you the connection?'

'Post-mortem photographs.' Idly playing with a wooden spatula and forestalling the next question with, 'In the mortuary office when I checked on a suicide.'

'What suicide?' Morrissey not wanting to let anything slip by him.

'Young girl in Brindley College lake. Not something that's news to you.'

'Who said she was a suicide? It hasn't been decided yet.' Seeing Reynolds's expression and making an accurate guess, 'Don't tell me—the grapevine again.'

'Source of all knowledge. How about some tit for tat—are you saying suicide isn't on the cards?'

'Certain things point in that different direction. Unless you know something I don't. Was she one of yours too?'

'No.' Looking at his watch face. 'John, I'm going to have to hurry things up. If it's just the file…?'

'A bit more than that now. More than the one file that is. I'd like a look at Leonard Lawson's too, if it's not too much trouble.'

'I'm not sure there is one,' said Reynolds, getting to his feet.

Morrissey rose with him, uncomfortable when he made his

third request because times were when police work put intol-
erable pressures on friendship, then he decided whichever way
he did it there wasn't going to be much room for diplomacy
and jumped in with both feet.

'And whatever you can give me on Eddie Dixon. I know
now that he was a patient of yours too. He kept an outpatient
appointment two or three days before he died. I'm surprised
that didn't come to mind when we talked about him.'

'It did.'

'But you didn't think to tell me?'

'I seem to remember you left rather suddenly...?' A smile
lightened his face. 'And it didn't take a lot of psychological
insight, John, to know you'd be back.'

'I don't suppose it did,' agreed Morrissey gruffly. 'Doesn't
take much insight to know you're going to say patient files
are confidential either, but like the two vagrants, he's dead,
and killed in the same manner.'

'There is absolutely nothing in his file that would help. I
only wish there was. Dixon came to me acutely depressed after
his wife died. He showed a very slow response to anti-
depressants and counselling, and over a period of five years
he's been back on the ''open door'' policy three times—the
last time he came he was happy in a new relationship and said
he wouldn't be seeing me again.'

'He was right about that at any rate,' said Morrissey grimly.
'Would he and Leonard have been in about the same time?'

'No.' Reynolds sounded impatient. 'What exactly are you
after, John?'

Finding a madman, thought Morrissey, and what better
place to look than a psychiatric unit? He put those thoughts
more diplomatically to Reynolds.

THERE WERE NO MESSAGES on Barrett's desk. Meaning, he
supposed, that Copeland and Woods had nothing worth re-
porting. What did he expect? Any student—or staff member
for that matter—who had nothing to feel guilty about would
have come forward long ago if they'd had anything to say.
His mind shifted onto Adrian Fletcher, still in his office when

the girl went missing, and that fact confirmed by Salter. He'd been out later though, because that woman tutor—what was her name? Rosemary something or other—had seen him coming back.

And thought she'd seen somebody else too but couldn't remember who.

He stared out of the office window at never-ending greyness and wondered why no one had owned up to being out, then went gloomily down to the canteen hoping he could think better on a full stomach. He was about to ask for a fry-up when Janet Yarby came in and he thought better of it. They hadn't progressed to a proper date yet but at least she wasn't looking down her nose at him anymore—and to Barrett, who had lusted for longer than he liked to think, that was a good sign. He settled for stew and dumplings but waved away the cabbage, busy with the coffee jug when she slid her tray along, his sideways look pretending he didn't know it was her.

She smiled at him, enough in itself without having her ask for him to pour one for her and then wanting to know where he was sitting, the unexpectedness of it making the jug slop hotly over his thumb so he had to resist sucking it even though it stung like hell. 'Far corner,' he said off-handedly. 'Take it over, shall I?' Hearing her ask for stew too confirmed he'd made the right choice even though it wasn't one of his favourites; he waited to pay with his back to her, tongue busy around the cuticle of his thumb.

Half an hour's uninterrupted conversation—just the two of them. He could have leaped into the air at the thought of it, but they weren't even over the preliminaries when Morrissey came in and spoiled it by playing gooseberry.

HOLLY WAS IN THE staffroom with her feet up when Philip walked in, gave her a huge smile, and made her think perhaps she hadn't done something terribly gauche after all.

'Hi!'

She smiled back at him. 'Hi.'

He dropped into a chair, lounging in it, legs stretched, 'I've been looking for you.'

She waved a hand. 'Here I am.'

'Feel like going out somewhere?'

'Tonight?'

'Unless you've other plans.'

Plans? Of course she'd other plans, like baked beans on toast and a pile of marking. She stretched and said, 'Where?' on a half-yawn because she didn't want to sound too eager.

'Umm…Cinema? Robin Williams?'

'Which one? *Mrs Doubtfire?* Is it on?' Hoping it was because she wanted to see it. 'Haven't looked at the paper yet.'

'It starts tonight.' He sat forward and looked less sure of himself. 'What about it then? Pizza House on the way back.'

'Mmm.' She slipped her shoes back on and grinned at him. 'It beats marking papers, that's for sure.'

'Pick you up at seven then.' He looked pleased with himself, up and moving in one movement. Not giving her a chance to change her mind.

WPC YARBY APPRECIATED that she should probably move but chose not to, eating solidly and exchanging pleasantries until her plate was empty. Only then did she pick up her cup, encompass them both in a smile and move to another table; saying something to Rosie Quinn as she pulled a chair out and both of them laughing.

Barrett sighed, fingering the neat hair on his top lip.

Morrissey brought him back to earth. 'Well then. How did the post-mortem go? Anything new?' The impassiveness of his face made it impossible to read what he was thinking, and Barrett had no choice but to bring him up to scratch when what he would rather have done was keep the results to himself—certain that once Morrissey knew, and word got up to Osgodby, he'd have to give up. Investigation closed—written off as suicide and easier all round.

Morrissey said amiably, 'Taking what Warmsby found into consideration, how do you want to handle it from now on?' He offered no comment of his own but let the detective sergeant do the hard work. Not something that Barrett objected to except that this time he was expecting to have his ideas overturned.

'We carry on the way we are,' Barrett said doggedly. 'There's nothing come out of the autopsy that's changed my mind about that. It'll likely be hard to sell to the super, but I'd say we keep on looking for who put her there.'

'Thought about giving a press release?'

'Treating the death as suspicious should hold them for now, sir.'

'Anything else?'

Barrett's mind went into overdrive again because that kind of question meant there was something he ought to have come up with and hadn't. Frowning he looked at Morrissey's empty cup. 'Think I could do with a refill, sir, how about you?' Anything to buy himself some time and Morrissey let him get away with it. Back at the counter Barrett poured coffee as slow as he could, turning over every piece of evidence he had in his mind. No point asking for witnesses on college property.

Cars parked on the road?

Something to be asked, he supposed—making it seem they weren't looking too close to home might be enough to disarm somebody. He turned back with a cup in each hand and saw Morrissey's eyes on him, then thought they could release the tape, hope for a positive response. He picked up speed, coffee slopping, and slid into his seat.

'Going back to where we were, sir, I'd like to release that message tape—local TV and radio, see what we can haul in.'

'Positive step.'

'Hope so, sir. Somebody has to be covering up, and we need to know who.'

'Take the release as authorised,' said Morrissey, swallowing coffee with a grimace, finding it overbrewed and pushing the cup away. 'That it?'

'Yes, sir.' Barrett watched Janet Yarby disappear through the canteen door and told himself there'd be another time, then took a look at his watch and thought he'd better get a move on too, because there was something else he had to do, something unpleasant that he'd pushed to the back of his mind, the need for it not spoken out loud by either him or Warmsby, but both of them, looking at Liz's gravid uterus, knowing it had to be done.

TWENTY-SEVEN

'SOD ALL,' SAID WOODS. 'That's what we've got. The both of us,' his eyes moved on to Copeland, busy with a student in the opposite corner. 'Don't know how the uniforms are doing, haven't had time to ask. I'll tell you one thing though, tutors have changed their tune. Now they can't have her nipping off and being unreliable they're singing suicide. Makes 'em feel safer, I suppose.'

'Students taking the same tack?' asked Barrett.

'Dead opposite. The ones that knew her, that is. Rest are dithering a bit, talking accidents. I've only had two buy the suicide angle. It's got the male students worried enough to start an escort service. Walking the women home and all that.'

'Be a good idea,' said Barrett, 'if it works.' Remembering other campuses where it hadn't.

Woods rocked back on his chair, scratching his nose. 'Post-mortem definite?'

'No.' Barrett answered short and snappy, not wanting to admit there might be a doubt but unable to find a way round it. 'Warmsby couldn't come down one way or the other.'

Woods with his hands behind his head looked up at the ceiling, there was nothing he liked better than to see Barrett discomfited. 'What do we do now then?' he said. 'Finish up and go home? Seems daft wasting time on a probable jumper.' He straightened up and pumped his arms a couple of times—primitive ape language that went straight up Barrett's nose. 'Looks like the tutors might have got it right after all.'

'Your opinion,' Barrett snapped. 'Not mine. Which means you're stuck here until I tell you differently—by which time, with any luck, we'll be done anyway.'

Woods shrugged. 'Don't see the point. All you've got's a scrappy bit of blue wool. Could have pulled that off falling.'

'Doesn't explain the answertape.'

'Might be anybody did that, there's always a hoaxer.' He saw the dark look on Barrett's face and raised his hands, palms out. 'All right! We keep on. Your head, not mine.'

'Yes,' said Barrett. 'And your arse if you don't ask the right questions.' He stalked off, leaving Woods behind him thinking he'd do that with pleasure—ask the right questions—if he knew what the sodding things were.

MORRISSEY WAS IRRITATED. Reynolds's hastily jotted notes on Eddie, together with Salter's borrowed files spread out before him on the desk, and nothing he could find in common except the manner of death—which fact alone meant he had to be missing something. Vexed at his inability to shake off the feeling that whatever the connection was, it lay in the unit, he rubbed at his temples and tried again.

What could Eddie, an ex-army sergeant with a medal from Korea and a bullet from Belfast, have in common with a pair of vagrants? He leant forward, disgruntled. There was nothing between Duffy and Lawson either come to that, except homelessness and a liking for alcohol. The idea came that one or both might have hung around the King's Arms—connected with Eddie that way—and he had Communications get the beat man to check. He was grasping at straws, and knew it, picking up the telephone when it rang and sighing when he heard Osgodby's voice asking for an update, gathering what he had together in the sure and certain knowledge that when he got upstairs he would have nothing that the chief superintendent would want to hear.

PAUL WASN'T DOING MUCH of anything. Didn't *want* to do anything, sitting like stone in the easy chair, head pounding, sand-ants gnawing at his eyes, red-hot coal where his gut used to be, making hangovers he'd had in the past pale into infant colic. Adey had called midday, pounding on the door, pain dancing in his head at the sound of it, and he'd covered his

ears until she went away, then staggered out of bed, peeing
and retching at the same time and having to clean up the mess.

Then Barrett came knocking and this time Paul had to answer it, unsteady on his feet, red tram lines where his eyes
used to be, unable to do more than turn the key before he had
to go back to the bathroom and add more pain to that he
already had. Ten pints of Tetley's and a half of whisky—
wondering if the other half would make him better or worse.
He washed his face, ran cold water over his head, and went
back to Barrett towel draped, and Barrett, aware that he'd have
to sober him up to get any sense, hoped a high blood-alcohol
wouldn't make any difference to a DNA test. Six cups of
coffee, hot and black, and three Panadol, followed each other
down Paul's throat before he tried to explain why he was
there—with Paul reaching for what was left of the whisky and
managing a long swallow before Barrett could take it away.

Paul said thickly, 'You didn't have to tell me that, you
didn't have to make it worse.' He cradled his head in his
hands. 'Liz didn't tell me. Why? If she'd told me...' he trailed
off, space gazing.

'What? What if she'd told you?'

'I'd have married her then, not waited,' he said dully. 'We'd
have been all right—exams over before...' Hesitating. 'How
far on?'

'Eight, maybe ten weeks.'

'Mine.'

'That's what I need to establish.'

'What?'

'That it was your sperm.'

'*Bastard!*' Anger in his eyes. 'Bloody bastard! She wasn't
a slag! You hear me? *Not*—a—slag!' Getting to his feet, shoving Barrett hard on the shoulder. 'That what you think, is it?
That what you're telling me?' Shoving again and Barrett
blocking it, hand half-raised, palm out, struggling to keep the
lid on and Hanson not taking any notice, standing his ground
hot-eyed.

'Don't be a bloody fool!'

'It was *mine*.'

'I know that.'

'What?'

'I said, I know that—it's you who's confusing the issue—this isn't about Liz, it's about evidence. Establishing whose child she carried could be critical. Think about it. If it's yours, would she have reason to kill herself?'

'No!'

'But if it wasn't, she might.' He said that flatly and watched Hanson's face tighten up again. 'If a coroner gives a suicide verdict my hands are tied—the investigation ends, whoever did it is home free.'

The other man's head swung from side to side in denial.

Barrett said, 'We need a blood test, Paul.'

'I don't see...' Hanson moved a step back to think about it.

'Yes, you do,' Barrett said. 'You don't want the world to believe she killed your baby, and you're going to help me prove different.'

Paul sat down again, anger dissipating, something close to despair taking its place. Bad enough before, now he was doubly bereaved, seeing the child in his mind's eye, wondering if it would haunt him for the rest of his life, the child, and Liz's ravaged, bloated face.

'What do you want me to do?' he said wearily.

TESCO SPENT A FEW minutes in the shop doorway taking a good look around before he went back to his pitch. Getting moved on didn't worry him all that much, but he didn't want to spend a night in the cells because he'd been begging. Anyway, he wasn't begging, didn't ask for anything, didn't say a word, just sat with his piece of cardboard and hoped.

Hunkering down he had some middle-aged hen tell him to find a job, then watched rain trickle past, himself saved from the wet by an overhang, and a stingy ninety-five pence gathered in by half-past three when police came in at a trot again from both sides. He got up fast, pocketed his cardboard, and dove in through the double doors, but this time the tactic didn't work. Pounced on inside the shop, neatly pinioned on both sides, Tesco realised that for once the police had been brighter than him.

HOLLY HEARD THE OFFICIAL press release on the six o'clock Calendar News and broke off ironing to listen. Cold wove around the nape of her neck. If they were treating Liz's death as suspicious, and questioning everybody at the college, then they must believe somebody there was responsible. Steam hissed as her thumb tightened involuntarily on the button. Then she heard the tape, louder, and its quality improved from when Barrett had played it back to her at the college. Almost, she thought, almost she could be taken in by it. She set the iron to her blouse sleeve and wondered if Philip had heard the news item too—something to ask him when he came—the chill coming back to her when she thought that it might be someone she knew, a student she taught, who had put Liz Pardoe in the lake.

She ran familiar faces through her mind, and wondered if she would ever see them in quite the same way again until Liz's attacker was caught.

At five to seven everything had been done and she had only her coat to put on when the doorbell rang. Philip surprised her with flowers, white pom-pom chrysanthemums, but Holly barely got out a thank you before rushing to tell him about the Calendar item, seeing first disbelief and then worry crowd over his face.

'It's so terrible,' she said. 'I just can't stop thinking about it, I mean—it's got to be somebody we know, hasn't it? Got to be. I keep going over the male students but it's so hard— you know—to think...?'

He held her coat, his eyes more distant than before. 'Not a student,' he said. 'I'm sure of it. Some trespasser, wandering through, looking for a short-cut, and just unlucky for Liz.'

'I don't know,' said Holly. 'All I really know is I don't think I'll ever feel good about the place again.' She took his arm, squeezing it as she looked up at him. 'Don't you feel that?'

'No,' he said, 'but I know what you mean.' Then changed

the subject and wouldn't let her talk about it again for the rest
of the night.

ROSEMARY WORE a sleek black number that finished two
inches above her knees. Shorter than she'd worn since the
seventies, but she didn't care, she had good legs, and maybe
if she'd shown more of them—been less well-bred and sensible—Robert might not have chosen to look elsewhere. Turning away from the mirror, annoyed that she'd thought of him
when she was meeting somebody else. How long would it take
to clear him out of her mind for good? She shrugged into her
long black coat, picked up bag, gloves and car keys, then
drove into town and pulled into the Primera's car park, to sit
behind the wheel for what seemed like ages before she could
make herself get out and walk into the restaurant. Suppose he
wasn't there? Or suppose he was, sitting in some concealed
place and not liking what he saw. Maybe the hem was too
short for forty—when was she supposed to start looking middle-aged? She allowed the waiter to take her coat, and when
he came back followed him across the restaurant to a table by
the window where a balding man—but thankfully with no
paunch—stood up to greet her.

His eyes examined and gave approval. 'I'm so glad you
could come,' said the voice she had liked. 'I thought you
might get cold feet.' Easy and comfortable, making her feel
that no, it hadn't been a mistake after all. Rosemary was laughing uproariously at something he said when she saw Robert
on the other side of the room with a hungry-eyed blonde, both
looking at her.

Was *that* what he'd left her for?

Rosemary raised her glass in salute, and not long afterwards
saw the argument start. Half an hour later they were gone, the
blonde with a face like a bird-pecked crab-apple and Robert
a thundercloud behind her.

The sight brought a *frisson* of pleasure. A full hour after
that before Rosemary and her new friend parted company.
'Yes,' she said in reply to his question. 'I'd love to meet again,
it's been the most fun I've had in months.' There was pleasure

on his face when he heard that. When they stepped out onto the car park both went their separate ways, and Rosemary was in her car and starting the engine when Robert appeared at the side of it, opening the door and bending almost double to talk to her.

'Rosemary, Rosie… I've been stupid. Bloody stupid and I know it. Can we talk?'

She turned the key and as the engine picked up said, 'About what, Robert? I thought everything had been said already.' Surprised how cool she could be.

'Let me follow you back to the college—we can talk there.'

'I don't think so, it's late.'

'Please!' The little-boy hurt look she had never been able to resist, and couldn't now, causing her to give in against her instinct for emotional survival.

'Five minutes, no more,' she said, setting down the rules.

'Whatever you say.'

His car headlights close behind her, all the way back along the Brindley road, his footsteps behind her on the stairs to her room. How many times since he left had she fantasised about just that? Wholly surprised that now it was happening it mattered so little, she poured them both white wine and listened to his tale of woe, to promises that he wouldn't keep, all of it stumbling into the old half-promise of marriage.

His face infused with scarlet anger when she turned him down.

The wine had been a mistake, he'd had enough already, his voice loud and argumentative when she made him go, becoming insulting as he slammed down the stairs. At the half-landing he turned to shout back, 'You always were a slut, Rosemary,' at her now-closed door, and Rosemary behind it felt the last tie to him slip away. Putting out the light she watched through the window as he left for the last time, reminded of that other night when Liz had died and Adrian had crossed the drive in his dark Melton. As she remembered that, the other image that had been hidden in her mind came into focus and took on a face.

Closing the curtains she put on a light, and told herself that even if it had been him it must have been entirely coincidental, because he was the last man on earth she'd expect to resort to violence.

TWENTY-EIGHT

MORRISSEY WOKE EARLY and lay for a minute, sensing his own depression without coming to a reason for it. At his side Margaret was still asleep, her breathing slow and even, and he eased out of bed carefully, trying not to wake her, gathering his clothes in silence and dressing in the bathroom when he'd washed and shaved. Rain spattered the kitchen window, ran down it in loops and whirls as he filled the kettle and put it to boil. Three slices of toast and two cups of tea inside him when Margaret came down yawning and the clock still not showing seven.

'I'm sorry,' he said gruffly as she pecked his cheek. 'I didn't mean to wake you.'

'You didn't, the bed got cold without you in.' Her voice was affectionate. 'Had anything but toast?'

'Don't want anything but toast. Not today.'

'Not enough to keep going on until lunchtime.'

'Enough for now, I'll get something later.'

'Chip butties,' she said derisively and made him smile as he pushed up from the table. 'You're not going yet?'

'Thinking time,' said Morrissey.

And needed. Another black Friday opening deep as a pit before him, and what was he supposed to do? Put a tail on every itinerant in town? He put on his jacket, shrugged into his car coat and kissed her goodbye, going out into the filthy morning still filled with foreboding. No longer *thinking* there might be another death but knowing it, seeing it being as inevitable as his car's damp plugs.

ADEY HAD CALLED AGAIN, shouting through the letter-box, 'If you don't let me in, Paul, I'll go around the back and break a window. I'm not fooling, I'll do it, I mean to get into the place somehow. Paul!—If you don't let me in I'll do it the hard way.' Pounding again. 'Paul? Paul?'

He pulled on his jeans and padded barefoot to the door. 'Adey, what do you want?'

'Open it, Paul.'

The dog started barking again. If the old man who owned it wasn't as deaf as a post... He pulled the door open and scowled at her as she pushed inside. 'God! You look awful again. When did you shave? Honestly, you've got to pull yourself together,' she shoved past him, rain from her jacket wetting his chest, a flurry of drops following her, driven in by the wind.

She took off the ex-army waterproof, shook it and hung it on the hatstand, making herself at home, scattering her belongings, scarf on a chair, bag dumped under the window, grabbing the kettle and keeping up a monologue he didn't want to hear, so he closed his ears to the words and wished he could shut out the sound of it too.

'Go on then,' Adey turned around and pushed him. 'Do whatever it is you do on a morning. And put on a shirt, for God's sake—it's freezing.' Turning to the fireplace she began to rake over cold coals, the bedroom door slamming behind her. She found firelighters under the sink but had to go outside to get more coke, making a quick dash without her waterproof and coming back shivering. There was a bright red glow when he came out towelling his hair, shaved and in a blue flannel shirt. She poured hot water onto Nescafé, pushed a mug towards him and sugared hers. 'Milk's off, want me to get some in?'

He shrugged, not caring one way or the other.

'Did you eat yesterday?' She peered in the fridge.

Maybe. Had to have or he'd feel worse. *Pie in the pub.* He repeated that to Adey.

'Cheese is mouldy, bread too.' She sighed. 'I'll go down the shop when it opens.'

'No need—I'll do it myself,' he avoided looking at her. 'I don't need you coming round, Adey.'

'Tough.' She sipped her coffee then got up to unzip her

bag, coming back with a letter and holding it out. 'From Dew-drop. I said I'd give it to you, maybe it's important.'

Maybe it was his dismissal taking over from suspension. He dropped it onto the table without looking.

'Open it,' said Adey. 'He'll want to know what you said.'

'Fuck him.'

'I'll open it then,' tearing the envelope, giving the letter a quick glance and folding it again. 'Better read it yourself.' When he didn't take it she spread it on the table. 'It's about Liz.' Only way to get his attention.

He read it and didn't care. A thousand apologies made no difference and they could stuff his course. So what if they'd lifted his suspension—so *what!*

'You'll come back,' she said. 'It'll take your mind off things, that's what everybody says—what we all want. Pick up where you left off.'

'How!'

She dropped her head. 'I don't know, but you have to.'

'No,' he said. 'I don't *have* to do anything,' and pushed the coffee away in favour of the whisky Barrett had taken from him yesterday, swallowing hard, telling her to close the door behind her on the way out.

HE HAD THE RIGHT to a solicitor. They'd told him that. He'd said no, why would he want one of them when he'd done nothing?

Should have known better. Said yes, he wanted one sharp-ish, and then shut up. Made monkeys of 'em, could have—if he'd kept quiet.

Now look where he was.

Knee-deep in shit.

Tesco felt he'd been fitted up. Scapegoated. Wouldn't be the first time but it could be the last. He'd told them how he got the coat from Oxfam, had said how he hadn't been any-where near Monk Street when Geordie Harry went under the bus—and then they'd got on about him killing Duffy. What else was he to think but he'd been fitted up? And that was before they dragged in the other two. Sneaked up on him from behind. Had he used the Monk Street gents? 'Course he had—who hadn't? So he'd know the lavatory attendant down there? Yeah, he knew him, shared a mug with him—two or three times.

That one with the two-tone hair looking smug, then barking at him—leaning halfway over the table to do it. *'What did you kill him for then?'*

He hadn't, wouldn't have, hadn't even heard about it, and he told them that—asking what did they bleeding think he did on a night? Go home and watch telly? That got him nowhere.

So he said he'd changed his mind, and wanted a solicitor, and shut up. Didn't even answer when they asked about Len. Scowling at the injustice of it all. And his knife gone too. His protection. That priggish sod with his flash clothes telling him it was an offence to carry an offensive weapon. Wasn't offensive, it was defensive. No point telling him that—wouldn't know what it was sleeping rough with a bloody loony running loose.

All right for some.

If he could just find his bike... Up on the saddle and away from the place. Out of the fucking town and looking for a job. Fat chance! Still... Had to be something. Somewhere. He found a spark of optimism, inserted himself into the line of fidgeting men dragged in off the street for an identity parade, looked left and right then changed his mind and moved two further down the line.

'Settled there are you or planning to move again?'

Tesco glowered in reply. Avoiding eye contact.

A woman came in, grey-haired biddy, the kind that put their noses up when they walked past. Tesco stood straight, fifth in line, and looked at the wall not at her. Never seen her before and if she said she'd seen him she was a liar, part of the fit-up. His hands oozed damply as she took her time, little and tubby like an overfed sparrow and him the crumb. Blinking, he prayed that this time would be no different, that she'd turn her nose up and walk past him like all the rest of her kind did when they saw his piece of cardboard, and him behind it invisible.

If he got out of here, if she didn't finger him…he'd need another knife.

WHEN BERNIE DEAKIN saw somebody else's rubbish in his kip it annoyed him. He saw it as symptomatic of today's ills, nobody respecting other people's property anymore. Not that the skip was his property, but he'd hired it, paid for it, and he didn't want it stuffed with somebody else's garbage when he wasn't looking. When he lifted the plastic bag by its tied-up neck and poked at it, it felt softish, like old clothes, and he took a squinty look at neighbouring windows to see if anybody was looking out, thinking if it was old clothes and he took a look he'd likely as not known which house they came from. With the bag at his feet Deakin got his pipe going and thought about it, tamping the tobacco with a scorched fingertip until it drew to his satisfaction, then coming back to the sack. Wasn't that the skip wouldn't hold it, it was the principle of the thing. He stared hard at the end house. Like as not be them with their tight smiles and new car. Lived here a year and her acting like Lady Muck from day one. He shoved the bag with his foot. Easy enough to tell their garbage—probably have a royal seal.

Get on with it then.

He untied the knot, bending near double to do it, legs spread to accommodate his paunch. Well tied—he'd give them that—six times round before the knot. Pulling it open he got the first sour whiff of contents. Not Lady M's after all, and that the one thing he was certain of before he went to get his gardening gloves so he could take a better look.

MORRISSEY WAS HOPEFUL, no more than that. Apples didn't usually fall off trees—not unless there was a worm in them, and that's the way he felt about Tesco.

It was bright of Sparrow to make the connection but too easy an answer to be right.

He watched Ida Jameson walk down the line of men, doing it carefully, having a good look—each in turn—front, left profile and back, not spending any more time on Tesco than the rest and not even Smythe trying to pretend it had been more than a wasted exercise. Morrissey thanked her for coming. Ida said, 'Fourth from the right is closest but not fleshy enough,' touching her jaw.

'Jowly?' Morrissey asked.

'No. Better fed, that'd be more it.' She beamed up at Smythe. 'Next time you're down my way,' she said, 'I've always got something cooking.' Morrissey's eyebrows hit roof level and Smythe went red, walked her to the door quickly and hoped the chief inspector didn't ask the whys and where-fores, the men behind him fidgeting as they waited for the next one and Tesco tossing up whether to move again, then deciding no, if he'd been lucky once he'd best stay where he was and hope it held. Eyeing the second woman warily and recognising her as more streetwise than the first, he squinted at the rest of the row, saw they were still standing straight and pulled his shoulders back, watching Jeanie Hawkes start a fast walk down the line and back again, over and done with in seconds, not stopping at all. Except that when she'd done they had to start turning round like a circus act while she repeated it all. When she stopped at him and took a good look, frowning as he pirouetted on his own, Tesco almost shat himself. Then she'd gone and his legs started shaking like a baby's. When everybody filed out he went with them, until he got stopped mid-way. 'I'm in the clear now,' he said aggrievedly. 'I can go.'

'When you're told and not before,' said the uniform who'd brought him there, and took him back to the cells.

'Sorry about that, sir,' said Smythe to Morrissey. 'I was hoping.'

'No harm in that. Let's just wait on what Forensic has to say about the knife. If it's clean we let him go and if it isn't we're happy.' Morrissey walked back to his office, telling himself if that happened he'd start believing in miracles.

THE SPOKEN MEDIA were doing their best. The tape played on the radio hourly with the news and on the local TV bulletin at lunchtime. It made him wonder how widely the broadcasts were disseminated. Just this area or further afield? If they put it out in Sheffield... The part-time pro he'd paid to do it didn't know who he was but she could give a fair enough description, would probably be down at the nearest police station in a flash if she found out what he'd used her for. He started to perspire, feeling his gut tremble as it had when he'd heard his father's feet, the memory so powerful that for a second he felt himself cower.

He couldn't risk it. Wondering if she always went to the same pub and if she'd be there tonight he rubbed his hands over his face and hair then stared in the mirror, marvelling that he still looked like everybody else, the voices in his head comforting him with the knowledge of what had to be done.

One of them was his mother, he knew that, even though he had no childhood memories of her, he knew she would want to help him—that's what mothers did. The other...he didn't know the other. Perhaps it was God.

TWENTY-NINE

MIDDAY AT BRINDLEY and Barrett knew no more than he had the day before, beginning to wonder like Woods if they were wasting their time. Wilson, poking his nose in for the third time that day, had no such worries; he'd said it was a waste of time and up to now his opinion had been vindicated—something he managed to point out in diverse ways at each visit. Barrett wished he could find something to spoil the college principal's day, didn't matter what, anything would do if it provided enough aggravation. He had spent five minutes stewing on his own in the corridor after the last visit, half-wishing he smoked, when the rumpus started upstairs. Overloud voices and—he cocked his head—one of them Paul's? The sergeant had begun a slow amble towards the staircase when the noise picked up. Definitely Paul and a fine, ripe choice of words. Wilson's, 'Calm down, calm down,' and—*Fletcher?*

Barrett took the stairs two at a time then but got there too late; an *ooof* of agony, the sound of bone hitting bone, and Fletcher about to hit the floor as Barrett made the landing.

Paul rubbed at his knuckles and Wilson wrung his hands. Typical of the man's approach to anything outside of normal. Barrett took a passing look at Fletcher, set himself in front of Paul, and said quietly, 'Back off.'

'His fault,' Paul said thickly, whisky fumes fanning Barrett's face. 'Killed her...my turn now.' Red-eyed and near insensate, gaining extra strength because he needed it, he shouldered Barrett and gained enough time to kick Fletcher, hard, in the testicles, Fletcher's scream, high as a woman's, bringing Copeland and Woods upstairs at a run, to get on either side of Paul, an arm each and him shaking his head, suddenly docile but defiant. 'Asked for it,' he said. 'Bloody asked for it. Killed her. Killed Liz.' Fletcher's hands had moved from clutching his stomach to clasping his groin, blood still pouring from nose and mouth and high pitched wheezes, snaking out between breaths. Wilson had his hands in mid-air, a frozen statue until Barrett snapped, 'Ambulance,' and watched him move away on puppet legs.

'Take him in?' said Copeland.

'Get a Panda out. Have him booked until we know the damage,' Barrett, incensed with himself for not having foreseen Paul's fast shoulder thrust, dropped on one knee beside Fletcher as Copeland and Woods moved Paul away.

'Had to do it,' Paul called back over his shoulder. 'Nobody'd take any notice.'

Wilson came back from his office, pasty-faced and rabbit-eyed, staring at Fletcher, knowing it could well have been him on the floor. His groin shrank with the thought of it, and Barrett, having seen his wish materialise for something to spoil Wilson's day, knew he would rather the cause of it had been anything but this.

BERNIE DEAKIN'S CALL was logged in by the incident room at 1 p.m. and referred to Smythe, who decided it was worth sending a Panda to investigate. At two o'clock the bag, and the string that tied it, was back at the police station, where Smythe took a look at grimed clothes and saw the dark stains that had caused Bernie Deakin to make his phone call. The clothes weren't Duffy's, Duffy's had been burned, and they weren't Len Lawson's because the same had happened to his, but they looked like they'd belonged to a tramp and the stains on them looked like blood.

A third body not found yet wasn't the most enticing thought Smythe had ever had, but he took it to Morrissey, who frowned at the ceiling and wondered if this was the thing his patchy sixth sense had warned him about.

'Where's the bag now?' he asked.

'Downstairs, sir, in a second bin-liner marked for Forensic. Thought that's what you'd want done.'

'It is. Do we know who's handled the bag?'

'Panda driver and the householder. And me.'

'Prints wanted from all three to go with it then,' said Morrissey. 'Get out there asking questions and take somebody with you, get the householder's prints at the same time. No more than a dozen houses, you say?'

'What I've been told, sir.'

'Shouldn't take long to get round them then, should it?'

'No, sir. Send the prints straight back, shall I, so Forensic get it all today?' Thinking on his feet for once, and trying to make up for past mistakes. 'Be useful if we matched up that half a thumb.'

Wouldn't it though, thought Morrissey, and more useful still if they knew who'd dumped the bag.

THE DOG-FOX SENSED danger. Ruff up and fur prickling with it. Two rubber-booted men had walked through Pel's Copse, loud-voiced, heavy-footed, poking in the underbrush finding rabbit holes and an old badger sett, swearing at scratches when they came to the thorn thicket where the vixen had made her earth, and then going away satisfied, looking no further. 'Reckon he was right then,' said one to the other. 'Good day's hunting there.' Across the field and into the green Land Rover, the fox on his belly watching them go.

THIRTY

BARRETT HAD EXPECTED Fletcher to insist on pressing charges, anticipating that he'd want the book thrown at Paul line by line, the loose teeth and broken nose enough to warrant that without the other. He felt squeamish at the thought of testicles big as oranges and hurting like hell. Not the sort of thing he liked to dwell on but difficult to get out of his mind. Then he wondered whimsically if such things could be classed as industrial injuries.

Looked at askance by the ward sister, told to keep his visit short because it was six o'clock and suppers were due in five minutes, he'd trotted briskly at her side to Fletcher's bed and then observed the damage in silence until she went away, uncharitably thinking she looked better from the back than the front. He hooked out the visitor's chair and sat, eyes drifting to Fletcher's splayed legs under the sheets.

'If you feel up to it I need answers to questions.'

Fletcher said flatly. 'Go away.'

'You were victim of a violent assault...'

'There was a brawl and I lost,' Fletcher interrupted. 'No necessity for police involvement.'

'A bit one-sided,' said Barrett. 'We have Hanson in custody. I thought you'd like to know that.'

'Get my revenge? Official Greek chorus? Won't do any good, you know, just serve to confirm what he already thinks. Let him go. Best thing all round.'

'Could be even worse—next time.'

'There won't be a next time if you do your job,' he said scratchily. 'For God's sake, if the girl killed herself come out and say so, if she didn't find out who did.'

Life should be that easy, thought Barrett.

'Sounds simple,' he said. 'Except nobody saw her after she

left the refectory, and so far the only person, besides her, known to have used the shrubbery path that night was you.'

'Which in your quaint police jargon "puts me in the frame". Is that it? Rosemary's ex-boyfriend was loitering that night, I noticed his car at the curb.'

'What time?'

'As I staggered home.'

'Was he in it?'

'I didn't look.'

'But you didn't think to mention it before.'

'I didn't expect to get beaten up,' he inched back up the pillows and grimaced.

'I thought Hanson came looking for you with his fists ready the night Liz vanished?' said Barrett.

Fletcher closed his eyes. 'I feel like hell, can we postpone this? Let him go and you come and talk to me later. Tomorrow or the next day. I'll still be here, undercarriage too bad for me to take off before then.' He found his buzzer and pressed the button. Barrett stood up and Fletcher's eyes opened again. 'Shall you let Hanson go?'

'I'm not sure,' said Barrett, watching a nurse come up the ward. 'I'll talk to you again.'

Fletcher moved a limp hand. 'Anytime,' he said peering beneath the bedclothes.

BARRETT HAD PAUL brought to the interview room, doing the whole thing properly, wanting to make it as unpleasant and intimidating as he could in the hopes of avoiding any further visits. Tugging down on his waistcoat he tried to emulate Morrissey's stone-face without quite managing it, but nevertheless got close enough for Paul to pick up the idea that this kind of experience wasn't exactly stacked high with pleasure. Sliding a tape into the recorder, Barrett stated date, time and who was there before he did his best to put the fear of God into a man he had every intention of turning loose.

'YOU LET HIM GO THEN?' said Morrissey.

'Seemed best when Fletcher doesn't want to press charges.

Should be safe enough in hospital. I don't think Hanson will try it again.' Barrett sounded more sure of that than he was. 'It's a shame we didn't get more from Brindley, but it's probably the weather to blame more than anything, I should think. More people about to notice things when it's less cold.'

'But not an explanation to sit well with Osgodby.'

'No, sir.'

'Best pull back then. Keep it open and wait for something to turn up. I'm sorry, Neil, I think that's the best you'll get now. The mood upstairs isn't good.'

'No, sir. Anything new on Duffy?' Barrett changed the line of fire, thinking that weekends got in the way of things, then remembered it was his turn on so who knew what might turn up?

'There's a bag of bloodied tramp's clothing in need of a body to fit,' said Morrissey, grim-faced. 'Could be hidden anywhere.'

And probably turn up that weekend, thought Barrett, and saw his own investigation going into mothballs.

MARIETTE WASN'T HER NAME, but it was the one she used when she sold herself to men to supplement her grant. Never on the street—that was something she hadn't been able to face yet—but discreetly in hotel bars, telling herself it would be safer that way, the men less likely to be violent, the cash reward greater, and the danger of AIDS less pronounced. Older and richer men were less averse to using condoms, the simple fact being that by the time they passed forty they'd learned a condom made them last longer.

At eight o'clock Mariette walked into the Plantagenet's bar with a pasted-on smile, hiked up onto a pink stool and looked around for a familiar face with money to spend. It felt better somehow, less shop-soiled, doing it with someone she'd already been with. She was sipping her way down a spritzer when a punter she knew made a bee-line for her, and her smile became almost genuine, because last time he'd bought her a drink this one hadn't wanted sex—just a crummy telephone call. She left the spritzer half-drunk in favour of a Manhattan and followed him to a quiet table. There she listened to what he wanted. Dinner and a chat he said, nothing else. Thirty pounds for a pleasant evening. Nice to be seen with a woman as attractive as her, better than being on his own.

Eat drink and be merry, and tomorrow fill up her meagre larder again.

She collected her coat and walked with him up the hill and down the alley where he said he'd left his car, passing three parked on the left, noses facing the street, and Mariette chatting to him, almost at the dark, blind end before she realised there were no more cars and the gloved hand blocked off her nostrils, and covered her mouth, his elbow firm around her neck, and her scrabbling fingers finding nothing to scratch, pull or tear as red-fringed blackness took over her mind.

HOLLY HAD STAYED LATE marking papers she should have marked the day before, anxious to have them in student pigeon-holes before she went home, warm in the staffroom and plenty of coffee to keep up her flagging interest. When Philip came in late she brightened, even though he was preoccupied again, getting himself a coffee and stretching out his legs, giving monosyllabic answers when she attempted conversation. He was still there when she left at ten o'clock, managing a smile when she said goodnight. Out in the hall Holly turned left and climbed the stairs to the lecture floor, sliding folded essays into mostly empty slots before walking along the first-floor corridor and down the back stairs to the car park. One of the lights was still out leaving a dark pool of shadow for her to cross. As she hesitated on the fringes of it, telling herself not to be a goose, she heard the quarrelling voices, and stepped back towards the hedge without thinking, trying not to be seen.

The last thing Rosemary would want was an audience.

HE WAS ON HIS WAY out again when he met Rosemary, colliding with her as he came out of his room, a hand reaching to steady her and Rosemary pulling back. 'I'm sorry,' she said, blowing her nose hard. 'I wasn't looking.' He hesitated. An appearance of normality was important, and the normal human action would be to ask if she was all right, and then, since the wet handkerchief and red eyes said she wasn't, to ask why she was upset. He struggled to quiet the clamour in his head so he could think. Things were happening he'd never intended to happen. He brought that thought to the front of his mind and said, 'Is it anything I can help with?'

'A shoulder to cry on? No, I don't think so. Counselling would drive me crazy.'

'A drink then.'

'You were going out.'

'A few minutes won't make any difference. Really. Come...' He held his door open and ushered her inside. 'Coffee or whisky?' Unsurprised when she chose the latter he went into the kitchen and came back with two glasses, saluting her with his. 'So? Still don't want to talk about it?'

'Nothing to talk about. Just someone I've had a long relationship with behaving like a pain. Not something I shan't recover from.' She took a drink, appreciated its warmth and took another. 'I needed this, thanks.' Rosemary studied him. 'You know, you seem quite a caring person. Involving yourself with students and everything. Getting to grips with community projects.'

He shrugged, felt a prickle of sweat, wondered where she was leading, hoping she'd finish the drink and go so he could be about his business. 'As far as students are concerned, from what I see and hear you don't exactly step back from problems yourself.'

'Robert—the man I told you about—used to say it was the frustrated mother in me. Who knows? He could be right.' She held out her glass so he had no option but to give her more. 'How do you see me? A disappointed uterus who drinks too much, or a human being with a normal quota of concern?'

'I think right now you're unhappy with your personal life, and that's what is clouding your judgement.'

'Could be right. How about Liz Pardoe?' She looked into her glass. 'Nice girl. I think everybody's really sad about her.

I know I am. What's your personal opinion—did she jump or was she pushed?'

'I don't know her state of mind.'

'Don't you? Happy. Happy and in love, and…' taking another drink '…also pregnant. Did you know that? She told me the day she disappeared, pleased as Punch about it, thought that as her designated tutor-counsellor I should know. I suppose it's something I should have told the police, but it seemed like a breach of confidence, you know what I mean? Now it doesn't matter, does it? No more secrets for Liz, everything laid open on a cold table. Do you think I should have told them before? Been more public spirited?'

His head thudded. 'I don't think it would have helped.'

'But if there was something you could tell them, you would, wouldn't you? Not hold back even if you thought it wouldn't help.'

'I don't know, I'm not in that position.'

Rosemary's glass was empty again. She held it up to the light. 'Cut crystal. I love the way it splits into rainbows. Why didn't you tell them you were out the night she disappeared? I saw you coming back—both you and Adrian—almost at the same time.'

'And told the police, I suppose.'

She shook her head. 'No, I don't suppose it's important. I mean, if you'd seen anything you wouldn't have held it back.' Smiling at him through an alcoholic blur, vaguely aware that the wine she'd drunk through the evening combined with whisky was making her indiscreet.

'No,' he said. 'No, of course I wouldn't.' Taking her glass, his head clear now. 'One more,' he said. 'A final nightcap.'

'Why not?' said Rosemary, leaning back and closing her eyes, thinking that was as good a way as any to a night's oblivion.

THIRTY-ONE

MORRISSEY WAS UP EARLY Saturday morning and out into his greenhouse, taking chrysanthemum cuttings, potting on pelargonium and fuschia that he'd grown from seed, hands busy, mind on other things, thinking that not long ago a murder hunt would have kept him working through until he got a result.

Before budget cutting became the Force's prime concern.

Cursing at disease spots on dahlia tubers he hunted out sulphur and dusted them liberally, killers in the plant world easily stopped. A pity that didn't apply where humanity was concerned.

Grappling with the problem of a sadist's motivation he found Reynolds's insistence that such mutilation always had a sexual basis hard to accept, asking himself where psychiatry ended and shamanism began. By what trick of mind did Reynolds see a sexually abused child wreaking vengeance as an adult? Crystal ball or genuine knowledge? He wished he had more confidence in such analysis, then told himself psychiatry was at best hit and miss, and with Freudian theory largely discredited all the whole thing came down to was intelligent guesswork.

He put the tubers back under the staging, the sulphur neatly on its shelf. A needle in a haystack and public apathy at a peak, and him looking for a man who looked and acted for most of the time no different from the rest.

At least Reynolds's theories were colourful; every crime attributed to a social ill and no place for evil. Forgive them their trespasses carried to the extreme. Gloom increasing, Morrissey brooded on the processes of law and punishment as he went back to the house, forcing himself into near cheerfulness as he washed his hands and breakfasted with his family, Mike in fine fettle, good humour all round and the chief inspector beginning to think a weekend at home wasn't such a bad thing after all. He was up from the table and headed back to the garden before the telephone's stridency stung his brain with the thought that the soiled clothes had found an owner. Morrissey turned slowly, and wished that just once the job would leave him time enough to concentrate on simply being a man.

As he barked his name into the receiver and heard Barrett's voice, distantly formal, a blackness of spirit settled.

The detective sergeant trod carefully.

'I thought you'd want to know this, sir, there's a second body in Brindley lake.'

WILSON WAS BESIDE himself, fidgeting, twittering about the good name of the college, saying, 'Can't we keep it out of the papers? This on top of the other is too much, what are people going to think?' Sweat sprang because there had already been talk of educational cutbacks and Brindley could end up a prime target, all it needed was bad publicity and a fall in applicants.

'Coincidence, do you think?' said Barrett. 'Two women ending up in the same lake?'

'How do I know? They both had their own individual problems and there can't be any question of foul play this time, can there?' *Foul play?* thought Barrett, staying silent and watching Wilson's mouth droop even further. 'You're not going to suggest there is?' said Wilson. 'No, I won't have it. It's too much. Everyone in the college knows how depressed she'd been.'

'For what reason?'

'Her fiancé chose another woman.'

'Would that upset her enough that she might take her own life?'

'Obviously. Of course, if I'd had any idea it was so bad...'

'You'd have done what?'

'Suggested counselling or a period of leave, some time for retrenchment.'

'But you didn't.'

'I tried to talk to her several times.'

'But she didn't want to confide in you, was that it?'

'She chose to handle things her own way,' then seeing Barrett's questioning look added, 'I had occasion to take her class one morning. She had drunk too much the night before. I pointed out it was a disciplinary offence and she didn't repeat the episode.'

All heart, thought Barrett. With him as top man staff morale must be at an all-time low. 'You have keys to her room?'

'Yes.'

'I'd like them,' he put out his hand, palm up.

'Surely there's no necessity for…'

'There's every necessity.'

'I don't see…' The frown cleared as he leapt at an idea. 'A note you mean? Of course, I should have thought of that, we'll go up now, Inspector.'

'Sergeant,' said Barrett. 'And just the keys themselves will be fine. No need for you to come.'

'Oh, but I…'

'The keys,' said Barrett, still holding out his hand. Wilson opened his top drawer, taking out a Yale key, the number ten stamped on its brass tag. 'This is always kept in that particular drawer?' asked Barrett.

'Yes.'

'And the drawer is locked?'

'Not always, no, there isn't a necessity.'

'Possible then for someone else to have access to the rooms?'

'For what purpose? Besides which if I'm not in the office the door is locked.'

'And no one else has access?'

'Except the cleaners.'

'Who come at what time?'

'Six in the morning.'

'They have their own key to your office?'

'One is kept for their use in the general office.'

'And could be available to anyone else who knew it was there?'

'I don't see where all this is leading.'

Neither did he, thought Barrett, except to show that some other person could have had access to Rosemary's room, could have surprised her there in the same way that Liz Pardoe had been surprised in the shrubbery. And then...? How persuade her to walk downstairs and out to the lake without making a fuss? Staring at the key and thinking it could be done in the same way he believed it had been done with Liz—by a man who carried a weapon to enforce silence.

HOLLY HEARD THE NEWS item on local radio and had to sit down fast. Her stomach did a quick flip-flop before settling like lead.

Rosemary?

God!

The thought came that if she hadn't stayed out of sight last night she might have prevented it—all she'd have needed to do was step forward, say something inane and try to diffuse things. Damn it! How come it was always so easy to do the wrong thing? Come to that, what had *he* been doing there anyway? Everybody knew he'd dumped Rosemary, so why hang around all the time and rub it in? She berated herself for driving blithely home, because even if she hadn't interrupted the quarrel she could still have gone back inside and made sure Rosemary was all right.

Moral cowardice, that's what she suffered from, walking away from things that might turn out to be difficult, and Rosemary depressed enough to kill herself. Holly scraped what was left of her egg on toast into the waste-bin because she couldn't face eating any more, and wondered if what she knew came under the heading of the 'relevant information' the news reader had talked about, not for one minute considering that Rosemary might have had no say in her own death.

HE'D BEEN AT THE LAKE, watching with the rest of the small crowd—ten students, four teaching staff and three women from the front office—face expressionless as Rosemary was lifted from the water. Less unpleasant this time, and that part

of his mind which allowed him to connect to society was glad
about that; he would rather not have caused her death at all
but she left him no choice. Like Liz and the young prostitute.
Rubbing his temples. He hadn't wanted to harm any of them,
the fault was theirs, not his. Seeing too much, hearing too
much, threatening his safety. If they hadn't done that they'd
still be alive. He fixed his eyes like everyone else on police
activity, presenting a picture of well-balanced normality, and
answered Barrett's questions when the time came without
quibble, even managing to stress how depressed Rosemary had
been these last weeks without offering a reason for it until he
was asked. Only then with seeming reluctance, did he tell Barrett of the speed with which Robert Sansom had dumped her
after so many years. 'Enough,' he said, 'to make any woman
doubt herself, especially at Rosemary's age.'

'What was her age?' said Barrett. 'She didn't look particularly old to me.'

'Forty. Not old from the three score years and ten viewpoint, but getting old for child-bearing. Rosemary felt it slipping past her.'

'She told you that?'

'In different words.'

He smiled to himself as he remembered the ease with which
Barrett had accepted that. Joyous in his cleverness, his path
protected, his work protected, the voices in his head exultant
that he was still free to kill.

HOLLY'S CONSCIENCE was like a heavy weight in her chest
that propelled her to Brindley and to Barrett's ear. She didn't
stop to put on make-up, simply picked up her car keys and
drove out of Malminster on the busy A63—almost coming to
grief on a twisty bend by the railway bridge and then driving
more slowly until her heart stopped trying to climb up her
throat.

She found her way into the college building barred until she
explained who she was and why she was there, after which
Barrett seemed to appear quickly enough for it to have been
telepathy.

It being Saturday he'd taken over both staffroom and cof-
feemaker, and had her in there drinking the stuff before he let
her start talking. Holly, not having seen her own pallor, didn't
know whether to be pleased or annoyed as she sipped the hot-
stuff and eyed the WPC who was Rosie-something-or-other
and didn't look anywhere near prosaic enough to be a policewoman. Barrett sat himself down so he could watch Holly's
face, said, 'When you're ready,' and looked expectant. Holly
was suddenly at a loss. Where was she supposed to start? With
last night's episode or the nasty comment Philip had overheard
two nights ago? Deciding that was just hearsay and so not
admissible—or was that only in court?—she frowned and began with what had happened last night, the WPC's pencil
moving fast.

'Did they both go into the building?' Barrett asked.

'I don't know. I heard Rosemary say, "Oh, go away, Robert, just go away," and then she started to run up the path.
He didn't go after her right away, he seemed to be hesitating,
then he called her name and he started running too.' She
looked at Barrett apologetically. 'I didn't think it was any of
my business so I got in my car and went home. I feel terrible
about it, if I'd gone after her I might have stopped her doing
it.'

'Doing what?'

'Throwing herself in the lake, of course. I mean, I should
have remembered how depressed she'd been, but it seemed
she'd been getting over it—you know—being more cheerful
again. I wondered if she'd found someone else. In fact,' a faint
pink coming into her cheeks, 'I hoped she had. I'm an incur-
able romantic.'

'But if she'd been getting over it,' said Barrett, 'why then
think she might throw herself in the lake?' He gave her own
words back to her. 'Unless something else had happened?'

'Well, I...' She took a deep breath, the words rushing out.
'I didn't hear this myself, but I'd been out with Philip Jacques
Thursday night, and when he got back here and let himself in
he heard Robert shouting up the stairs at Rosemary, calling

her a slut. And she wasn't that,' Holly said earnestly. 'I promise you. The last thing in the world anyone would think to call Rosemary was a slut.'

THIRTY-TWO

ZIPPO HAD BEEN in the army—until he got tossed out like
some reject penny.

He'd never got over that, and never managed to get a job
either, with the wildness in his eyes and a chip on his shoulder.
After a while he gave up trying and hit the road with a black
and white fox-terrier and an ex-army greatcoat from an army-
surplus shop. When the dog died he didn't have the heart to
get another.

That was ten years ago.

Christmas 1990 he'd gone back home to Manchester, cleaning himself up in the gents' washroom before he went down
Throstle Street and knocked on his mother's door, blinking at
the shiny new paint. But it hadn't been his mother at the door,
it had been a young couple looking at him suspiciously, and
he'd thought they must have forced their way in because his
mother would never have left—not when she knew he'd come
home one day.

When he'd turned nasty a neighbour called the police and
got him a ride to the cells in a Panda car.

He was still there, staring at the cracked ceiling, when the
social worker came and took him to his mother's grave.

That was a shock.

He hadn't been back to Manchester since.

Saturday night the Burger King on the Middlebrook Road
closed at eleven, and at ten to midnight Zippo slipped into his
usual place between the big square refuse-bin that supplied
him with food, and the kitchen's back wall, well hidden under
flattened-out cardboard boxes. One time the kitchen boy had
found him sleeping there and doused him with cold water.
Zippo had needed to go down to the citadel to dry out. That
was how he knew the face that woke him a little after two.

FROM AN INVESTIGATIVE viewpoint Sundays are not good days; people object to being broken off from late breakfasts, car washing, and Sunday dinner. Students object to being broken off from other things. Those that haven't taken dirty washing home to Mum, that is. Barrett knew all that; knew too that this time the lake really did seem to have swallowed up a suicide, and that Monday's post-mortem would probably confirm that. What else was he to think when students and staff alike reported the same depression? And then there was the empty dihydrocodeine bottle on the table in her room, next to an uncapped bottle of whisky with a third gone. Part of him gloomily thought suicide would be the best thing all round because two serial killers loose at the same time belonged in a nightmare.

But some things continued to niggle him.

Like why a woman that depressed by breaking up would cut out a lonely hearts ad? And he knew she had. She had left the square of newsprint marking Thursday's journal entry. *Martin 7.30,* and beneath that, *Finally got Robert out of my system.*

Which meant he shouldn't have been there Friday night— or Thursday either, come to that, Philip Jacques having readily confirmed what Holly said, and from the sound of it carrying his own share of guilt in not sorting Robert Sansom out there and then.

Rain dripped depressingly past the window, and Barrett thought morosely that one Sunday activity at least would be out of favour, only a duck would wash a car in this weather and it'd have to be masochistic at that. Wandering into the big CID room where Copeland and Woods were as idle as he, he asked Copeland if he fancied a ride, and then the two of them drove out to Robert Sansom's address and leaned on his bell, staring at the blonde who opened the door while Barrett thought that anything further away from Rosemary's quiet containment would be hard to find.

'Robert Sansom,' he said curtly. 'Is he in?'

'Depends,' she said, looking the pair of them up and down with measuring eyes. 'You don't look like any of his friends

I know about, and I'm not fetching him out for a couple of Mormons.'

Barrett showed his warrant card. 'This help?' Putting a hand on the door. 'We'd like to come in, if that's all right,' he shoved a little against the wood.

'Not unless he says so, so take your hand off, you can't force entry without a warrant.'

Barrett took his hand away. 'You'd know about that, would you?'

'I watch *The Bill*,' she said. 'It's amazing what you can pick up. If you want to wait I'll go and tell him.' Shutting the door whether they liked it or not. Copeland said, 'Want me to go round the back?' Barrett shook his head.

'Shouldn't think he'll have his mind set on running out yet. We'll give him two minutes and then pound hard enough to get the neighbours interested. In this kind of expensive conversion it isn't the kind of thing he'd want.'

Copeland said, 'I think I've seen that one before, the girlfriend, but I'm not sure where. Let's hope it comes back.'

Getting the last word out as Sansom came, got a look at the warrant card, and asked, 'What's the problem?'

'It's about Rosemary Dwyer. We really need to come in.'

'Rosemary?' A mix of emotions crossed his face. 'She isn't in any trouble? No, of course not; the worst Rosemary could ever do would be slam a door.' Answering his own question but still puzzled enough to frown as he allowed them in. 'Not the car. Not a road accident?'

'Not that,' said Barrett.

'What then? Through there,' he pointed. Copeland said politely, 'After you.'

'You didn't hear a local news broadcast yesterday?' Barrett asked.

'I wasn't here yesterday. I took the children to Alton Park.'

'Children?' Both Barrett and Copeland looking around and not seeing signs of any.

'My wife—my ex-wife, has custody. Jenny and Jamie, they're twelve and ten.' He scowled at Barrett, daring criticism. 'I get to see them Saturdays. Something to look forward to, they're nice kids.'

Copeland stared across the sitting-room. The blonde had a foot on the coffee-table edge, painting her toe nails a bright scarlet. Barrett said, 'It would be best if we could speak to you alone, sir.'

Sansom looked at the raised foot and bent head. 'Susie was about to go home—weren't you?'

The small brush stopped in mid-air. 'But I'm in the middle of…'

'You just started.'

She screwed the top back on the varnish bottle and said petulantly, 'You'll have to take me then, there isn't a bus for half an hour and I'm not standing around getting soaked.'

'If you catch it on the main road there's a shelter.'

'I'd look like a drowned rat by the time I got there, and I just got my hair done. Yesterday!' Her glare encompassed all of them. Barrett looked at the ceiling and Copeland looked at the floor. Sansom said, 'Then go in the bedroom and shut the door.' Susie moved slowly, taking her varnish with her, leaving a six-inch listening gap. Copeland wandered across and closed it.

Barrett said, 'When did you last see Miss Dwyer?'

'A couple of days ago. Why? What's happened to her? If it isn't the car, what is it?'

'I'm afraid she's dead, Mr Sansom. Drowned in the college lake Saturday night. I got your address from her diary.'

For perhaps a minute Sansom simply stared, then he said, 'Oh…my…God!' and sat down. If his reaction wasn't genuine he was a remarkably good actor, Barrett thought, but where law-breakers were concerned that wasn't altogether uncommon. Leaning forward, elbows on knees, Sansom dropped his face into his hands.

Copeland said, 'Can I get you a drink?' Sansom lifted his head.

'Whisky. Please. Over there, in the cabinet.'

Copeland opened up the burr walnut, found a bottle of Glenfyddich and a whisky tumbler, poured a stiff measure and brought it to Sansom.

Barrett said, 'Glenfyddich. Nice and smooth. Do you always drink that particular brand, sir?'

'Mostly.' He took a long swallow and leaned back. 'Why? If you'd like a drink, help yourself.'

'No thank you, sir, it's just that I noticed Miss Dwyer drank the same brand.'

'Probably the bottle I took over there at Christmas. Rosemary rarely drank whisky except to be social. When she drank alone she always preferred white wine.'

'Always?'

'As long as I've known her.'

'And that was?'

'Almost ten years. Look, are you sure this isn't some mistake? I can't believe Rosemary... She wouldn't have had any reason to...'

'Really, sir? I understood that you and she had parted rather acrimoniously, and that the break-up was one she would have preferred not to happen.'

'It wasn't like that.' Sitting up abruptly he took another drink. 'I didn't break it off—not finally—I simply said I wasn't ready for the next step yet. I needed time to get my bearings.'

'Perhaps Miss Dwyer misunderstood. The impression she gave friends and colleagues was that you had ended a long-standing relationship, and she was extremely depressed.'

'Not fatally so. Rosemary was with another man on Thursday night, dining at Primera's. I saw her there myself.'

'And felt a little jealous?' Sansom looked at him suspiciously. 'The reason I say that, sir, was that you were both seen and heard on college premises late on Thursday night.'

'No, I don't think so.'

'You were heard to call Miss Dwyer a slut.'

'Not like that. I mean, yes. I did go there and Rosemary made me a coffee, which I drank. If you must know I went to persuade her to get back on the same footing. I knew I'd made a mistake, I mean...' He dropped his head and said almost inaudibly, 'I asked her to marry me, I thought that was what she wanted.'

'And it wasn't?'

'I don't know, she turned me down, said she'd met someone else.'

'And that angered you?'

'Wouldn't it you? Ten years forgotten just like that.'

'It seems to me you were the first to do the forgetting,' said Barrett. 'For example, where does...um...Susie,' waving at the bedroom door, 'fit into this?'

'None of your damn business.'

'Yet.'

'Never.' Draining the glass Sansom stalked across the room, Barrett and Copeland raised eyebrows behind his back.

'So when you met her Friday night that was to try to change her mind about it, sir?' Barrett pursued mildly. 'Recoup lost ground.'

Sansom still had his back to them, elbow bent, glass almost at his lips, and for just a second seemed to freeze before he came back to his chair. 'What is it about Brindley? Do they have a spy system?'

'You were overheard, this time in the car park. I believe Miss Dwyer ran from you in tears, and that you went after her. Would you like to tell me what happened after that?'

'Nothing happened; by the time I got to the back door she was inside and the door was locked.'

'You didn't speak to her again?'

'No.'

'You didn't go back later?'

'No.'

'Are you sure about that?'

'Of course I'm bloody sure,' he shouted. 'If you must know I came home and got sodding drunk.'

'Can anyone confirm that?'

'No! What difference does it make? You said she'd thrown herself in the lake, do you think I'd have let her do that if I'd been there?'

'I didn't say that, sir,' Barrett corrected. 'My actual words were that Miss Dwyer had drowned in the lake. How she got in there is exactly what I'm trying to find out. So you can see how important it is that you remember if anyone saw you after you left Brindley College.' His eyes were steady on Sansom's face, watching the whisky flush turn pale.

THIRTY-THREE

SUNDAY NIGHT HE STILL had Zippo's clothes in the boot of his car, and it worried him that until then he hadn't been able to find a place to burn them. The worry continued to gnaw until he remembered the derelict house, isolated mid-way between Malminster and Brindley, a weather-scarred and haunted-looking place half-hidden by overgrown hedging and empty for years. He drove past, cut his lights, and pulled into the side of the road. Two cars went by with dipped headlights, heading towards Malminster; a bus lumbered up the hill, windows thick with condensation. He waited until the road was clear of traffic then opened the boot.

Bag of clothes in one hand, can of petrol in the other, he trod carefully around the side of the house looking for entry and found a broken sash. That another person had at some time or other gained entry by the same means—might be in the house even—didn't worry him. Everything he did was pre-ordained, of that he was certain. He threw the bag inside, reached down the can, and let it drop the last six inches. Straddling the sill, his torch beam picked out walls curtained with grey mould. Damp, ancient paper hung in limp strips. He swung the beam and found an ancient and black cast-iron fireplace. The faint, rotting smell of decay touched his nostrils. He set both feet on the floorboards and took his bundle and the petrol can to the fireplace. The smell of petrol drifted between bare ceiling laths, and the petty thief upstairs who had needed to leave Bradford fast crawled out of his sleeping-bag and felt for his boots, while below him petrol soaked through Zippo's clothes and trickled across the hearth, some of it seeping onto the floorboards.

Once lit it made a glorious pyre.

He was outside and running for his car when he realised he

still had Zippo's lighter in his hand and stopped, considering it. Nothing there that could give him away. Sure about that, the black leather of his gloves giving it a final rub before he threw it from him, the silver arc of it reflecting moonglow.

MORRISSEY SEEMED to have balanced on the brink of something all weekend. Not the second drowning at Brindley—like Barrett he was keeping an open mind about that until after the post-mortem. No point in doing anything else with Osgodby ready to flare at the next perceived provocation. Mulling over the chief superintendent's increased volatility, he wondered if it was frustration, or pressure from above, that served to increase Osgodby's tetchiness. Or perhaps it was neither. Osgodby too could be plagued by personal problems. No one was immune. He joined the traffic on the Middlebrook Road plagued by his own demons, the day still dark, but in Morrissey's book better to make an early start and simmer with foreboding in his office than at home. He marched into the police building, dark expression causing raised eyebrows, the chief inspector coming in this early twice within a week begging speculation that Inspector Beckett's marital problems might be catching.

A cleaner dusting around Morrissey's desk gave a second's thought to saying she hadn't finished yet, then recognised a lost cause and saved her breath. No skin off her nose and it saved her a good ten minutes—she chirruped a cheery good morning as she went and got a grunt in reply.

He stared out of the window, Katie's voice in his head. *'Think three cheerful things before breakfast.'* Well, at least the rain had stopped, something to be grateful for, but impossible right then to be positive about much else. He sat at his desk and turned the key, then locked it again before he'd even opened a drawer and went downstairs to the canteen, catching a few sideways looks but everybody staying clear as he brooded in a corner, two coffees and a chip butty inside him before his premonition came home to roost.

SEVEN A.M. AND KEVIN Lester wishing he were back in bed—
especially when Karen was still in there, tucked up warm.

Only the third time he'd slept with her and both of them
needing not much more than a touch to boil over. Swelling
when he thought about it and turning his back, searching for
something non-existent in his locker until his penis shrank,
then going out of the back door for a quiet smoke before the
delivery lorry came; Mark behind him shouting, 'Shut the
fucking door, there's a flaming draught,' and Kevin not taking
any notice. Half a dozen drags then pinch out the tab. Quarter
past seven and no sign of the lorry, ducking back inside for a
warm and Mark with the chip pan going for fries all round
while they waited.

Ten to eight before he heard the lorry backing and got ready
to unload, Kevin wondering why he had to be there at seven
and not half-past. Not something he planned on asking though,
only a month in the job and two years unemployed.

Last box out, lorry gone and Kevin tidying up the alley
before the smell really registered, fouler near the big square
bin. Going back in and telling the manager because they'd
have to get it emptied fast before any customers got a whiff.
Jimmy Webster going back outside with him and wrinkling
his nose, sending Kevin inside for a pair of steps then pulling
on the handle and opening the heavy lid, trying to think what
they'd put in there that could have gone off. Putting one foot
on the bottom tread of the steps before he changed his mind.
No point being manager and doing the dirty work when he
could send Kevin up instead.

'Don't see the point,' said Kevin, not fancying getting any
closer. 'Why not just get it emptied?'

'Because I need to know what's gone off, that's why. Whatever it is, shouldn't have—not that fast, so I'll have to do a
report, won't I?' Holding the steps. 'Go on then, up you go.'
The two of them and the bin like a tableau under the big wall
light, Kevin on the second step and leaning over the bin edge,
then backing off and near falling as his feet hit the ground.
Shaking his head, bile coming up in his throat and making
him gag, Webster staring at him as if he'd gone mad until

Kevin told him what was in there, and then the both of them going in through the back door faster than they'd come out.

THE ALLEY BEHIND the Burger King was cordoned off and remained so for most of the day, while the whole of it was painstakingly searched, inch by inch, and everything it contained bagged for forensic examination. Morrissey had few hopes that anything would come of it, the whole scene now depressingly familiar. He had stood with Copeland looking at the bulk of the lidded skip, while Copeland voiced a mutual thought.

'Not looking for anybody undersized, are we? Lifting him up there, dead weight.' Copeland hefting an imaginary burden. 'Need some muscle on him. What about the shop, sir? Do we let it open or keep it closed?'

'It stays closed until we have a statement. Get Woods to give a hand and make quite sure the staff know not to talk about what's happened. We can do without rubbernecks.'

'Got a few already,' said Copeland, tilting his head at a knot of women loosely gathered behind the blue and white tape. 'Something to go home and tell the old man—unless he's in there,' nodding at the skip.

'Another vagrant,' said Morrissey with gloomy certainty. 'And the sooner he's identified the better. Head only pictures run off as near to now as possible. Make sure the photographer knows we want that.' He moved away, scattering the women with a blunt, 'Nothing for you here, get about your business,' as he went.

BARRETT WAS GOWNING UP in the low mortuary building before Morrissey got back to headquarters, Rosemary's postmortem scheduled for nine o'clock that morning. Warmsby wasn't there. Barrett wasn't unduly worried by the Home Office absence; Gibson, the hospital pathologist, rarely let anything slip by him and—lacking Warmsby's macabre sense of humour—didn't crack ghoulish jokes that got under Barrett's skin.

Gibson was both taller and thicker-set than Warmsby, settling to work with nothing more than a mild grumble about the amount of space CID's problems were taking up in his department. Barrett forbore from mentioning that another of those problems was on its way, and tried to detach his mind from the fact that he had known Rosemary, because knowing her somehow made the indignities worse than observing the same procedures practised on a stranger.

'Superficial bruising of the right upper arm and right wrist, a small abrasion over the left patella—there were splinters of wood there that I've already taken out—and...' turning her so that Barrett could see, 'a larger bruised area over her lumbar spine. If I had to guess I'd say she's been pushed hard back against something solid, probably with a scraping movement. Ring any bells?'

'The lake bridge,' said Barrett. 'Ever known a suicide go in backwards?'

'It's possible. Doing it that way she wouldn't have seen what was waiting for her.' He moved the body again, laid it supine and dropped the top of the table, tilting the head and extending oesophagus and trachea, making the first long incision as he asked, 'Did she have good reason to go in?'

'She had better reasons not to.' Wondering what he would say if asked to list them, thankful that Gibson just nodded and got on with his work. Butcher-shop smells drifted up. Barrett lifted his eyes to the tiled wall.

'Alive when she went in, and death by drowning. That's the one certain fact I can give you but I suspect it won't be enough. There are no signs of violent struggle—nothing to suggest she was fighting for her life, but it's always possible she might have taken drugs—either voluntarily or forced on her. We won't know that until results come back from blood and tissue samples. I'll ask for the process to be speeded, but...' shrugging '...might as well ask for the moon.' Head bent, he concentrated, fingers busy. 'Last one was pregnant, I believe?' He caught Barrett's nod and said, 'This one isn't, so suicide or not that particular cause is ruled out.' He refolded the rib cage over the empty chest cavity and rinsed off his hands, checked the clock and found it a minute short of an hour since he had begun. 'From my point of view, that's it. There's nothing more concrete I can give you until Forensic are done with the specimens.' He took off the plastic overall and peeled off his gloves, eyeing Barrett speculatively. 'What's your opinion? Suicide or something else?'

'Open mind,' said Barrett. 'Have to have, but it won't stop me asking questions. There's a lot I still want explained.'

'Good luck then.' Gibson crossed to the scrub sink, glad to be a pathologist and not a policeman.

PLENTY OF NEW REPORTS on Morrissey's desk, including one that interested him greatly—a thumb print lifted from the black plastic bin-liner dumped in the rubbish skip matched the partial from the Monk Street washroom. It didn't bring him any closer to finding the thumb's owner, but might be one step in the right direction.

More importantly still it proved the man he was after could be as careless as anyone else.

THIRTY-FOUR

AT THE SALVATION ARMY citadel the long trestle-table with its urn and soup kettle had been set up as usual, but Malminster's homeless were thin on the ground. Smythe did a fast head count of ten and headed towards a haggard-looking Captain George. Sister Mary snapped, 'It doesn't help, you know, coming here all the time.'

'I don't suppose it does,' said Smythe. 'But we haven't much choice.' Then looking at Webber. 'I'm sorry, sir, but...'

'If you went out on the street at night instead of bothering with questions all day, you'd do better!' She glared as if she held him personally responsible. 'I suppose that's what you're here for again?'

'No,' Smythe said. 'Not this time, that'll come later.'

'Well I...'

Webber said, 'That's enough, Mary.'

'We need help identifying a body,' Smythe said. 'Chief Inspector Morrissey wondered if you might come down to the mortuary with me and see if he's one of your regulars.'

George Webber sighed. 'It's right then, there's been another. They've all heard about it.' Nodding at the huddle of bodies. 'It's started an exodus.'

'Might be a good thing,' Smythe said. 'Better than risk being the next. How about it then, sir? Shall you help us with identification?'

'Yes... Mary can manage. I don't suppose it will take long.' When he picked up his peaked cap from behind the table Sister Mary's eyes fixed on him with a look that Smythe wished he could see in Zoe's. Unrequited? Have to be or she'd have eaten him alive. He wondered if Webber knew about her secret passion, speculated on how long she might have nourished it, but was wise enough not to mention it to the other man.

'Where was this one found?' Webber asked as he got in the car.

'Back of the Burger King. Warm spot between the kitchen wall and a skip.'

'No identification?'

'No, sir, nothing.' Silent then, the both of them, on the ten-minute ride, until Smythe parked under the tall trees near the mortuary building. 'Shouldn't take more than five minutes altogether, sir, if you still feel up to it?'

'It's possible I won't know him,' Webber said getting out. 'Not all the homeless come to the citadel; some stay away because we are who we are.'

'A fear of being preached at? I can see that.'

Webber sighed. 'We call it offering the way of the Lord.'

'Yes, sir, as I remember he died too, and not very pleasantly.'

Webber broke his step, then strode on again, saying nothing else.

AT THE SAME TIME as Zippo was being identified, Tesco found himself released. 'How about an apology then?' he said as he got signed out. 'And a bit of cash to compensate for mental trauma? Oh yes,' seeing the custody sergeant's quick look. 'I know all about that; doesn't take a solicitor for me to know I got banged up for nothing. Haven't you got a contingency fund? I've lost two days' earnings being in that cell.'

'And got two days' board and lodging. There's your belongings, check 'em and sign there.'

'I want me knife.'

'Confiscated.'

'What for? What d'you expect me to eat with? You ever tried peeling a spud with a thumb nail? Eating utensil, that knife, and I want it back.' Folding his arms.

'Well, you're not getting it.'

'And I'm not signing.'

'Looks like you're stopping here then,' said the sergeant.

'I want to see that detective, him in charge, tall feller. I'm not budging 'til I do.' He fetched a chair and sat with folded arms in front of the desk.

'He's in charge of a murder inquiry—not the custody room.'

'Then that's what I need to see him about, isn't it?'

'Information?'

'Right.'

'Didn't think to pass it on before?'

'No, I didn't. All right?'

Staring each other out but Tesco with the upper hand. 'It'd better be good,' said the sergeant picking up the phone.

Tesco grinned.

'NO POINT FRETTING about it,' Morrissey said. 'Osgodby won't wear any more effort going into it without blood results. It's different from the Pardoe girl, you said that yourself.'

'Won't hurt to trace the lonely hearts' box number,' said Barrett.

'Won't hurt if you wait a day either,' said Morrissey, adding to the frustration. 'Keep your eye on the first one and wait and see what happens with the other.'

'Yes, sir.' He sat at his desk, knowing when not to argue, and caught up on paperwork.

ADEY HAD BEEN TO SEE Paul again. She didn't pussyfoot this time but tore a strip off him instead, and asked what Liz would have thought to him getting drunk and felling Fletcher. She wouldn't have liked it, Paul knew that, but it was for her he'd done it. 'Heard the local news lately?' Adey snapped. 'No? Thought not. Rosemary's dead. Now don't you feel ashamed of yourself? Because you ought to.' Glaring at him. 'What have you been doing all weekend? And look at yourself—honestly, the place stinks. Go on.' Pushing him. 'Go and get a shower while I start cleaning up.'

'Rosemary?' Paul said without moving.

'She drowned in the lake, just like Liz. Friday night. And that can't be down to Fletch, can it? Not when you put him in hospital.'

'Didn't hurt him that much, he'd be out in half an hour.'

'Really?' The word loaded with sarcasm. 'Well, for your information, he's still in there.' Adey pushed him again. 'Go! Get cleaned up.'

Paul turned, shaking his head, trying to remember exactly what he'd done to Fletcher. Couldn't have been that bad or they wouldn't have let him out of the cells. Adey had got it wrong, had to have, telling himself that over and over as he took off his clothes and got in the bath, forgetting to turn on the hot tap and gasping as cold water rushed down the make-shift shower and hit his skin.

When he was through, he went back to Adey, sober but with a headache.

'What happened?' he said. 'Were you there? Did you see it?'

'I just found out last night.' Adey rinsed the last pot. 'I went home for the weekend. Josie told me about it when I got back.'

Paul grabbed her arm. 'It's somebody here then, don't you see it? Not a stranger—somebody here.'

'Not this time,' said Adey. 'Don't you remember how depressed she's been? It's no use going on, Paul; this time everybody knows it's suicide.' She put mugs on the table for coffee while Paul hunted out the Panadol, thinking to himself he didn't believe any of that and wondering why Barrett hadn't been to see him. He tipped four tablets into his hand then put one back. Behind him Adey watched coffee granules turn into a dark liquid under the swirl of hot water and wondered if she ought to tell Barrett that she had lied about the night Liz died.

MORRISSEY STARED impassively at Tesco. 'The custody sergeant tells me you have information—is that so?'

'It might be. Depends.'

'On what?'

'On whether I get me knife back. Like I told him out there, it's either that or I buy another and I've no money, have I? Can't cut me food up without it.' Or protect himself, but he wasn't mentioning that.

'Let's hear it then.'

'Give us your word on it first.'

'If the information is useful I'll see about having the knife released. That's all I'm prepared to say until I've heard it.' Morrissey sitting back trenchantly and folding his arms.

'Have to talk to Zippo then, because he reckons he knows who's doing it—who done that lavatory attendant anyway. Wouldn't come here in case he got picked up for something else.'

'Like what?'

'He's a bit light-fingered.'

'But he told you?'

'Said he was going for a pee and this feller locked up right before he got there. Wouldn't tell me who it was but he hasn't been down the Sally Ann's since, and that's why.'

'Somebody he'd seen there?'

'Has to be.'

'Another vagrant?'

'I told you—wouldn't say—but I reckon if you forgot his thieving, he would. Just don't tell him it was me that put you on to him, OK?'

'Where do I find him?'

'Can I have me knife?'

Morrissey went out of the room. Five minutes passed before he came back with the knife and set it on the table, keeping it under his hand. 'Now,' he said. 'Where do I find Zippo?'

'Got a place behind the Burger King,' Tesco said. 'That one on Middlebrook Road. Plenty of boxes and a warm wall. Gets to scavenge throwaways too, been wishing I'd thought of it myself.'

Morrissey took his hand away from the knife, staring at Tesco as if he were a dead man.

THIRTY-FIVE

TUESDAY MORNING passed with nothing but Zippo's post-mortem to give it significance. Every officer on the street from the newest constable up had an eye out for anyone lighting up with a Zippo lighter. A flash of silver was likely to earn a tap on the shoulder and an, 'Excuse me, sir, may I see your lighter?' Unlikely though it was the killer would have made the mistake of keeping it, anything was worth a try. On the same basis, skip-hire firms were asked for customer lists and the skips themselves searched for Zippo's missing clothes. The town dump teamed with council workers and police on the same errand. Nothing turned up.

Barrett, faced with big enough troubles of his own, questioned Robert Sansom again, and hoping to find some discrepancy of story came back from different angles to the fact that Sansom's car had been parked at the roadside the night Liz vanished. The questioning got him nowhere—after half an hour he still had to go away empty handed and fighting his old habit of leaping at the easiest solution. One more coincidence though—just one—and he'd take Sansom in for questioning. Barrett was sure about that, and consciously willing it to happen.

At midday Morrissey was summoned upstairs to have Osgodby, sucking teeth and cracking fingers, invite him to speed up progress because higher-ups were asking questions he couldn't answer; at the same time slipping in a complaint of his own that adverse press reportage didn't exactly brighten his life. Morrissey stoically allowed the other man's angst to dissipate itself before he put up an idea for the chief superintendent to ponder. Osgodby's gut reaction was to shake his head and snap that it was too risky. Morrissey pointed out that it was the only option they had for a quick result. 'It isn't just bait,' he said. 'It's getting information. We need somebody in among them that they'll talk to, and we need it now because they certainly aren't talking to us yet.'

Sucking in more air, whistling it through his teeth as he considered what Morrissey had said, Osgodby stared at a spot above the chief inspector's head. If it went wrong, turned into a balls-up…? He said brusquely, 'Got anybody in mind for it?'

'PC Sparrow is the man I'd like. He's already been accepted at the citadel as someone jobless and helping out. If he now says he's lost his digs and needs to sleep rough for a bit, they'll wear it—he's a good young officer and he'll pull it off nicely. It'd have to be put to him as his choice though, and without coercion. If he doesn't like the idea, I'll put it to Woods.'

'And what if it goes wrong. Whose head?'

'Yours and mine,' said Morrissey. 'No escaping from that, is there? But we'll take all reasonable precautions; we'll know where he is and he'll maintain regular radio contact. Safe as we can make it without actually arming him, and I doubt if the CC would sanction that.'

Osgodby's bark of a laugh. Hard enough to get shields and helmets—not needed often but Saturday nights got lively at times. He said, 'Do my best, John,' as he cooled down, straightened his pen and flashed a brief smile. 'Leave it with me.' His hand went to the telephone. 'Anything else?'

As good as dismissed, Morrissey went back to his office, sitting morosely in his chair and thinking that risks couldn't be entirely eliminated. If Sparrow did agree to go undercover and things went badly wrong, chances were that neither Morrissey's office nor Morrissey's rank would remain his for very long.

The thought of that paling besides the risk that would be Sparrow's.

'SO WHAT DO YOU THINK?' A long silence and Holly looking at him exasperatedly. *'Philip?'*

'Mm? What?' Coming back from thoughts that didn't concern her, and not having heard a word she said. 'Sorry, Holly, what did you say?'

'I said, did I do the right thing? Telling the police about Robert Sansom?'

'What about him?'

'You know—the argument.'

'I suppose. Probably.'

'Would you have?'

'I don't know. Depends.'

'You don't think I should have.' Said disappointedly, because no matter that she liked him when sometimes she didn't feel she knew him at all.

'I didn't say that.'

'You didn't have to.' She curled deeper into the chair. 'Is it because I told them what you heard? Is that it? Did they ask you about it?'

'Holly…I've got other things on my mind now. If you felt you should tell them, then it was right to tell them. Can we leave it now? Please?'

'Yes, of course,' she got up and walked past his chair. He put a hand up and caught her arm.

'How about a meal tomorrow night?'

'I don't…' She looked down at him, thinking his face was pale, like a poet in decline for love, and felt a prick of conscience because he was worrying about something and not burdening her with it. 'It would be nice,' she said. 'Really, really nice,' and left him alone to solve his problem.

FLETCHER LOOKED BETTER, sitting in a chair in the day room without any sign of discomfort until he got up—and then wincing as he moved. 'Stitches,' he said. 'Bloody nuisance.' He walked back to his bed in short steps, the beds on either side empty, occupants in the day room. 'Suppose you wanted a bit of privacy.' He hoisted himself up against the pillow, legs stretched. 'Another couple of days and I should be out. Think you'll have solved it by then?'

'You know about Rosemary?' Barrett asked bluntly.

'Sad business. I liked the woman, always knew where you stood with her.'

'And where was that?'

A laugh that was almost a giggle. 'Respected my brain and despised my libido—that's where I was with Rosemary. Didn't much care for my drinking habits either. What you call an open and honest relationship, eh?'

'Did it anger you?'

'Why should it? Still enough cherries to pick elsewhere.'

'Like Christine Raines.'

Fletcher waved a hand and didn't answer.

'Did Rosemary ever talk to you about the night Liz Pardoe vanished?'

'No, not specifically—except to say she'd seen me coming back to the college.'

'That didn't worry you?'

'Why should it?' Narrowing his eyes, fixing them on Barrett. 'You don't believe the gossip then? Don't think she got tired of the world and found a quick way out? No, of course you don't; you want somebody to collar and you know it can't be me.' Crossing his ankles and then changing his mind and bending one knee.

'Couldn't have been you the first time, could it? You were in your office.'

'Let you into a secret,' said Fletcher. 'I lied.'

'What?'

'The first time Hanson came I wasn't there. Oh, I know I should have said so at the time but I panicked—easily done in my position—and then Alan Salter made it necessary.

Barrett bristled. 'Where were you?'

'On the throne.'

'How long?'

'All the intimate details? Need the number and size? Fifteen to twenty minutes—possibly longer, if you were a martyr to constipation you'd understand. Salter's sound, you'd have had me hanged by now without him—or castrated—not sure which would be worse.'

'What makes you think it's safe to tell me now?'

'Rosemary.'

'Depressed after losing her lover, and suicide very likely.'

'Never! Too much fire to take that way out. Wouldn't have given him the satisfaction.'

Barrett stared at him. One voice contradicting many but which was the lie? He said, 'If you were responsible for Liz Pardoe's death that's what you would want me to believe.'

'But not that my alibi was a load of crap—pardon the pun. What about Rosemary's ex? It'd be nice to pin it on him, and if he has a penchant for something younger, well…he might have seen Liz as meat on a plate.'

'Except that at the relevant time he and Rosemary were together. Liz was already missing before he left.' Leaning forward. 'The relevant time is the period that you were out of your office, and I'd like to know why Salter gave you an alibi if you weren't there.'

'So would I,' said Fletcher, 'but it isn't something that keeps me awake nights.'

'YOU DON'T HAVE TO do this,' Morrissey said. 'Refusing won't go down on your record.'

But it would go down in Morrissey's memory, and that wouldn't suit Sparrow at all. The PC said cheerfully, 'I know that, sir, but I'd like to do it. Make a change from routine. When would you want me down there?'

'Tomorrow. That suit?'

'Yes, sir.'

'If you're certain about doing this I'll let Captain George know what we're about. It might be best to give a helping hand like last time, let them get used to your face before they hear the hard luck story.'

'Yes, sir.' Sparrow let his shoulders slump. 'Got behind with the rent, DHSS won't help, and I'm out on my ear dossing like the rest of them. Thing is though, not having done it before, I don't know where I'm at. Any advice would be much appreciated.' Exactly the right note in his voice and Morrissey smiling, thinking Sparrow might have chosen the wrong career.

'You know not to discuss this with anyone.'

'Yes, sir.'

'Tomorrow morning then. My office, ten o'clock.'

'Sir,' Sparrow saluted, then walked out straight backed, wanting to whoop as he went downstairs because everything was working out just the way he wanted.

THIRTY-SIX

HE HAD BEEN RIDING two horses, striving to keep them together, sweating and in agony from the effort of it when he woke up and found the sweat at least was real. He knew the meaning of the dream, knew the horses were in his head, out of control. Getting up to turn the duvet, rubbing his body with yesterday's shirt, part of his mind still engrossed with the dream and the voices silent, himself on a small island of sanity and seeing with the utmost clarity that it all had to end, he curled back on the bed, the duvet over his head, crying in the thin pathetic wail of a child.

ROSEMARY'S BLOOD analysis report was on Barrett's desk Wednesday morning. On first reading depression settled; obviously he had been wrong about her, it was there in black and white, high levels of dihydrocodeine from the empty bottle on her table—and a forensic report that said no fingerprints on the bottle except her own.

'Not even the chemist's?' said Morrissey, deceptively mild. 'Surprising, that. Or maybe she'd given it a good polish,' he added kindly.

Barrett ducked his head, smarting that his mind hadn't moved fast enough to come up with the same thought.

'Chloral hydrate,' he said. 'That's a sedative, isn't it?' Puzzled because he'd found none in her flat, and where else would she keep it? He perked up again when he thought of that. Maybe he was on to something after all.

'A Mickey Finn,' said Morrissey. Barrett stopped reading and swivelled his head.

'What was that, sir?'

'Chloral hydrate mixed with whisky—a Mickey Finn. Knock-out drops.' He saw light dawn.

Barrett searched among the litter of papers for a stomach contents analysis and found it. Whisky in abundance—overkill to jump in the lake even if she'd been capable of it—and he didn't believe she had. That he might not have misjudged Rosemary's resilience after all brought elation. It also brought a sense of anger at the waste of twenty-four hours.

'I'll need to talk with Gibson again,' he said. 'See if he's changed his mind about the PM report.' He gathered everything he had into a folder, eager to prove his hunches could come good too.

SPARROW WORE THE SAME clothes he had worn the last time he went to the citadel, with the addition of a scuffed canvas parka that had seen better days. Dark mouldy-green and a sagging hood. 'Borrowed it,' he said defensively. 'Next door's kid. Gone off to college and left it behind.'

'Can't think why,' said Morrissey dryly, 'but at least you'll look the part. Got everything straight in your mind?'

'Yes, sir. Look like I'm sleeping rough, call in every half-hour, home at 6 a.m. for a sleep, and back at the citadel tomorrow.'

'Not too early,' said Morrissey. 'Don't want you looking like an eager beaver. Radio in if there's anything important, and don't take chances. See or hear *anything* unusual once you're on your own and I want to know about it. Now...' Giving him a last chance. 'If you want to back out it won't be held against you.'

'I know that, sir, but I still want to do it.'

'Right.' The chief inspector reached down and lifted a battered zip-top holdall onto his desk. 'Spare clothes, might not fit but they look the part. Food at the bottom and a thermos. Tomorrow's refill is up to you. Got your radio? Good. Captain George knows what you're up to but nobody else. Let's keep it that way.'

'Yes, sir.'

'Go on then, what are you waiting for? Good luck.' Watching Sparrow walk out full of confidence and hoping neither of them ended up with a bloody nose.

GIBSON SAID, 'I've been expecting you. Been reading this, I suppose?' He waved his copy of the blood analysis. 'Thought as much—and now you want me to come down finally on one side or the other. Right?'

'It'd certainly be a help,' said Barrett. 'I found the empty codeine bottle but no chloral hydrate.'

'Intriguing in itself. Suicide is still a possibility, everything depends on the sequence of events. If she took the pills, swallowed chloral hydrate, and drank the whisky in her room, there is no way she would have been capable of walking as far as the lake. *However,* if she only drank the whisky and walked to the lake before swallowing the rest...' He shrugged. 'That's what the coroner will have to decide—if you don't get to the right solution first.'

'The chief superintendent will want to see something more definite before he sanctions another investigation.'

'Put my own head on the line?'

'Something like that. An addendum to the PM report.'

'No need, I haven't sent out the first one.' He tapped the papers in front of him. 'It's here, ready to be typed up—cause of death, drowning, contributory cause, drug overdose coupled with high alcohol intake,' ticking off on his fingers. 'Chipped left lower incisor, dorsal abrasion of lower lip, laterally elongated bruising over lumbar region of spine, bruising to right arm and wrist.' Gibson dropped his hand. 'I've seen examples of that type of mouth injury from enthusiastic force feeding, and as for the lumbar bruising—how high did you say the bridge parapet is?' Watching Barrett's hand hover around waist height and nodding. 'Yep. Be about right.' Relaxing, hands behind his head, he looked up at Barrett and asked innocently, 'Think that'll be enough for him or would he like me to run a demonstration?' Barrett's face grinned wide with pleasure at the thought.

OSGODBY HAD HEMMED and hawed, pressured from above for results and from below for resources, but he had finally given way under one more piece of forensic evidence. Scrapings from the bridge parapet had disclosed fibres from Rosemary's black wool coat, and flakes of green paint that matched that on the parapet had been taken from the back of the coat itself. When the report had come in mid-morning Barrett had almost crowed.

'Wouldn't have done it that way herself. Parapet waist-high, half-comatose from pills and lever herself backwards? Given the circumstances I'm not even sure it could be done.'

'You mean somebody held her upright and then tipped her backwards? Why not pick her up and drop her in? Not a big woman was she?'

'About the same size as WPC Quinn. Five four-ish. Maybe he wanted a last look at her face before she went in.'

Morrissey sighed. 'He, Neil? We keep coming back to he. Anybody in mind?'

'Fletcher had the right track record—sexual harassment, other things—but he's ruled out for Rosemary. Couldn't have crawled out of bed to save his life Friday night, poor sod.'

'Who else then?'

'I don't know, sir, it's a question of motive. The ex-boyfriend—Rosemary's, that is—seems to have been set on causing her trouble and I haven't got a good explanation out of him for that, but couple it with him being at Brindley the night Liz Pardoe died and he looks like a possibility. Timings are all wrong, but that doesn't count him out, and with Rosemary dead there's only his word on any of it. She could have told us the wrong times in the first place, covering up for him—if so, when they split up it could have put him in a panic, worried him enough to quieten her for good.'

'So you're looking at him now for both women?'

'I'm just saying it's a possibility, sir,' Barrett said carefully.

'Something to tell the chief superintendent, you mean.'

'Better than nothing, sir. Let him think we're getting somewhere…'

'Even if we're not,' finished Morrissey, but didn't repeat that when he got upstairs. Enough for Osgodby to see the evidence and be offered a crumb of hope for a fast ending than raise his blood pressure with the bare truth.

SPARROW DUMPED HIS BAG and made a song and dance about DHSS and the way they'd messed him around. Lost his digs and all their sodding fault for not sending his money right, getting into the spirit of his part and feeling proud of himself as his audience sat up and took notice. 'So,' he said. 'Thing is, I could give you a bit of a hand again if there's a cup of tea in it. I mean, I don't want hand-outs, charity, soon as I get another place I'll have a Giro.' Leaning forward a bit. 'You'll be booked up solid, I suppose? No chance of sleeping here tonight?' A minuscule shake of his head to that last bit so Captain George got the right message.

'No bed, but we'll be glad of help again. Want to put your bag back here?' Motioning Sparrow round behind the table. 'Get yourself a soup while it's quiet.'

'Ta, thanks,' putting the holdall behind the trestle, getting a pot of soup and a piece of bread and taking them over to the table where the early birds were. 'Looks like I've joined the club tonight, lads, me for a nice comfy pavement and hope it doesn't rain. Anybody got ideas on a place to doss?' Looking round with the right mix of hope and angst and having five bodies inch intimately nearer, wondering how long it would be before he picked up the authentic smell.

ADEY WAS THERE almost before Barrett had set up shop, stepping into the room he had commandeered as a makeshift incident room and looking nervous as a cat. 'Is it true?' she said. 'Everybody's saying Rosemary was murdered, and that's why you've come back. Is that right?'

'We're looking very carefully at both deaths, and yes, this is now a murder inquiry. But you knew it would be that all along where Liz Pardoe was concerned, didn't you?'

Adey flushed. 'I suppose so. I just didn't expect...I mean, Rosemary? We all thought she'd got depressed and—you know?'

'That's what someone hoped would be believed.'

'Paul knew. He said right away we were wrong. He was going to come and tell you that but I persuaded him not to.'

'Why?'

'I thought you'd think he was just...you know.'

'Whistling in the wind.'

'Sort of. Thing is, I didn't tell you the truth—right at the beginning, I mean.' She went bright red. 'I was here, I hadn't gone home, we were having a party, sort of, upstairs in one of the student rooms, and, um, well we didn't want it to get out or Dewdrop would have gone spare.'

'And you saw her? You saw Elizabeth Pardoe?'

'No! I'd have told you that!'

'What then?'

'Well... There's a light missing on the car park and I'd left the Mini round the side so I could go out the front door and not the back, okay? So, about half-past ten everyone wants fish and chips and I got the short straw. I was in the Mini, belting up, hoping the engine would start, when I saw this man walk from the shrubbery—well—two actually but you know about one of them.' Looking at Barrett. 'Adrian Fletcher. He came out as I went through the front door. The other—I think—was Philip Jacques.' She shifted her feet uncomfortably. 'I'd have told you before except... Well...you know, he's really nice, with everybody, and I didn't think it mattered, only when I knew what had really happened to her, I started worrying about why he hadn't said he was there. Or perhaps he did and it's just college gossip that he didn't?'

'You're sure about that, sure it was Jacques?'

'I think so.'

'Only think?'

'Well, he definitely had dark hair and a dark overcoat, and it couldn't have been Fletcher because I'd just seen him going in the front door, and Salter, you know, the psychologist, his office light was on, and none of the men students wear overcoats so I don't see who else it could have been.'

Convicted by a process of elimination, thought Barrett, but it tied in with Rosemary's half-memory of a second man.

'Thank you for telling me now,' Barrett said. 'It's helpful of you to come forward.'

'It isn't something I feel good about,' said Adey. 'I mean, I really like him, he's the best tutor we've got.'

THIRTY-SEVEN

BARRETT WENT LOOKING for Jacques, then remembered the Wednesday sessions at the citadel and realised he was wasting his time. Holly was there though, having to leave her tutorial group to their own devices and come out into the corridor to talk to him. 'I know it's important,' she said crossly. 'But why couldn't it wait?'

Because there were two dead women already and he didn't want a third. He told her that and watched clouds trail across her eyes.

'You said you wanted to talk about Philip,' she said. 'And I don't see how the two things connect.'

'How well do you know him?'

Holly started to say very well, then stopped because it wasn't true, not exactly. She knew him better than she had two weeks ago—but that wasn't very much help, was it? She knew him well enough to know he was good company and that she liked him. Liked him very much, in fact, enough so to quietly dream about a totally different kind of relationship.

She said slowly, 'I know he's very well liked by both students and staff, and he's an excellent tutor.' Then she frowned and added emphatically, 'If you want me to say he's kind to old ladies and animals then, yes, I suppose he is. I mean— you know—he never zaps flies even, he just lets them out the window. That should tell you something about him.'

Not a lot, thought Barrett, except that Jacques might like flies better than he liked women.

He said, 'You've been seeing him socially. I remember your telling me that, and you mentioned you had a meal together. Was that just the once or do you see a lot of each other?'

'We've been out twice to a restaurant, once to the cinema— and I cooked a meal for us at my flat. Once. Just a meal, nothing else. All right? I want to know why you're asking all this, why can't you talk to Philip instead of going behind his back?'

'Because he isn't here,' Barrett said reasonably. 'And in his absence you make a good advocate.'

Holly snorted. 'He needs one?'

'Do you think he does?' Pushed into offering an opinion on that, Holly sidestepped.

'Not unless you can give me a good reason.'

Barrett said, 'Do you keep a diary?'

'Yes, I do. And it's private.' A bite of anger came when she thought he might ask to see it. 'Look, I want to know where all this is leading.'

'I want to place Philip Jacques's movements on certain dates, and of course if you can say he was with you I won't have to bother him. Do you have the diary here?'

'In my handbag.'

'Fine. Perhaps you'd go and get it?'

'I don't need to, I have a good memory.'

'Good enough to remember when you were with Jacques?'

'Yes, I think so. Why don't you tell me which particular dates you're interested in?' said Holly, her mind buzzing around the practicality of giving Philip an alibi. Then Barrett took that option away from her.

'We like to do it a little differently,' he said shortly. 'It saves any confusion. Suppose you just tell me the dates you and he were together?'

Holly felt her cheeks heat up. It was one thing to think of subverting the police process and another to be found out. Flustered, she gave Barrett the dates he needed, telling herself that since Philip had done nothing wrong it didn't matter. When he had finished writing she said sharply, 'What exactly is he supposed to have done?'

'On the night you stayed home and cooked supper,' said Barrett. 'What time did he arrive?'

She shrugged. 'Ten o'clock-ish.'

'Was that the time you expected him? It seems a little late for an evening meal.'

'It was an open invitation,' said Holly. 'He had a lot of papers to mark and we left it that he'd come if he could. Why? What would it have to do with either Rosemary or Liz?' Folding her arms and feeling angry. 'I suppose that's what this is all about?'

Barrett looked at the list of dates. 'The last time you went out with him was Saturday, the day after Rosemary died. Did he seem any different? Less talkative? Moody? Something on his mind perhaps?' All of those things, Holly thought, and stayed silent. Barrett kept his eyes on her and bided his time.

'He was tired,' she said at last. 'Planning lectures and reading thirty essays on the same subject isn't exactly relaxing, you know? And then there was the news about Rosemary...' She trailed off, remembering how Philip hadn't wanted her to talk about it, and ended lamely, 'We were neither of us exactly jolly.'

'The night Liz Pardoe died—did you see him then?'

'No. I went home at six. I told you that.'

'And you didn't see him later?'

'We weren't going out together then. Look, I'm not going to say anything else until I know what Philip is supposed to have done.' She folded her arms even more tightly, a lump of misery inside her. 'It isn't fair expecting me to talk behind his back.'

Murder wasn't fair either.

He pointed that out to her as kindly as he could.

SPARROW THOUGHT he was doing well, plenty of sympathy and nobody anywhere near guessing what his real business was. Two or three places suggested where he might kip for the night too, but one of them offering to keep him company. Not that he could blame any one of them for that. All very well him coming in with a hard-luck story but he could as well be carrying a knife as the next man. No. Given what had been happening he wouldn't have fancied a night laid alongside a stranger—not if he was one of them. He grinned at Tesco and offered a humbug, watching him take one and nod, then putting the bag on the table, seeing it empty faster than he could count.

Tesco was the only one keeping his distance, taking it all in and saying nothing. Sparrow didn't force it, time spent in police cells quietened a lot of people; if he'd been recognised Tesco would have said something before now. He collected half a dozen empty mugs and took them back to wash, getting a frosty smile from Sister Mary as he put them in the sink.

He was back at the table, settling into his place again when Barrett arrived with Woods in tow, and Sparrow's ears flapped like everybody else's to hear what was said without quite catching it. He squinted round furtively, anxious not to have his cover blown, feeling relieved when they headed for the little room where Tolly Martin had gone to recite the story of his life, their eyes not turning to him at all.

IT WAS THREE NIGHTS since Jimmy Purvis had watched fire leap across the hearth in the old house and feed on a trickle of petrol, and that had been his mistake. He should have stamped it out instead of following the other man over the windowsill. In the few minutes he'd been away the old wood had gone up like tinder and stopped him getting back upstairs for his belongings. For the first time in his life he felt like the robbed rather than the robber. It really irked that all he took away with him was a discarded Zippo lighter, and a memorised number plate that he now trailed around car parks looking for. He didn't think he was wasting his time doing that; instinct said whoever set the house alight would pay good money not to have it known. And besides, trawling car parks brought other perks.

He was going after one of them Wednesday afternoon, reaching for a handbag on the back set of a Peugeot 106 when he got careless. The traffic warden was big and burly and would rather have been a policeman except he'd left it a bit late. Grabbing hold of Jimmy Purvis marked the crowning point of his life, as he would later recount to anyone willing to listen, and his only regret was that he hadn't been able to bang Jimmy up in a cell himself instead of just handing him over.

BARRETT'S WAS THE MOST perfunctory of knocks and he didn't wait for an answer. On his way to the citadel he had called in on Robert Sansom again and this time had met with a flat refusal to answer any more questions. The only thing pushing had achieved was for Sansom to pick up the phone and ring his solicitor. Failure would have worried Barrett less if Woods hadn't been there as a witness, and he didn't plan to have a repeat performance with Jacques. As it was, Tolly Martin was up from his chair and slithering out the door before surprise had properly settled itself on the face of the man he'd been talking to. Salter said, 'I hope you have a good explanation for this; it takes us long enough to coax them in without being broken off halfway through. God knows if we'll ever get Tolly back, and where's the therapeutic value in that?'

'Seems to me if he'd wanted to do it he'll come back,' answered Barrett. 'And if he didn't—well, you wouldn't want him in here under duress, would you? No therapeutic value in that either, I would imagine. I did knock, Mr Salter, and I'm sorry to interrupt, but now, if you wouldn't mind going with Detective Constable Woods, I'd like a private talk with Mr Jacques.'

Salter looked at Jacques. 'If you'd rather I stayed put, Philip, I'll do that.'

Jacques shook his head. 'No, can't think what this is about but it can't be anything much. Have a word with Tolly while you're out there; let him know they're not after him.'

'Now, why would you say that?' Barrett asked when Woods and Salter were gone. 'And why would he think it—unless life histories include criminal confessions? But if they did—anything serious—you'd pass it on, wouldn't you?'

Jacques didn't answer.

'Do I take silence as a no?'

'Not necessarily, but to the people we're here to help,' nodding at the door, 'you're the enemy. Not you in person, the police. Fact of life. It's a thankless task keeping law and order, almost as bad as being a teacher.' He turned in his chair a little, stretching out his legs and crossing his ankles, letting Barrett know he was relaxed. 'What can I do for you?'

'I've been given certain information about your movements on the night Elizabeth Pardoe died, and it doesn't tally with the statement you gave me. Miss Pardoe left the refectory at nine o'clock and started to walk home through the shrubbery. I'd like you to tell me again where you were at that time.'

'In the refectory myself. A lot of people saw me there.'

'You left after Miss Pardoe?'

'We've been through this before. No, Liz was still at the counter when I went out.'

'And where did you go then? Out? Up to your room, or where?'

'I went to my room, I marked some papers, I watched a little television, played some music, and went to bed.'

'You seem to mark a lot of papers.'

'We all do, there's a lot of students.'

'We have a witness who saw you walking away from the shrubbery at ten-thirty that night.'

'Then it's a mistake, I didn't go out of the building.'

'You're quite sure about that?'

'Positive.'

'But you could have gone out without being seen, it wouldn't be difficult?'

'No more difficult than it would for anyone else. Look— I've told you I didn't go out, but I can't prove it—all I can say is your witness made a mistake.'

'The night Rosemary Dwyer died you were also marking papers and you talked with Holly Havers in the common room. You were there when she left. Is that right?'

'Yes.'

'So you'd hear Rosemary come in the back entrance?'

'No, I don't think so, should I have done?'

'Miss Havers overheard a quarrel between Rosemary and a friend of hers, a Mr Robert Sansom. I'd be interested to know if the quarrel continued after she came indoors and if Mr Sansom came in with her.'

'I don't know, the common room door was closed, I didn't hear anything, if I had I'd tell you. What would be the sense in keeping quiet?' He watched Barrett's face and felt jolted when he read the answer. 'You know something I don't,' he said slowly. 'That's why you're here; you don't believe she killed herself.'

'I never did believe that,' said Barrett. 'The difference is we now have forensic evidence to prove she didn't.' Watching Jacques drop the casual pose and sit straight. 'So you can see, sir, why I'm interested in what you may have seen and heard that night.'

'No,' said Jacques warily. 'That isn't why you're here at all. You think I did it and that's what you want to prove.'

'And did you do it, sir?' asked Barrett. 'Was it you who put two women in the lake?'

'God!' said Jacques, rubbing both hands over his face. 'I can't believe you've even asked.'

THIRTY-EIGHT

WOODS, KEEPING SALTER out of the office, had studiously ignored Sparrow and listened with only half an ear to the psychologist's pacification of Tolly. 'I been in there once,' said Tolly. 'Waste of breath it is, so bugger off.' He belched by way of punctuation.

'Looks like you've got yourself a lost cause with that one,' said Woods as Tolly wandered off.

'He'll come round,' said Salter, not that bothered because he knew what he wanted to know. 'More intriguing than Tolly, would be knowing what's happening in there.' He turned and looked back at the office.

'I can't help you with that, sir.'

'Don't know or won't tell?'

'Just routine inquiries, sir, nothing else.'

'About Rosemary, I suppose?'

'Nice woman from what I've been told. Can't think of anyone at the college who'd do something like that, can you, sir?'

'I thought suicide had been accepted.'

'Things change. Be nice if they didn't sometimes.' Meeting Salter's eye. 'You're a psychologist, sir, so you'd know better than we do what makes a man kill.'

Salter shrugged. 'Are you asking me?'

'I suppose I am. Yes. I mean, we all get angry or want things we can't have, but we don't kill because of it,' said Woods. 'So there has to be another factor. I mean, take what's happening to this lot.' He looked around and dropped his voice. 'It's nasty, twisted, and the latest thinking is there's likely to be some bodies we haven't found yet. Could have been going on years—different places even—and us not knowing. Then whoever's doing it decides to let us find a few.

Think that means he wants to be caught or he's just showing us he's clever?'

'I think it all sounds like conjecture.'

Woods grinned. 'Too right it is, but it doesn't change the question.'

'Be sure to ask it then—when you catch him,' said Salter.

'Oh, we'll do that, sir, catch him I mean, but I'd still be interested in your opinion. I mean slaughtering old men, there's got to be more behind it than I picked up in basics, hasn't there?'

Slaughtering thought Salter. Woods had made a good choice of word. He watched the office door open and Barrett come out alone. 'Everyone believes the human mind to be a complicated mechanism,' he said easily, 'and so they look for complicated answers, but the truth is simple—when a man loses his taste for life he develops a taste for death, and it doesn't often matter whose. Does that answer your question?'

He strolled away without waiting for Woods to reply, interested only in knowing what Barrett and Jacques had been talking about.

MEN HAD BEEN IN PEL'S Copse again, two of them, pacing the ground round the thorn patch and walking the field edge, one standing on the bonnet of his Land Rover to get the lie of the land, and both of them leaving their scent behind. The dog-fox, coming back close to dusk with the vixen, picked up the ripeness of stable and kennel and, ears flat, nipped and harried his mate back to the better safety of the old culvert on the far side of the college lake.

The vixen, now in cub, bared her teeth but didn't bite.

JIMMY PURVIS DIDN'T SEE any point in denying what he'd done—not much point when he'd been caught handbag in hand—instead he did what he always did on such occasions and confessed to a small string of petty crimes that made the two constables who interviewed him feel good, and also earned him a word in court about how he'd cooperated. It wouldn't stop him going down for two or three years but it might earn him a softer spot.

The paperwork was done and Jimmy back in his cell when Copeland wandered downstairs to see if any minor crimes on the petty thief's list were outstanding on his own. Unlucky with that, he asked for the list of items found on Jimmy's person.

'This,' he said, sticking his finger on the sheet of paper. 'Did you get a good look at it?'

'I didn't get a good look at anything,' said the custody sergeant. 'All I did was list it. I'd another three waiting to book in and a fight breaking out. It gets hectic down here, believe it or not.'

'I believe it,' said Copeland. 'Purvis's things still handy?'

'Should be.' Peering down. 'What is it then? Something off one of yours?' Starting to prise open the packet before the penny dropped. 'Christ!' he said watching the Zippo lighter slide onto his desk and anticipating the earful he'd get from upstairs. 'And knowing my luck it'd have to be the right one, wouldn't it?'

'Good thing you spotted it,' said Copeland, letting him off the hook and telling himself that was another favour he could call in when he needed it.

MORRISSEY HAD CLOSETED himself with Reynolds again and strained their friendship even further. It wasn't something he'd looked forward to and he had accurately anticipated Reynolds's distemper, but he'd needed links and for the past two days his mind had been giving him back the same answer. Morrissey didn't like it any better than Reynolds did, but it was the only one that had presented itself. 'Four dead men in less than three weeks,' he said bluntly. 'I can't pussyfoot. I don't feel any happier about it than you do, but that can't make any difference. Same basis as Occam's Razor. Strip away everything superfluous and whatever's left has to be the answer—however unpalatable.'

'Unpalatable?' Reynolds slamming back in his chair and looking at the ceiling. 'Damn it, man! You know better. Professionally I shouldn't even be listening to this!' Angry that Morrissey could get him into that position, and angrier still because he couldn't fault the logic behind it, not when he had seen the same thing himself days ago and struggled ever since to redraw the line between professionalism and public duty.

Morrissey said quietly, 'If it was one of mine I'd feel the same way. I'd want to protect until I had absolute proof, but I wouldn't balk at looking for it, and that's all I'm asking you to do. Give me names and addresses and I'll do the rest—it won't come back to you. If he's innocent he need never know we've looked. The only involvement you'd have had would be in saving me time.'

'You haven't shown me any evidence.' Reynolds kept his eyes on the ceiling. He had told Morrissey that for ninety-nine per cent of the time the man who killed Duffy and the rest functioned normally in society, probably held down a job, and was accepted by his peers. The common profile of a psychopath that he'd been trained to recognise. He pushed up abruptly from his desk. 'Under duress,' he said grimly. 'Not friendship, not this time,' rummaging through files in the top drawer of his grey file cabinet and coming out with the information Morrissey needed, their parting handshake less firm, and on Reynolds's part at least, almost perfunctory.

SALTER HADN'T BEEN ABLE to get much out of Jacques and that annoyed him. That Tolly maintained his refusal to return also annoyed him, as did the fact that no one else took his place. At exactly five o'clock Jacques cleared his papers and left, still without talking about Barrett.

Salter followed him, but only as far as the kitchen where he kept his jar of Columbian roast. Sister Mary set a thermos she'd been rinsing on the table, eyed him with her usual degree of disapproval, and asked if the police had found out who was killing vagrants yet? Salter told her that wasn't the reason for Barrett's visit; it had been something altogether different the police had wanted to talk about.

'It's to be hoped they know what they're doing then,' she said sagely, 'before somebody gets hurt that isn't *supposed* to get hurt. There's a lot of mice gets away with the cheese and who's crying then?'

Salter was still working that out when Sparrow carried in a load of pots, pushing up his sleeves and getting stuck into the washing-up, keeping on Sister Mary's good side. She took her eyes off Salter's coffee-making and turned her attention to him, her voice not losing any of its brusqueness but her eyes softening. 'I've got that spare flask,' she said. 'I knew I'd put it somewhere. What would you like?'

'Ta,' said Sparrow. 'Bring it back tomorrow. Coffee'd be nice.' Stacking the last wet pot, wiping off his hands and going out for more—nodding at Salter as he passed.

'Now that's a nice young man,' said Sister Mary. 'Not many like him, more's the pity.'

'But still a vagrant,' said Salter. 'No different to the rest except for age.'

'I wouldn't say that,' said Sister Mary. 'I don't believe he'll be out on the streets for long.'

'Yes, well, I think you'll find what the rest of us have found, you can get the man off the street but not the street out of the man. Don't invest too much time in him, it's a slippery slope.'

'I thought you were supposed to be helping them?'

'Only if they're willing to accept it.'

'Well, you needn't worry about him,' opening a jar of supermarket own-brand coffee, 'because he isn't one of them at all.' She moved her head around like a gaunt bird. 'He's a policeman, but them out there aren't to know it.'

Rage brimmed. Salter didn't let it show. 'Here,' he said offering his Columbian roast. 'Make him some good stuff, least I can do considering what he'll be up against.' He watched the ritual of its making and forgot about Tolly's intransigence in the light of this new turn of events. Going back to his briefcase for saccharin he returned with that and what was left of the chloral hydrate—making a show of sweetening his own coffee and managing to get the chloral hydrate into Sparrow's when Sister Mary's back was turned.

COPELAND WOULD HAVE liked to have had Purvis hauled out of his cell and shoved into an interview room so he could extract the whole story out of him before passing it on up the ladder, but that was a pipe dream best left on television. Real life dictated that he take the new piece of information upstairs and in Barrett's absence knock on Morrissey's door, after which any interviewing would be done by the chief inspector himself, with Copeland merely allowed in for window-dressing.

Not that it made any difference.

The sight of Morrissey, in black mood and granite-faced, his height reinforced by rugby-sized shoulders, was normally enough to intimidate any thief, but Purvis was an exception.

'I found it,' he said, 'and that's the truth, lying there it was like somebody had dropped it. I mean, if I hadn't have picked it up somebody else would have. What's so special about it anyway?'

'Depends where you were on 22 January,' Morrissey said with deceptive quietness.

'How am I supposed to remember that? What was it. Monday, Tuesday, what?'

'Saturday. *Last* Saturday. Night,' Morrissey added foreseeing another time-wasting question.

Purvis slid forward on the chair and relaxed. 'Oh, right, well, that's easy then, isn't it? Bradford. Banged up, drunk and disorderly. Good way to get a night's kip, pissing down outside it was,' Grinning across the table, knowing that was all he had to say and let them whistle for exactly *where* he'd found it. Of course, if a bit later on he thought the extra bit of information might do him good then he'd bargain with it, but meantime—whatever sized monkey they brought on—they weren't going to get it.

BARRETT HAD CALLED in to see Fletcher again and come away still juggling times. Fletcher had been out of his office, he'd admitted that, but Salter had alibied him—*why?* Not to establish his own presence because Paul Hanson had already done that. And Adey claimed Salter had been in his office when she went for fish and chips. *No!* She'd said the light was on

in his office—not the same thing. And then she'd seen someone she thought was Jacques cross the drive from the shrubbery path. Setting Jacques and Salter side by side in his mind.
Possible to mistake them in the dark but for him Jacques and
Sansom were still odds-on favourites. He parked neatly in the
yard and wondered how Morrissey was getting on, hoping the
chief would be in his office and ready to talk, then he heard
the story of Zippo's lighter from the desk sergeant and headed
for the canteen, beating Morrissey back upstairs by a hair's
breadth and Morrissey thinking one of the two chip butties
was his.

TESCO HAD STUCK to Sparrow and Sparrow didn't like it.
'Look,' said Tesco. 'There's safety in numbers.'
    'Except I'd rather be on my own.'
    'Unless you meet the knife man.'
    'I'll handle him,' said Sparrow.
    'Except that's what Zippo thought, him being ex-army.'
    'I can look after myself,' said Sparrow. 'And I'm not look-
ing for company.'
    'Might be after you more than me if he's twigged who you
are.'
    Sparrow stopped walking. 'I don't know what you're on
about.'
    'Come off it. Marks & Spencer's, last week. Doing all right
there before you come and moved me on—not that I harbour
a grudge—wouldn't have to do it if I had the bike back.'
    'Great,' walking another couple of steps. 'So who else
knows?'
    Tesco shrugged. 'Nobody I've told. It's right, no need to
look like that. What'd be the point? Sodding hell, I want him
off the streets as much as you do. Where will you doss?'
    'Railway bridge on Marsh Street,' said Sparrow who hadn't
been trying to keep it secret. 'He'll not be able to get behind
me there.'
    'You want me to piss off then?'
    'Something like that.'
    'Fair enough,' Tesco veering off down a side street but still

reaching the Marsh Street bridge five minutes ahead of Sparrow, stowing himself out of sight in the dark behind the Heineken hoarding, hoping it didn't begin to rain.

THIRTY-NINE

HOLLY HAD WAITED for Philip to return to Brindley, guessing that Barrett would have interrupted the afternoon session at the citadel to ask his stupid questions, and guessed too that Philip would have found the process unsettling. One look at his face told her she had made the right assumptions. She said, 'There's nobody in the common room and the coffee is fresh—well, reasonably. You really do look as if you need one,' she touched his arm impulsively, the worry on her face stopping an automatic 'no' in its tracks. 'Look,' she said, 'I know they've got it all wrong; I mean, it's obvious. I just don't know why they can't see how stupid it is.' He followed her into the common room and slumped in a chair, letting her wait on him. If the world were as fair a place as Holly wanted it to be, none of this would have happened. Liz would be taking her finals and Rosemary would be out with her new man.

'God!'

He took a gulp of coffee, found it wasn't all that fresh but still better than nothing, and raised the mug in salute. 'Thanks.'

'I'm not doing anything tonight,' she said awkwardly. 'I'd really like it if you came back to my place and had supper with me?'

He gave her a tired smile and a compliant, 'That'd be nice.'

And it was—until the adverts came on before the ten o'clock news and his face suddenly grew tired again. Through the window she watched him cross over the road and get into his car, still no closer to knowing if he liked her as much as she liked him.

JIMMY PURVIS had been giving the lighter a lot of thought. In his experience chief inspectors didn't waste their valuable time talking to small timers like himself, not unless something big was on the line. He lay on the hard bench, hands behind his head, working out the best way to cut a better deal. Wasn't as if he could lose anything by it. Staring up at the light wondering what time it was, shifting his position, thinking a good soft mattress wouldn't go amiss, he got up on his feet and banged on the door. Then had to do it twice more before he heard the rattle of keys.

'I want to see the top man,' he said when the window flap opened. 'One I talked to this afternoon. Fancy giving him a call?'

PC Watts, fresh on duty, hadn't caught up with the news. 'Who was that then?' he said. 'CID or one of our lot?'

'CID of course. Chief Inspector. You tell him I want a word.'

'You must be joking, sunshine, he's home with his feet up.' Starting to close the flap until he caught the word Zippo and decided he'd better hear Jimmy out. 'What about Zippo?' he said.

'Don't you know nothing?' asked Purvis. 'That Zippo lighter I had when they picked me up. I know who had it before I found it.'

'Better tell me then.'

'Not sodding likely,' Purvis shook his head. 'That bit of information's worth something. Him or nothing, suit yourself. Wouldn't like to be in your shoes though if he misses out on it. Still—probably wouldn't have had much of a career anyway even if you hadn't got on the wrong side of him.' He watched the flap slam shut and stretched out on the bench again while he waited.

SMYTHE HADN'T GIVEN UP on Zoe, but she'd been playing hard to get, turning down invitations with a soft voice and a 'maybe next time'. In a spare minute that morning he'd used the canteen pay-phone to try again, and this time she'd said yes and set out the conditions. He could take her to the new Italian place but she wanted to be home by ten. And perhaps—if he behaved himself properly—she'd go discoing Saturday. Dis-

coing wasn't what he'd been campaigning for but it was a
start, always supposing Morrissey didn't cock it up again.
He'd hoped she wasn't serious about the ten o'clock business,
or that if she was she'd ask him in for coffee, but that didn't
happen. She touched a finger to her lips, then put it on his,
and was inside with the door shut before he had wit enough
to grab her. Luckily for him he was in the Crown drinking
Kalibar and not feeling any better for it when she tripped out
again at ten-thirty. It would have really hurt his pride to recognise the H reg Jag she got into with such familiarity—
although it might have prepared him for another disappointing
Saturday night.

THE CUSTODY SERGEANT had been apologetic, not mentioning
there'd been a half-hour wasted already while he and PC Watts
debated the pros and cons, still feeling uneasy at relaying
Purvis's message in case there was nothing in it, but not willing to risk Morrissey's wrath next day if it was kosher. By
then Purvis had tired of waiting and was quietly snoring.

When the phone rang at Barrett's place he was half-minded
not to answer it. After months of inviting Janet Yarby to drop
in for a coffee and look round his new flat she was there, and
had been for a half-hour, sitting near the arched window ad-
miring the high view over Malminster, and both of them getting on like a house on fire. 'Might be important,' she said.
'Want me to get it?'

That idea didn't appeal, a female voice could spoil things
completely. Barrett turned off his reluctance, lifted the receiver, and found that spoiling things didn't need a female
voice after all—Morrissey could do it equally well. By the
time he hung up Janet was on her feet and ready to go.

'Sounds important,' she said settling the strap of her shoulder bag into place. 'Time I went anyway. Thanks for the coffee, Neil.'

Halfway into his jacket Barrett took the car keys from his
mouth and said, 'The coffee invitation's always open, I'd like
it if you came again.' Hopeful but not really thinking it would
happen, he turned the lights off as they went out of the door,

then clattered down four flights of stairs behind her to the outer door.

'It's been nice,' she said as she got into her own car. 'Next time I'll bring some buns,' starting the engine and waving a hand through the window as she drove off, leaving Barrett with 'Next time' buzzing in his head all the way into Malminster.

PURVIS SAT FIRM. Getting impatient with him wouldn't speed things up and it's time they knew it. He looked at the two of them. 'I know what I said, and I'm not going back on it,' he stated. 'What I'm saying is, I want a deal. I mean this Zippo business; well, it's got to be important to bring you two running, so there's room to manoeuvre, work something out between us. Lucky I'm not a snout, else you'd have to pay me too.'

'Don't push your luck,' said Morrissey. 'Think about what we could tack on for obstruction.'

'Better still,' said Barrett. 'Ask yourself why we shouldn't just book you for murder.'

'What murder? I don't know anything about a murder, we're talking about a sodding lighter here not a corpse.'

'The lighter came from a corpse,' said Morrissey. 'But you'd know that, wouldn't you? How else would you have it?'

'Come off it. Wasn't any corpse there. Person who had it chucked it away.'

'Who was it?'

'How would I know? Looking for him, aren't I—to give it back,' he added quickly.

'Like you intended giving back the handbag?' said Barrett.

'Can't prove I wouldn't have.'

'I can't promise anything,' said Morrissey. 'You know that. All I can say is that if you cooperate, I'll do what I can.'

'And if you don't you'll be in bigger trouble than you thought,' said Barrett.

'Bloody double act.'

Purvis stared at them and Morrissey began to grow impatient.

'Murder?' said Purvis.

'More than one.'

Purvis gave in.

'I was hitching for Barnsley when this truckie dropped me off, middle of nowhere, pitch dark and bloody freezing. Country. You know, trees, fields and not much else—except this house, boarded up and on its own.'

'Where was the house?' asked Barrett.

'I don't know, I'm just passing through.'

'But somewhere on the way to Barnsley?'

'He turned off, said he was going for the M62.'

'Can you show us? On a map?'

'Shouldn't think so, I don't come from round here, best bet's the fire brigade.'

'Why is that?'

'Because this nut I'm trying to tell you about burned it down, didn't he? The house. And me in it if I hadn't got myself out. Fucking lunatic. All me stuff went up—sleeping-bag, the lot.'

'You saw him?'

'Went after him, didn't I, would have kicked his bloody head in if he hadn't had a car. He chucked the lighter and I picked it up.'

Morrissey leaned forward. 'Describe him for me.'

'Come off it, it was pitch.'

Wild-goose chase, thought Barrett. Come haring down for nothing.

'You said you could identify him,' Morrissey said softly.

'I got his registration number,' said Purvis. 'When his lights come on. Thought that'd do you nicely. Like American Express.'

IT WAS QUIET when the buildings were empty, he could hear a TV faintly through the walls, snatches of music too, but only when the orchestra reached crescendo. He knew where Sparrow was and he knew what the voices wanted him to do, but for the moment he was weary, as the child in him was weary, crying its thin, high cry and no one hearing. Sweating as the wail grew louder and drowned the clamouring voices, a small boy rocking in pain, shrunk small inside the man, hiding where his father would never find him again. Squatting on his haunches, sucking his thumb until the voices grew stronger than the wait.

MARSH STREET was off the normal thoroughfare, a narrow back street without shops or houses, lined by tall warehouses and patches of waste ground, with a pair of hoardings strategically placed to catch the eye of passengers on passing trains. On dark winter nights pedestrians avoided it, and its only asset was the bridge that provided a dry place to sleep. Since Duffy died, and Len not long after, Sparrow's new friends had given such isolated spots a wide berth. Sparrow had been given no choice in the matter, the Marsh Street bridge was an excellent place for a decoy duck and there were plenty of empty yards where police units could wait nearby in dark secrecy.

Smythe came out of the Crown at ten-thirty, and knowing where Sparrow was meant to be, walked towards Marsh Street, telling himself a little moral support wouldn't go wrong. Cutting down between the high station wall and a brewery, the skin of his ears taut for other footsteps, he knew that he wouldn't have taken Sparrow's job on himself—not without a lot of persuasion. He strolled, collar up, hands in pockets, thinking about Zoe and taking his time.

Wedged in a cut-back under the bridge Sparrow was asleep, the coffee in his flask laced with enough chloral hydrate to keep him that way until morning. Tesco had tried a little rough shaking but the tactic hadn't worked, and he had gone back behind the hoarding with the knife blade open in his pocket just in case. He had his head down on his arms and his eyes closed, dozing at the wrong time when Salter came down Marsh Street from the town end, his hand on a knife that was sharper than Tesco's. Eyes and mind fixed on Sparrow he didn't see Smythe coming out of the darkness of the brewery wall, and the first Smythe saw of Salter was a bending figure and a flash of metal reflecting an overhead light. He was running before the scene had fully registered but he didn't get there in time to save Sparrow; Tesco did that with less ground to cover and a cry like a banshee. Salter had Sparrow's head back when Tesco sent him off balance, the blade missing the great vessels but still slicing open Sparrow's trachea. Blood and air bubbled. Salter rebalanced, voices exploding in his head, slashing blindly and Tesco's knife sharp across his arm, then Smythe's footsteps echoing as he came under the bridge and Salter running away.

Tesco on his knees and Sparrow's rasping gurgle scaring him half to death.

MORRISSEY HAD ORDERED that Sparrow be pulled in off the street but the message had gone out too late. Another thing to add to all the others that lay heavy on his conscience. Barrett's journey to Brindley with two squad cars in tow had been abortive, and every available police officer was out hunting for Salter. Morrissey didn't expect him to be found that night, in the dark there were too many hiding places. Daylight would bring a different tale.

He tried to convince himself of that as he waited at the hospital with Sparrow's mother.

FORTY

THE CUT ON SALTER'S ARM was deep. He bandaged it as best he could but it had bled profusely, dripping down his clothes and onto his shoes, and by the time he got back to his car there was a white police Escort pulled up behind it. He backed away and caught a bus on the outskirts of town, intending to get off at the college until he saw there were police there too, and stayed on, getting off a mile up the road instead. Finding himself disorientated by the almost absolute darkness. Salter started walking back towards the college, found a farm track and followed that until he came to a mish-mash of buildings, the largest of them a barn that he slept in until morning.

THE HUNT HAD PLANNED a small meet, to get the hounds back onto form as much as anything, the Huntsman and his whippers-in anxious to be away, the Master making the most of the hospitality, his big chestnut snorting and blowing steam as it waited. Four scarlet coats and a mix of blacks and green, the hounds leaping, whimpering to be away and across the open meadow to the sweet tone of the horn.

Over behind Bailey's farm the foxes had been hunting, ranging separately over their newly marked-out territory, free as the night, sharp, barking calls carrying across the stillness, until now, fed and rested, they were heading back to Brindley—the farm and its fields between them and the college, and themselves between the hunt and the farm, peaceful until the copper horn sent the hounds streaming over the brow of Beech Hill and down across the meadow, the riders already ragged behind them and the vixen breaking cover, panicking, stretching her legs towards the safety of home, the hounds picking up her scent and crying in pursuit, the double note of the horn spurring them on.

The dog-fox came from the west side of the farm, running towards not away from the hounds, stronger and older than the vixen, crossing the field behind her in full sight of hounds and riders, tail streaming, cutting her scent and the pack dividing, the bigger half swerving to follow the bolder prey and the rest called in by horn or whippers-in. The vixen didn't slow her pace, through a thicket, across four fallow fields, onto ploughed land and then to Pel's Copse, trembling in the thorn thicket.

Salter, moving without any clear purpose back towards the college, heard the horn and stopped, watching the hunt come over the hill and down the meadow, amused at the ease with which the dog-fox subverted the chase to his own purpose, looking bare over his shoulder, tongue lolling, before vanishing into leaf-bare woodland. Behind him Salter moved on, his arm throbbing, the pain reaching from his hand to his shoulder. He saw no police, no evidence of any search, guessed that although a watch would be kept on the college the main search would be concentrated on roads leading out of Malminster and in the town itself, and when they didn't find him they would look further afield.

He was crossing the last field when the fox swung back through Bailey's farm, still running fast, wiley enough to snake through the farmyard, scattering hens, the farm dogs barking, whippers-in struggling to keep hounds from crashing in among buildings and pens and the farmer coming out with his shotgun, swearing at the chaos around him, two sows breaking out of a sty and lumbering in panic and three hounds off after the farm cat.

The dog-fox skirted the barn, picking up a remembered sour scent and following it towards Pel's Copse. Salter turning on the fringe of it and seeing the animal fleeing towards him, hounds closing fast and riders left behind. His back close against the thick bole of an old oak Salter watched them come, expecting the fox to veer, to run for cover and take the pack with him, but the grinning face came straight at him and Salter felt automatically for the knife, its blade doing no more than nick the fox's haunch as it launched itself at him, scrambling up over his body and into the tree, sprinkling him with droplets of blood. He might still have been all right if he hadn't in panic slashed out at the hounds, but the scent of fox blood mingling with his own, and the yelping of injured dogs, sent the pack into a frenzy of snapping, leaping jaws, the hunt ending in chaotic disorder as the sweating, cursing Huntsman, joining his whippers-in, frantically attempted to turn the dogs away from the man.

Unnoticed, the fox dropped down into the copse, moving at a loose trot through the undergrowth, then showing himself, a patch of red-brown fur crossing the field and up over the collapsed college wall to his mate.

TESCO HAD BEEN TREATED royally, a comfortable bed for the night and a fry-up in the canteen for breakfast. It was a new experience to have policemen acting like friends. 'This mean I don't get moved on then?' he said chirpily. 'Going to turn a blind eye when I'm outside Marks & Spencer's?'

'Don't push your luck,' said Woods. 'Tell me about this bike you lost.'

'Not lost. Some thieving scumbag took it. You've got it written down somewhere. All right if I go now?' standing up and starting to move off.

'So long as you don't go too far,' said Woods. 'We'll want you back as a witness.'

'If you catch him,' said Tesco, then thought of something else. 'Don't suppose,' he said, 'you've got a piece of spare cardboard?'

MORRISSEY WISHED he hadn't needed to look at Salter. Soft tissue damage was so extreme it was impossible to recognise the body with any certainty, and although some primitive justice might have been served by the manner of his death, Morrissey could wish there had been a different end to it, recognising there were questions he would never now have answers to, and grateful that what he saw as failure was viewed less critically by those above him. Grateful too that Sparrow would survive, unable yet to do much more than nod his head and raise a thumb. The shout of relief at being alive would have to wait a while.

Inquests were held, files were closed, and some digging into police pockets provided Tesco with a replacement bike on which he headed home to Sunderland.

A month after the disastrous hunt, two men with shotguns went back to Pel's Copse to look for fresh fox debris, ready, if they found it, to dig out the earth and kill the fox that had turned their sport into a shambles. The dog-fox had been back before them, digging through soft, damp soil to the source of a smell that had tantalised, uncovering a half rotted hand. When the men came, treading wet earth, looking for fox faeces, they found instead the turned back soil and a hand that had by then lost two fingers.

UNTIL THE END OF TIME
Polly Whitney

An Ike and Abby Mystery

IN DYING COLOR

Roller-blading duo Ike and Abby return—still divorced and still working together. Ike is the gorgeous producer of "Morning Watch," Abby is the director.

Abby is mugged walking to work by a man who promises a story. Abby suspects his attacker knows something about a crime wave sweeping Manhattan: the Yellow-Man murders. The victims are homeless, their faces are painted yellow, a cryptic message left behind.

But when a "Morning Watch" guest becomes a victim right outside the studio, Ike and Abby are drawn into the murders, trying not to kill *each other* in the meantime.

"...clever, effervescent, and jam-packed with acid-spiked tidbits about broadcast news." —*Mystery News*

Available in April at your favorite retail stores.

WORLDWIDE LIBRARY ®

TIME

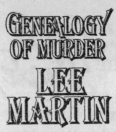

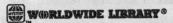

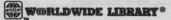

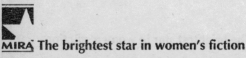